Praise for *No Judgments*

"Meg Cabot is best known for her books for younger readers, but her adult fiction is a total delight."

—PopSugar

"The ever-delightful Cabot charms in her latest, which is equal parts sweet and steamy."

—*Booklist*

"As in Cabot's previous adult romances . . . our heroine's wit and humor and determination to stay the course shine through in this breezy story that is a pure delight to read."

—*Library Journal*

"You know the woman who wrote The Princess Diaries series (and a dozen other series adding up to more than 80 novels for middle-grade, YA and adult readers) will deliver a happy ending, along with engaging characters, lively dialogue and plenty of plot twists."

—*Tampa Bay Times*

"I don't know if Little Bridge Island is a real place or not but it officially has a place in my heart."

—LibraryReads

"Cabot, best known for her Princess Diaries young adult series, shows that her work for adults can be just as frothy and entertaining."

—*Publishers Weekly*

"Cabot has a long, successful track record of writing entertaining stories that allow readers to escape from the realities of life by bringing levity, wit and a host of surprises and happy endings to the page. *No Judgments* is further testament to her appealing, winning style."

—Romantic Between the Lines

NO OFFENSE

Also by Meg Cabot

The Princess Diaries series
The Mediator series
The Boy series
Heather Wells series
Insatiable
Overbite
Ransom My Heart (with Mia Thermopolis)
Queen of Babble series
She Went All the Way
The 1–800-Where-R-You series
All-American Girl series
Nicola and the Viscount
Victoria and the Rogue
Jinx
How to Be Popular
Pants on Fire
Avalon High series
The Airhead series
Abandon series
Allie Finkle's Rules for Girls series
From the Notebooks of a Middle School Princess series

NO OFFENSE

MEG
CABOT

wm
WILLIAM MORROW
An Imprint of HarperCollins*Publishers*

This is a work of fiction. Names, characters, places, and incidents are products of the author's imagination or are used fictitiously and are not to be construed as real. Any resemblance to actual events, locales, organizations, or persons, living or dead, is entirely coincidental.

HarperCollins books may be purchased for educational, business, or sales promotional use. For information, please email the Special Markets Department at SPsales@harpercollins.com.

FIRST EDITION

Designed by Diahann Sturge
Molly chapter opener art © Khabarushka / Shutterstock
John chapter opener art © MSSA / Shutterstock

Library of Congress Cataloging-in-Publication Data has been applied for.

ISBN 978-0-06-289007-8
ISBN 978-0-06-300712-3 (hardcover library edition)

20 21 22 23 24 LSC 10 9 8 7 6 5 4 3 2 1

NO OFFENSE

CHAPTER ONE

Molly

The program wasn't going the way Molly had planned.

Oh, the children were delighted with the cookies that Island Bakery had provided. They were having fun slathering on the frosting and sticking on the different-colored candies. Most of these were going into their mouths, actually, but that was fine. That wasn't the problem.

The problem was who else had shown up to the program besides the children and their parents.

"Boom chicka boom boom boom," Elijah Trujos said, manipulating a gingerbread man he'd decorated to resemble an extremely well-endowed male adult-entertainment star into French kissing an equally well-endowed gingerbread woman. "Get a load of this, kiddies!"

The children, not having any idea what Elijah was doing, laughed delightedly.

The few parents who'd squeezed into the tiny child-sized

chairs around the play table in the children's section of the Little Bridge Island Public Library did not laugh. They stared in horror at the teenage boy.

"Elijah," Molly said in a firm tone. "Could I have a word with you in private, please?"

"Not right now, Miss Molly," Elijah said, forcing his gingerbread cookies to do something sexual that Molly was fairly certain was illegal, even in the state of Florida. "I'm busy enjoying this lovely children's program you've set up."

Gritting her teeth, Molly wished she'd listened to Phyllis Robinette, her mentor and predecessor, who'd warned her, "Never do any children's programs involving food. They don't end well."

But what could possibly go wrong with cookie decorating? Molly had asked herself. The cookies she'd ordered were gluten-, dairy-, and nut-free, and so couldn't trigger the allergies of any of her known patrons.

And the dough had been cut and baked into human shapes—completely androgynous. She'd even been careful to ask for no gingerbread women (in skirts), as that might be perceived as sexist. Her gingerbread persons were completely gender neutral.

And yet somehow Elijah Trujos had found a way to pervert even this.

She leaned over Elijah's shoulder and said, as patiently as she could, "That's the problem, Elijah. This is a *children's* program. You're sixteen, and so technically a young adult. Wouldn't you be more comfortable over in the *young adult section*?"

"At what age does childhood end, Miss Molly?" Elijah asked, pausing the gyrations into which he'd been twisting his festively decorated cookies to give the farmyard mural on the children's room's ceiling a thoughtful glance. "The Jewish faith says childhood ends at thirteen, when a boy achieves adulthood through his bar mitzvah. Here in Florida, eighteen is considered the legal age of consent, at which we can also vote and join the army to sacrifice our lives for our country. But neurologists now say the human brain isn't fully mature until the age of twenty-six. So shouldn't the Little Bridge Island Public Library allow their patrons to remain in the children's section until at least that age?"

Molly narrowed her eyes, and not only because of the excessive amount of cologne Elijah was wearing. She'd heard all of his speeches many times before. "You do know that if a patron engages in disruptive behavior, the librarian has the right to ask him or her to leave?"

"How am I being disruptive?" Elijah asked. "I'm following the program guidelines—decorating cookies." He held up his obscene gingerbread man and woman. "Although I'm a little offended by the fact that *you're* so offended by my humor, Miss Molly. You really need to loosen up."

Molly restrained an urge to say something she'd regret. This was not her first tangle with Elijah Trujos in the five months since she'd taken the job as children's media specialist at the Little Bridge Island Public Library.

But she was determined that it would be her last.

"Fine, Elijah," she said calmly. "If that's the way you want it."

Then she walked back to her desk and picked up the phone.

"Ooooh," Elijah cried, delighted. "Calling the po-po, are we? Gonna get me sent to the big house for cookie porn? Overreacting much?"

Molly hesitated. How could Elijah think she was calling the police? Did he not know her well enough by now to realize that she would never dial 911 on a minor, particularly one who wasn't being violent, particularly *him*? Elijah's mother had once confided to her how grateful she was to Molly for allowing him to hang around the children's room, since—now that she and his father had split—he spent most of his time when he wasn't at the library in his room, playing video games. His mother preferred him to be at the library. (Mrs. Trujos seemed unaware that the library had a wide and extensive collection of video games and consoles.)

Truth be told, Molly did find Elijah amusing . . . even the cookie thing was kind of funny. Under other circumstances, Molly would have laughed.

But the parents of the small children at the play table didn't seem to find the cookie thing funny or think she was overreacting. They were all gazing at Molly with approval as she punched buttons on her phone's keypad.

Elijah looked slightly less sure of himself, though he maintained his air of righteous indignation.

"Go ahead, Miss Molly," he said, his mouth full of Red Hots and chocolate sprinkles. "Call the po-po! What are they gonna charge me with . . . being the only person here with a sense of humor?"

"Yes, hello," Molly said, as someone on the other end of the phone picked up. "This is Molly Montgomery from the children's section of the Little Bridge Island Public Library. We have an individual here who is being—"

"—hilarious!" Elijah shouted. "We need an officer to come down and arrest him for making us all feel great!"

Molly eyed Elijah sternly as she went on to describe his skintight denim jeans, black hoodie, camouflage backpack and baseball hat, shaggy brown hair, and general height and weight.

Elijah, meanwhile, began rapidly to eat the evidence against him.

"The po-po," he exclaimed, spraying cookie crumbs everywhere. "The po-po'll never get me!"

"Wouldn't it make more sense," one of the weary-looking fathers asked Elijah, "for you simply to leave?"

"I got as much right to be here as you do, man," Elijah said, biting into the head of his male cookie.

"No, you don't," the father said. "I'm here with my four-year-old. And I'm not subjecting the rest of us to pornography."

"Pornogwaphy," echoed one of the toddlers at the activity table in a delighted voice.

"The First Amendment defends my right to free speech," Elijah cried.

"Not in front of my child," said the mother of the child who'd repeated the word *pornography*. "At a cookie-decorating program in the children's section of a public library."

Molly felt as if she'd barely hung up the phone before Henry from the reference desk came running in, looking pale but determined.

"I got your call," he said to her. His gaze focused on the back of Elijah's head. "This the kid?" Then, when Elijah turned around, Henry's enormous shoulders slumped. "Oh, it's *you*."

Elijah, who'd been licking icing off his fingers, looked similarly disappointed.

"Wait," he said, throwing Molly a disgusted look. "You called *Henry*?"

"I didn't want to," Molly said. "But you pushed me too far this time."

Elijah laughed. "I should have known you'd never call nine-one-one on a kid."

"No," Molly said. "I wouldn't. But next time, Elijah, I will call your mother."

He rolled his eyes, unimpressed. "I can't believe I ate all that frosting for *Henry*. I feel sick."

"Serves you right," Molly said.

Henry placed a heavy hand on Elijah's shoulder. "Come on, kid. You're going back to YA."

All the fight had left Elijah. He and Henry, the reference librarian, had tangled often in the past, and Henry always won, due not only to the nearly one hundred pounds—most of it muscle—he had on the boy, but to his endless patience.

"Fine," Elijah said, rising from his chair. "But I want all of you to know that what you witnessed back there was one of Elijah Trujos's finest performances, and one day, when I have my own comedy special on Netflix, you'll say to yourselves, I knew that boy back when he did cookie porn at the library."

"I'm sure we will, Elijah," Henry said, still keeping a hand on Elijah's shoulder. "Don't forget your backpack."

"I enjoyed the show, Elijah," Molly couldn't help calling after him. "It just wasn't appropriate for a younger audience."

"Ingrates," Elijah said, allowing himself to be steered from the children's section just as a voice called, "Miss Molly?"

One of the younger children's mothers waved to Molly from the direction of the restrooms.

Molly wondered what could possibly have gone wrong now. This was not the first time, of course, that a parent had expressed concern to her about the condition of the restrooms, although there was something more urgent than usual in this particular young mother's expression.

"Yes, Mrs. Cheeseman?" she asked.

"Oh, Miss Molly." Mrs. Cheeseman steered her five-year-old daughter, Bella, back toward the play table. "There's something wrong with the last stall in the girls' room. The door is locked, but no one is in there. I couldn't see anyone's feet, and no one answered when I knocked."

Molly forced a smile onto her face.

"Of course, Mrs. Cheeseman," she said. "I'll take care of it."

Molly had already sensed from Mrs. Cheeseman's expression that it wasn't a lack of toilet paper or liquid soap that was upsetting her, but something of a more dire nature. The average citizen would probably be surprised to learn how often librarians—many of whom had masters degrees—were called upon to dispose of diapers or unclog toilets, though this was not listed anywhere in their job description. It usually happened because no one else would do it. The cleaning staff at Molly's library, for instance, stated that union regulations would not allow them near biohazardous materials, which all bodily fluids were considered.

Therefore, if a diaper was not properly disposed of, Molly, as head of her department, was usually forced to dispose of it herself, since she could not bear asking a subordinate to clean up for her any more than she could bear the mess.

The fact that the door to the stall was jammed told Molly that they were facing a DEFCON 2–level diaper situation, or possibly worse. Worse could include an intoxicated or sleeping displaced person. Little Bridge Island was a charming resort town in South Florida, known for its year-round warm weather. . . .

But that same warm weather drew a large indigent population who occasionally used the restrooms of the local library for purposes for which they hadn't necessarily been designed.

Molly's fake smile disappeared the moment she hit the girls' room. She winced at her reflection in the large mirror above the three sinks beside the hideous orange metal bathroom stalls, surrounded by equally hideous orange tiles that had not been updated since the nineties. She'd been working so hard all morning to set up her program, she hadn't yet had a chance to check her mascara, which had flaked and given her raccoon eyes.

It didn't help that since moving to Little Bridge she'd been staying up way too late—even when she didn't have to—watching true crime shows, eating ice cream in bed, and trying not to go on Instagram and look at the photos her ex's new fiancée, Ashley, had posted of their engagement party. Molly couldn't believe that Eric had gotten engaged already. Should she write to Ashley and warn her what she was getting herself into? It was possible she had no idea the kind of person Eric truly was. It had taken several years for Molly to find out, after all.

But what if Ashley knew and liked that kind of thing? What if she couldn't wait to quit her job and spend the rest of her life cooking and cleaning for Eric (as it had turned out he'd expected Molly to do)?

Molly should have been relieved at her lucky escape. Instead, she had dark circles under her eyes and had somehow managed to smear white cookie frosting across the front of her new blouse. There appeared to be some in her hair, as well.

Oh, God. Maybe she really was turning into a cliché of a spinster librarian, like her sister was always saying. She didn't even have the guts to call the cops on a child.

But how could she? Part of her job was to help and protect children.

And anyway, spinsters were cool. The word descended from the late Middle English and originally meant a "woman who spins," a respectable occupation for any woman, and one that was usually so profitable, the woman needn't marry at all if she chose not to. It was only later that the term became derisive.

"Hello?"

Molly was sure she'd heard a noise . . . a sort of snuffling sound, similar to a sob.

There was, of course, a third reason the stall door could be locked: not someone passed out or trying to hide a mess about which they were embarrassed, but a child—a child sitting on the toilet, her little legs too short for her feet to reach the floor. Molly occasionally found one sulking—sometimes even reading—in the stalls when she went to check the restrooms before locking up at night.

When asked why they chose to sit there instead of in the (admittedly well-worn) furniture provided for this purpose in one of the reading rooms, the answer was always, "I wanted to be alone."

How well Molly understood the sentiment.

"Hi, it's Miss Molly, the children's librarian," she said in a gentle voice through the stall door. "I don't want to disturb you. I just want to make sure you're all right. If you say you are, I'll leave you alone."

No answer. Just another faint snuffle.

Molly hadn't been hired to babysit or clean, but most days, she found herself doing both in some capacity. It was the price she paid in order to do what she loved for a living.

So, with a sigh, she dropped to the restroom floor—

ancient linoleum, but mostly unstained, since the cleaning crew mopped it every night—and peeked beneath the foot-and-a-half-wide gap between the bottom of the stall door and the floor.

There was no one in the stall.

There was, however, a fairly large box of industrial-sized trash bags sitting on the toilet seat. The snuffling seemed to be coming from inside it.

Molly's heart began to pound with excitement. Her first thought—ludicrously, she realized in retrospect—was *Kittens!*

Someone had left a box of adorable kittens for her to find in the bathroom.

Why not? Everyone knew that Molly loved cats, and she'd been lobbying for a resident library cat ever since her arrival. The only reason the rest of the staff had vetoed the idea was because of the move. It made sense to wait until they were in the new building.

Still, it wouldn't be *her* fault if someone decided the library was the perfect place to leave their cat's litter.

Swiftly, fantasizing about what she was going to name the kittens—of course they'd keep only one; it was difficult to rationalize having more than one library cat, with the number of patrons claiming dander allergies—Molly slid beneath the stall door and awkwardly climbed to her feet, then peered into the box.

But instead of the adorably fluffy black-and-white or even orange tabby kittens that Molly was expecting to see, she saw a doll swaddled in a blue-and-white beach towel.

Oh, no, she thought, lifting the edge of the towel to get a better look at the doll. *I'll have to find this doll's owner. She's going to miss her—*

It was only when the doll moved that Molly realized what she was truly seeing.

And suddenly, for the first time in her career, she found herself calling the police because of a child.

CHAPTER TWO

John

Sheriff John Hartwell was having lunch at the Mermaid Café when the call came through.

Specifically, he had been trying to decide between a Harpooner—a half pound of Grade A ground beef with bacon, grilled onions, and your choice of cheese—or a Mermaid chopped salad.

Obviously the salad was the healthier option, though he wasn't entirely sure about the blue cheese and bacon.

What he really wanted was the signature bone-in rib eye over at Island Steak House, but they weren't open for lunch, and besides, Doctor Alvarez had warned him that he needed to start eating cleaner. His weight was fine, but his cholesterol wasn't, and if it continued on this trajectory, the doctor had said, he'd soon have to go on medication.

What John hadn't mentioned to the doctor was his suspicion that it wasn't his eating habits that were causing his cholesterol levels to go up, but stress. Like the recent spate of home burglaries over by the old high school—not so unusual given that half the island's residents neglected to lock their doors at night (or at any other time).

Even his living situation was stressful—more stressful, in fact, than being the youngest sheriff in the history of Little Bridge, or the bar fights he frequently had to break up over at Ron's Place. John would happily take a drunken brawl over being a single parent to a teenage daughter any day.

"Hi, Sheriff." Bree Beckham, the Mermaid's most popular waitress—thanks to her bright pink hair and even brighter smile—came up to the counter to wait on him. "What'll it be today? Burger?"

John looked down at the menu and sighed. Who was he kidding? He was never going to eat a salad, not even one with locally caught shrimp.

Bree seemed to sense his dilemma. "How about the fish sandwich?"

Well, that was a nice compromise, just in case the doctor was right. "What's the fish today?" John asked.

"Yellowtail," Bree said, with an approving nod at John's caution. "Caught fresh this morning. We can fry, blacken, or grill it for you."

John was saved from having to grapple with this decision—obviously he'd prefer it fried, but neither his daughter, Katie, nor his doctor would like this—when his radio crackled.

"Chief," Marguerite, over at the station, said. "You at the Mermaid?"

"'Scuse me, Bree," John murmured, and lifted the hand radio on his shoulder to his mouth. "Yes, I am, Marg. And stop calling me Chief. What've you got?"

"Sorry, Sheriff. Craziest thing. We just got a call about a baby being abandoned in one of the bathrooms over at the library. EMTs are already on their way, but—"

"I'll be right over," John said, and gave Bree an apologetic smile as he refastened his radio. "Have to take a rain check on that fish sandwich."

"A *baby*?" Bree shook her head, not even trying to pretend she hadn't been eavesdropping. That wasn't the Little Bridge way. On an island with a population of nearly five thousand, everyone knew everyone else's business. "Who leaves a baby in a library? Must be a tourist."

John didn't want to ruffle anyone's feathers by mentioning that in his experience, the incidents of child neglect in Little Bridge were spread evenly across the board, tourists and locals alike. So he only murmured a laconic, "Yep," then laid down a five-dollar bill to cover the cost of the café con leche he'd consumed while perusing the menu.

"Oh, Sheriff." Bree pushed the bill back toward him. "You know your money's no good here."

John smiled as he put on his wide-brimmed hat. "Put it in the donation jar for all those animals you like to save, then. And give my regards to Drew."

Bree grinned happily at the mention of her boyfriend's name and pocketed the bill. "I will. Thanks, Sheriff."

The library was only one block away, but John drove, lights and siren blaring, because a lost baby was an emergency. So it was less than a minute before he was pulling up before the squat, office-style building that looked so out of place beside its statelier neighbors. Through some fluke in city planning, the town library had ended up in the middle of one of Little Bridge Island's oldest and most expensive residential neighborhoods, each house built in the Victorian style, with wraparound, veranda-style front porches trimmed with gingerbread and dotted with comfortable-looking rattan sofas and chairs (about which his daughter, who'd spent her formative years on the mainland, had once asked, "Why doesn't anyone steal them, Daddy?").

The owners of these homes weren't bothering to contain their excitement that the library—an architectural horror built in the 1960s—was scheduled for demolition in a few short months. Thanks to the generosity of a single, very wealthy donor, the eccentric but universally beloved widow Dorothy Tifton, the books were soon to be moved to the old high school, which was being renovated to accommodate them, and a center for Floridian history was to be constructed in the old building's place.

As he pulled on the glass-and-metal doors and heard the familiar squeak of protest, then smelled the even more familiar scent of mildew, paper, and dust, John wondered if the librarians were as wistful about this move as he was. It's true that the old library was small and cramped, and the new one was going to be a vast improvement.

But it sometimes seemed to John as if too many things were changing too fast . . . and not necessarily for the better.

"Hey, there," he said to the extremely old woman sitting at the reception desk. John thought he recognized her as the librarian who'd worked in the building when he'd been a boy. But that woman had been so old then, she must surely be dead by now. "I'm Sheriff Hartwell. We got a call about a—"

The old woman nodded.

"I know, John," she said in a creaky voice. "Although I suppose I should be calling you 'Sheriff' now."

So it *was* her. She wasn't dead! And somehow she'd remembered him after all these years. He must have made quite an impression as a boy . . . probably not a good one.

"Thank you, ma'am," he said, politely doffing his hat. *Phyllis Robinette,* read the nametag pinned to her blouse. Of course! If it wasn't for Phyllis Robinette taking him in hand that rainy day so many years ago, when he and his friends had staggered into the library, looking for something to do (or, more correctly, destroy), and showing him the biography section, he might never have discovered all those books on the people—sports heroes, military heroes, aviators, and lawmen—who later became his role models.

It was because of this woman that he'd discovered reading for pleasure, which had caused him to perform better in school, make good enough grades to get into college, major in criminal justice, and become what he was today . . . the county sheriff.

Should he tell her what a remarkable impression she'd made on him?

"I don't suppose you'd be able to hurry this along?" the old woman asked, tartly. "The presence of so many persons carrying firearms is going to make quite a few of our patrons nervous."

No, he was not going to tell her. At least, not today.

"I'm sure we'll have this all straightened out shortly, ma'am."

"Mm-hmm. The way you've *straightened out* those burglaries over by the old high school?"

He took the criticism in stride. It wasn't as if he hadn't heard it before. "Well, we do our best, ma'am. Those particular break-ins—"

She didn't wait for him to finish. "Right in there, John. You know the way."

Dismissed, he turned and walked in the direction in which Mrs. Robinette was pointing, a fresh wave of nostalgia washing over him as he entered the room in which he'd spent so many hours as a boy. It looked—and smelled—exactly the same, down to the mural on the ceiling of friendly barnyard animals. (Why barnyard animals on an island in South Florida that was closer to Cuba than it was to the mainland, he'd always wondered. Why not sea creatures? Perhaps because so many children growing up on Little Bridge knew how to avoid jellyfish stings but not that milk came from cows.)

The EMTs were already there. John was pleased to see it was a particularly competent team, who worked well together and rarely gave his deputies any guff.

Bearded, tattooed Max was kneeling beside an attractive young woman whom John had never seen before—unusual, since, aside from tourists, he was acquainted at least by sight with nearly everyone on the island. The young woman was holding a baby in her lap. Max had a stethoscope pressed to the baby's chest.

"Good, strong heartbeat," Max said after a moment.

"Thank God," the young woman said. The people gathered around her—men and women, boys and girls, many of them holding heavily decorated gingerbread men, for some reason—all echoed the sentiment, letting out a collective sigh of relief.

"Wade," John said quietly, since it was a library and there was a baby and Max seemed to have the scene under control. The baby wasn't even crying, but John had enough experience with babies not to take that as a positive sign. Wade noticed him and quickly came over.

"Hey, Sheriff," he whispered. "Can you believe this?"

"Not sure," John said. "What *is* this, exactly?"

"Baby, abandoned. New librarian found her," Wade said, nodding in the direction of the attractive young woman. "Molly, er, Montgomery, I think her name is? Anyway, somebody stuck the baby in a box and left her in a toilet stall in the girls' room."

"Hmmm." John narrowed his eyes. There was a box

advertising industrial-sized trash bags sitting on a tiny, child-sized table a few feet away. "That box there?"

"Yeah. Whoever did it wrapped her up in a towel, but she was cold anyway on account of the AC in here. Librarian did the right thing by picking her up and trying to keep her warm till we got here. We're gonna get her over to the hospital now, but she seems to be doing okay, considering."

John nodded. "Good. How old do you think she is?"

"Newborn. Hours. No more than a day, for sure."

John nodded again. He'd said, "*Good,*" but he didn't actually think any of this was good. Bad enough to abandon a baby, but to abandon one in a box meant for trash bags, and in a *library*? Especially when the fire station, a state-appointed safe haven for newborns under a week old, was just down the street.

He counted a dozen people in the room, not including himself and the EMTs. Of that, six appeared to be women of child-bearing age. It was doubtful from their demeanor that any of them was the mother, but he'd need to question them all.

This included the librarian. She was handing Max the baby, whom the EMT began to address in gibberish. John knew that Max had two dogs at home that he adored, so speaking in gibberish to any creature smaller than himself wasn't unusual for him.

Still, the librarian apparently didn't know this. She looked slightly concerned as she watched Max bundle up the baby in an emergency thermal blanket from the ambulance. In her early to mid thirties, Molly Montgomery was neatly dressed in black slacks and a floral top, her dark hair cut in what John's fashion-conscious daughter always referred to as a bob. The librarian had a slim figure, not one of a female who'd given birth recently, and it would be odd—though not unheard of—for someone who'd just delivered a baby to report it as if she'd "found" it.

But neither of those things was enough for John to rule her out as the mother. He was going to have to question her. He was going to have to question her most closely of all.

"Marg," he said into the handset on his shoulder. "I'm gonna need some help over here at the library." He glanced around at the crowd, noting that their gazes were still fixed on the baby. People sure did go nuts over babies. "A lot of it."

His favorite sergeant's voice was as unruffled as usual. "You got it, Sheriff. Castillo and Martinez are on their way."

That task completed, John stepped forward, deciding that he should start with the new librarian, since she was the one who'd found the baby, and not at all because she was so attractive and a possible, though not likely, suspect.

"Miss, er, Ms., ma'am?" They'd recently gone through a four-hour sexual harassment–awareness training program at the department, at John's own request, after what had happened with the last sheriff. But even with the training and a teenage daughter at home to constantly remind him when he was saying something that could be construed as sexist, he was never sure when he might be offending someone. "Ms. Montgomery?"

As the librarian tore her gaze from the baby and brought it to his face, he was startled by how large and dark her eyes were. This had to be some kind of trick of the makeup she wore. No one's eyes could possibly be that wide and beautiful on their own.

"Yes?"

"Sheriff John Hartwell." John touched the rim of his hat, nodding politely, his standard greeting toward all members of the public. "I understand you're the one who found the baby. If I could just ask you a few questions?"

"Oh, of course." The librarian turned from the baby and began walking toward a cluttered desk a few feet away.

"Thank you, ma'am."

John observed several things at once, the first being that Molly Montgomery's voice was quiet but pleasantly melodic, exactly how a children's librarian's voice should sound. Mrs. Robinette's voice had sounded that way, back before time and dealing with a constant stream of badly behaved children like himself and his friends had robbed it of its youthful vitality.

The second was that her desk was one of the messiest he'd ever seen. Piled high with books of all different sizes and thicknesses, it was also littered with scrap paper of assorted colors and the kind of stubby pencils they gave people at bowling alleys—and golf courses—to fill out their scorecards.

More upsetting to a type A individual like himself was the plethora of brightly colored Post-it notes stuck everywhere, including on the librarian's computer screen. Post-its like that would leave a sticky residue on a computer monitor that could be hard to clean.

If the desks of any of his deputies back at the department had ever grown even remotely this disorganized, he would have referred them to human resources for counseling immediately.

But none of these was the most disconcerting thing John observed. The most disconcerting thing he observed was that the librarian's backside was every bit as appealing-looking as her front side.

He quickly averted his gaze, however, as he knew from both his sexual harassment training and his many years of experience on the job that eyeing the physical attributes of witnesses was inappropriate.

"Would you like a seat?" the librarian asked, gesturing to an empty chair beside her desk. Unfortunately, it was a child's chair. Everything in the children's department was child-sized, except for the librarian's desk. "Or something to drink? We have sparkling apple juice today. We were having a cookie decorating party when one of the mothers came out and said she thought there was something unusual in the restroom."

"Uh." He eyed the small table littered with cookies and frosting. "Gingerbread cookie decorating? In April?"

"Oh." She glanced in the direction of the table and gave a rueful little smile. "Yes, well, I wasn't here during the holiday season. And I've always wanted to do a cookie decorating program. So it was a non-holiday-specific cookie decorating party. Though I'm not sure now that it was the best idea."

He raised his eyebrows. "Why not?"

"Well, it got a little messier than I was expecting." She pointed at the tile floor beneath the table, which was littered with cookie crumbs and a rainbow of sprinkles. "And though the program was intended for younger children, we had a teenager show up, which ordinarily would have been fine, but this particular teenager—"

It could not possibly be this easy. "Any idea of her name?" He drew his notebook from his belt.

"Oh, no." Smiling and shaking her head, she said, "Elijah's a he. And the baby couldn't possibly be his. Elijah's sixteen, but there's no way he . . . I mean—" The librarian sank down into the chair behind her desk, the smile gone, her hands fluttering a little nervously. "Sorry. What I meant is, Elijah is a wonderful boy, but he couldn't have anything to do with the baby. He barely has any friends, let alone a girlfriend. And besides, he was here with me the entire time."

John nodded. Of course she was nervous—not because she was guilty of anything, but because of what she'd been through. It wasn't every day someone found a newborn baby in their workplace bathroom and then got questioned about it by the authorities.

He knew it wasn't helping that he was towering over her in his uniform. It was time to sit, even though every bone in his body cried out at the thought of folding his six-foot-three frame into that tiny little chair beside her desk . . .

especially remembering how, twenty odd years ago, he'd easily fit into similar chairs in this very same room. Now the chair creaked beneath his weight.

The librarian didn't appear to notice the great sacrifice he was making, however, just as she didn't appear to notice that she had white frosting smeared across her black floral top, and a little bit in her dark hair, too. She was simply too upset.

"She's going to be okay, right?" she asked him anxiously. "The baby?"

"Oh, yes," he said, shifting his weight in the tiny chair. "I have it on excellent authority that she's going to be fine. Are there security cameras in this building?"

She nodded. "Yes, of course—"

His heart leaped, until she added, "But they don't work."

"Excuse me?"

"We're having state-of-the-art ones installed in the new library, of course, to help enhance the safety of our patrons and to prevent theft and vandalism. But the cameras here are ancient, and stopped working ages ago, and since we were moving anyway, we figured, why spend money on new ones—"

He decided it was best to skip to his next question.

"And you didn't notice anything—or anyone—out of the ordinary this morning?"

"No. But it's been so busy, because of the cookie party. And honestly, anyone could come in anytime holding a box that size and I wouldn't give them a second glance.

We accept donations year-round." She must have noticed his puzzled look, since she elaborated, "Of books. We have a used-book sale every other weekend, so people are constantly dropping off boxes of books. We do a very brisk business in paperbacks, especially romance novels and thrillers, what with all of the tourists on vacation."

He nodded like he knew what she was talking about. "And you're certain the box wasn't there when you arrived this morning?" he asked, opening his notebook so he could record her answer, trying to appear professional in his absurd position in the children's chair, with his knees sticking up higher than his elbows.

"Oh, yes," she replied, her large eyes huger than ever. "I always check all the rooms when I get in, just to make sure there isn't a *From the Mixed-Up Files of Mrs. Basil E. Frankweiler* situation going on. And the box certainly wasn't here then."

"A *what* situation?" he asked, more confused than ever.

"*From the Mixed-Up Files of*—oh." She flushed a little when she realized he didn't know what she was talking about. "Nevermind. It's a children's book about a girl and her brother who run away and hide in—it doesn't matter. The box wasn't here, but the cleaners had come overnight. So far, since I've been here, they've never missed a night."

This was his chance to find out why he'd never seen her around before. "And how long have you been in this position?"

"Oh, not long." She shook her head, the ends of her black hair—some of which were coated in white cookie frosting—swaying. "I only got this job at the end of December."

"And before that you were?"

He told himself he wasn't asking out of personal interest. He definitely needed to know for the investigation. Due to her accent—flat and inflectionless—he suspected she was from somewhere in the Midwest, and so he wasn't surprised when she replied, "Denver. I've known Phyllis—Mrs. Robinette, the former children's librarian—for ages. We met at ALA." She said it as if she expected him to know what it was, but he had no idea. American Lung Association? Alaska Airlines? "When Phyllis told me that she wanted to retire but was having trouble finding a replacement due to Hurricane Marilyn—you of all people must know about the housing shortage here since the storm—well, I just jumped at the chance to apply, especially since my mother's best friend, Joanne Larson, owns the Lazy Parrot Inn. Her husband, Carl, hasn't been doing so well lately, and they've really needed an extra hand. They've got a spare room since the night manager quit, and, well, everything just fell into place. Who wouldn't want to live and work in paradise? Especially now, with the new library opening up soon."

"Yes," he said, again nodding as if he'd understood a word of what she'd just said. "Completely." Except for the part about the Lazy Parrot—it was true Joanne and Carl Larson had lost their night manager a while back. John himself had arrested him for petit theft in the second degree—and about Mrs. Robinette. She was the type to stay on volunteering long after her "retirement," to make sure everything continued to run smoothly, which explained why she'd been at the reception desk to greet him.

The darkness of Molly Montgomery's huge eyes made sense now, too. It wasn't only the result of makeup, but the purple shadows that came from a lack of sleep, working as a children's librarian and the live-in night manager at a popular local hotel.

Still, there was more to her slightly-too-chipper story than she was admitting. That faint white line on her left ring finger attested to that. He'd noticed it, especially because it matched the one on his own exactly.

Although he was very curious, he wasn't going to bring it up. It wasn't pertinent to his investigation.

"Well, Ms. Montgomery," he began, but she interrupted quickly.

"Oh, please, call me Molly. Or Miss Molly. Everybody here does."

"Okay, well, Molly, then—"

"What's going to happen to her?" Her gaze was worriedly following the baby, whom Max was carrying out to the ambulance. "Where are they taking her?"

"To the hospital. They'll check her out, and if she's okay—which the EMTs seem to think she is—she'll go to Child Protective Services, and then into foster care."

The librarian looked troubled. "But what about her mother?"

"Well, obviously, we're going to try to find her so we can question her."

This was clearly the wrong thing to say, since those large dark eyes grew even larger, and she visibly tensed. "Question her? About what?"

"Well, for starters, about why she abandoned her baby in an empty trash-bag box in the bathroom of your library."

"But you don't know that she did. That baby could have been kidnapped."

"Kidnapped?" John had thought he'd heard everything in his line of work, but this beat all. "And the kidnappers just happened to forget her in the bathroom of your library?"

She glared at him. "Stranger things have happened in this town, from what I've heard."

He wasn't going to argue, since that was perfectly true. It was Florida, after all. "Well, if that's what happened, we'll find out—after we find the mother and question her."

"But even if she did leave her baby here, I'm sure it was for a very good reason—clearly she doesn't feel able to care for her right now. I know I haven't worked here all that long, but maybe this library is a place where she's always felt safe, and so she thought her baby would be safe here, too."

"Uh," John said, struggling to come up with a reply to this. "Well, now—"

"And she *was*. We found her and made sure that she got the help she needed. People don't come to the library simply to check out books anymore, you know, Sheriff. People come to the library for all sorts of reasons—to use our computers, to look for jobs, to take classes, to socialize, and even as a place to get help when they're hurting or feel as if they're in danger. Helping them in that way isn't exactly what we've been trained for, but it's still our job. I'm sure wherever that baby's mother is now, she's feeling very frightened and alone. So I hope, if you do find her, that you won't file charges against her. I personally feel very sorry for her."

John cleared his throat. That had been quite a speech, and it had certainly put him in his place.

What was worse, he realized with dismay, was that she looked even more attractive when she was angry.

"Well, I do, too," he said, finally. "And of course I'll pursue all lines of investigation, including that this baby might have been kidnapped from her mother and then abandoned here in your library"—even though nothing like that had ever happened before in all of John's many years working in law enforcement—"But no matter how frightened or unable to care for her child she felt, the mother could easily have left her at the hospital or my office or even the fire station right down the street from here. All of those places are designated safe havens for anyone who feels overwhelmed with a newborn, no questions asked. The library isn't."

"But—"

"*But* she didn't do any of those things, did she? She—or someone—put that baby in an empty trash-bag box and abandoned her in a chilly library bathroom. That is a crime. And it's my job to investigate when a crime has been committed, and that's what I intend to do, if that's all right with you, Miss Montgomery."

The librarian's mouth pressed into a thin, straight line, as if she were willing herself not to say something she might regret. "Of course that's all right with me."

"Well," he said. "Great."

"Great," she said. "I hope you have better luck solving this mystery than you've had solving the mystery of the High School Thief."

He felt his jaw tighten. Of all the blows she could have delivered, this was the lowest, and he doubted she even knew it.

"Thanks," he said. "I'm sure we will, considering the high school thief hasn't left a single shred of DNA evidence."

"Great." She swept out from behind her desk with a queenliness that reminded John of her allegedly retired boss, Phyllis Robinette. She'd probably learned it from her. "Let me know if there's anything else I or the staff here can do to help. In the meantime, if you're through with your questions, I really need to get back to my patrons."

John knew he'd made a mess of things with the pretty librarian. He wasn't sure how, exactly, except by saying that he intended to do his job.

But since she was a woman, and he seemed always to make a mess of things with women, he wasn't surprised.

John had no idea what to do about the situation, so he simply unfolded himself from the tiny child's chair—too late, since Molly had already marched from her own chair to where her patrons were being questioned by his most competent deputy, Ryan Martinez.

Well, this wouldn't be the last time he'd see her, he supposed. He could come back and bring her an update on the case. No one could abandon a baby on an island as small as Little Bridge and get away with it. He'd be seeing Molly Montgomery again, and next time, he'd be more careful not to say the wrong thing.

Whatever that was.

CHAPTER THREE

Molly

News of the baby abandoned at the library spread across the island quicker than word of a tasty new taco truck. By the time Molly left work that day, everyone seemed to know about it, even the tourists staying at the bed-and-breakfast where she was living (and working part-time) until she could find an apartment that was semi-affordable.

"Is it true?" one of the guests asked from a chaise lounge as Molly passed the pool on her way to the kitchen, where she was headed to help Mrs. Larson assemble the hors d'oeuvres for happy hour. "Did the mother really leave the baby in a toilet?"

Molly nearly dropped the tote bag of groceries she was carrying from Frank's Food Emporium.

"No, that's not true," she said. "She was on a toilet in an empty box."

The tourist—Mrs. Filmore, a regular who'd been coming

to the inn the same week for years—gave her husband a triumphant look. "I told you! That's why they're calling him Baby Boy Sacks—as in garbage sacks. It was an empty box of trash bags."

Molly was appalled but bit back a retort. The guest was always right—even guests like Mrs. Filmore, who used the white washcloths in her room to wipe off her copious layers of makeup instead of the black washcloths and hypoallergenic makeup-removing towelettes that the Larsons provided for this purpose. Molly knew, because she found Mrs. Filmore's bright red lipstick and black mascara-stained washcloths in the laundry every morning. They reminded her of the scary clown from Stephen King's *It* (a problematic but still highly popular, if slightly dated, read. She had to remember to show it to Elijah. It might appeal to him, since it was both humorous and gory, but also featured young people finding their true calling through helping others).

"Moses," boomed Mr. Filmore, from the other end of the pool.

Molly had been heading back toward the kitchen, but now she paused. Mr. Filmore rarely spoke, perhaps because it was easier to allow his gossipy wife to do all the talking for him. So when he did open his mouth to say anything, it was usually worth listening to.

"I beg your pardon?" Molly said.

"Moses." Mr. Filmore brought his frozen drink to his lips—Molly couldn't tell what it was, exactly, but it had a festive umbrella and also a slice of lime clinging to the side, so possibly a margarita. "They oughta call the baby Moses, on account of him being found on the water."

"Oh, Mel." Mrs. Filmore playfully splashed a spray of pool water at him. "Didn't you hear? He was found on a toilet, not on the water."

"Don't toilets have water in 'em? Oughta call 'im Moses. Better'n Baby Boy Sacks. Sacks ain't even a proper name."

Mrs. Filmore shook her head, clearly disgusted by her husband's joke. But as Molly made her way back into the kitchen, where Joanne was busily assembling canapés, she wondered if Mr. Filmore's joke didn't have a ring of truth to it. Except, of course, the baby was a girl, not a boy.

"Oh, thank goodness you're here." Joanne was an elfin woman in a hot-pink beach cover-up and matching leggings who had spent enough time tanning in the sun to make her age indeterminable. She could be anywhere from forty to seventy, though her cigarette-roughened voice and leathery-looking chest suggested the latter. "Did you get them?"

"I did." Molly swung her grocery tote onto the counter where Joanne had already laid out several trays of tantalizing-looking cheeses and crudité. "But do you even need them? Surely what you have there is enough."

Joanne snorted. "Are you kidding me? When that group that was on the sunset sail comes in from being out on the water, they're going to be famished. Not to mention the Walters family. They went out on a deep-sea fishing charter."

Molly drew one of the cucumbers she'd bought for Mrs.

Larson from the tote. "But they all have dinner reservations. I know—I helped some of them make them last night."

"Of course, but we don't want to send them to dinner hangry. I like to keep them well-fed and happy so they'll behave themselves when they go out into town. That way I won't get any complaints from my fellow business owners that I haven't been taking care of my guests."

"That makes sense." Molly had been at the Lazy Parrot—whose owners were far from lazy—long enough to know how to pitch in when needed. She threw on an apron over her work clothes and began peeling one of the cucumbers—on which dabs of homemade fish dip would later be spread—as Joanne opened the oven to check on a tray of goat cheese tarts. "So I guess you've probably heard what happened at the library today."

Molly didn't really want to talk about it, but then again, she was dying to talk about it—especially with someone who might understand how disturbed the incident had left her. If she'd been back in Denver, she'd have processed the incident over drinks with her colleagues at her old job. They'd have gone to the Cruise Room in LoDo and gotten nicely toasted.

But she wasn't in Denver anymore.

And though both Henry and Phyllis Robinette (bless her!) had asked if she was all right, and invited her to go to Uva, the nearby wine bar they often frequented after work, Molly had said no, not only because she had to get back to the inn to help the Larsons, but also because she had a walk-through in the morning at the new library with both the architect and the donor who was making the new library possible, Mrs. Dorothy Tifton herself (as well as her miniature poodle, Daisy, who followed her owner everywhere). Molly wanted a drink, but she also wanted to stay in and prepare herself for this important meeting.

As if she'd known what Molly was thinking, Joanne whipped around, pulled a bottle of red from the wine fridge, and expertly cracked it open.

"Poor dear," she said, pouring two generous glasses before sliding one toward Molly. "I completely forgot. What a terrible thing. Here, drink up. Was he really found in a trash bag?"

Molly accepted the glass gratefully. "She. And it was a box. A trash-bag box. Where is everyone hearing that it was a trash bag?"

"Facebook community page," Joanne said, simply.

Of course. Molly nodded, then took a sip of wine before turning her attention back to her cucumbers. She knew all about this page. It was supposed to be private, run by the former mayor's wife and restricted to residents of Little Bridge only, but anyone could get on it. It tended, like most of social media, to be a little more gossipy than Molly thought healthy. This was why she both hated and loved it, though she'd managed to cut down the amount of time she spent visiting the page, just as she'd managed to cut down the amount of time she spent cyber-stalking her ex and his new fiancée.

Except that she hated to call it stalking. The people on those true crime shows she liked did actual stalking. All she had was a healthy curiosity about the motives behind her ex's very sudden engagement to this woman he'd met only two months ago, who probably had no idea what she was getting herself into.

"Well," Molly said, giving her cucumber skin a particularly vicious swipe, "you shouldn't believe everything you read."

"No." Joanne was enjoying her own deep swigs of wine. "Of course not. Ah! Now, that hits the spot. I knew that wine rep wouldn't do me wrong."

Molly nodded toward the bottle. "It's very good."

Joanne grinned. "That's why I save it for myself—and the staff, of course. I wouldn't waste it on guests, unless of course they asked for it, which none of them ever do. All they ever want is margaritas and rum and Cokes. Which, I don't blame 'em, being on vacation. Anyway, I heard you met the sheriff. What'd you think of him?"

"Excuse me?" The sudden change of subject had Molly blinking.

"Our new sheriff. What'd you think of him? Well, now that I think of it, I guess he's not that new. But he's very young, and a lot better than Sheriff Wagner, the last fella we had. He turned out to have a whole other secret family living up in Tallahassee."

"What?" This was so much like something that could have been on one of the crime shows she liked to watch that Molly accidentally dropped the scraper.

"Oh, yes. It turns out Wagner was siphoning department funds to support 'em. County asked John Hartwell to leave his fancy detective job up in Miami and run as sheriff just because everyone here had lost faith in the old sheriff's entire department. John grew up here. He's only been in the job a couple of years, but I have to say I think he's doing all right. That's why I was wondering what you thought of him when you met him today."

Molly couldn't help scowling at the memory of the too tall, too full-of-himself man she'd encountered. "Do you want my honest opinion?" she asked, as she ran the scraper under the faucet.

"Well, of course I do. I wouldn't've asked if I didn't, would I?"

Molly didn't hold back. With her mother's old friend, she didn't have to. "I don't think too much of him. He seems pretty arrogant."

"Really?" Joanne sounded surprised. "I've met him several times, and he's always seemed real nice."

Molly snorted. Although she'd been shy around the Larsons at first, as she didn't know them that well—Joanne had grown up living next door to Molly's mother, then moved away after college and had been out to Denver only a handful of times to visit since—in the few months she'd lived with them in Little Bridge, she'd quickly grown to think of them as family.

"Do you know he thinks that baby's mother, whoever she was, abandoned it there in that bathroom?"

Joanne took a sip of her wine before answering, her gaze

not meeting Molly's. "Well, he's probably right. I read that, before the safe haven law, there was something like ten thousand babies abandoned a year up in New York—"

"But that's New York! I'm sure no one in Little Bridge would do something like that."

Joanne quickly began stacking Molly's canapés onto the tray with the rest of them. "Oh, honey, I know you're new here and so you have kind of an idealized view of the place. That's normal. Everyone falls in love with Little Bridge when they first get here. But let me tell you, crime happens here same as it does every place else. They're just a bit—*odder* kinds of crimes. You've heard about this thief we've got over by the old high school—now the new library—who just waltzes into people's houses and helps himself to whatever he likes? Which, shame on us, we've all got to learn to lock our doors. This isn't Mayberry. And of course we're fortunate that he's never hurt anyone—no one's ever even seen him, since he only seems to strike in the middle of the night while everyone is asleep. But what about our own former sheriff having a whole second family, and trying to pay for it out of our tax dollars!"

"But that's different," Molly said. "There are always going to be thieves, and men—and women—in power who try to take advantage of the system. All I'm saying is that it's hard to believe anyone would deliberately endanger a child if there wasn't some mitigating reason—"

"Listen to you." Joanne chuckled as she lifted the tray of canapés. "Mitigating reasons. You really are Patty's daughter, all right. She was always spouting off big words like that when we were kids. I'm real glad to have you here, Molly. It's like having Patty living next door again. I feel about fifty years younger. Now be a doll and grab those cocktail napkins over there, and let's go get these people's drink orders."

"Sure, Jo." Molly obediently seized a pile of the Lazy Parrot's signature cocktail napkins, each depicting a brightly colored parrot snoozing on a perch in a palm tree, large letter *Z*s coming out of its beak.

"And don't you worry about that baby" were Joanne's parting words to her as she backed her way through the swinging door from the kitchen out toward the pool. "If anyone can find the mama, it's John Hartwell."

Molly was glad her mother's friend couldn't see her grimace as she followed, muttering, "That's what I'm worried about."

CHAPTER FOUR

John

The last thing John felt prepared to deal with when he got home that night was mother-daughter drama. But that's exactly what he encountered, even though his daughter's mother lived one hundred and fifty miles away.

"Hi, Dad." Katie was waiting for him in the dining room. This was a bad sign. If she was not in her room, on her phone, texting with her cousin Nevaeh, it meant something was wrong.

John, being a trained investigator and also a father, could tell that even more was wrong than usual, because Katie had cooked. Katie did not enjoy cooking and usually ate at Nevaeh's house or waited for him to bring home takeout.

But tonight, she obviously wanted something from him, since she'd not only set the dining room table using all of their best china—his ex, Christina, guilt-stricken over leaving him with primary custody, had also left him with all of their wedding presents and all of the furniture they'd collected during their thirteen years of marriage—but also thrown something into the oven that smelled suspiciously like Katie's go-to emergency healthy-dinner recipe, chicken marinated in salad dressing.

John realized it was going to be a long night and threw off his hat and tie, undid his belt, and went to the refrigerator for a beer.

"What's up, Katie?"

"Dad." Katie followed him into the kitchen. "I know you've had a busy day. I heard about the baby. Is he okay?"

"She. And the baby's fine."

John opened the oven door and glanced inside. Yep. There it was. Assorted chicken parts floating in store-bought low-calorie Italian salad dressing. Not that it wouldn't be tasty, even if it was fairly healthy. It's just that she only made it when—

"Well, that's good. I heard people are calling her Baby Garbage Sacks—"

"What?" John cracked open his beer with more force than he'd meant to, startled by her words.

"Baby Garbage Sacks," Katie said. "On account of her being found in the library in a garbage bag?"

"Of all the—" Now John was annoyed. "Where did you hear that?"

Katie shrugged her thin shoulders. "It's all over Facebook."

"Well, please inform your Facebook followers or friends or whatever they are that the baby was not found in a garbage sack but in a box, and—oh, hell." He took a swig from his beer. "I'll have Marguerite do it in the morning."

In addition to being an excellent sergeant, Marguerite Ruiz also ran the sheriff's web page, on which John kept the public up to date on important information such as who had been arrested for what lately. The discovery of this baby at the library would fall into that category. He couldn't have misinformation floating around, especially given the fact that, upon pulling into his office earlier, he'd found his desk almost literally covered in boxes of diapers, pacifiers, and baby clothes and toys. And not just his desk, either, but the desks of his deputies, all of whom seemed to think the donations were a hilarious joke.

But it wasn't a joke. The good people of Little Bridge—and even neighboring islands—were donating this stuff for the infant he now knew they referred to as Baby Garbage Sacks, or some such nonsense. They were donating the things out of the kindness of their hearts, of course, but it wasn't necessary. The infant was in perfectly good hands at the NICU, and as soon as she was deemed healthy enough—which the doctors had assured him would be soon—she'd be transferred into foster care, probably with the Russells, who were damned fine people. There was no need for all this donated formula and Tickle Me Elmos. It certainly didn't look professional around the office, especially since his deputies kept tickling them and setting them off for laughs.

"Well, that's good, Dad," Katie said. She was hovering

around him as he pulled off his boots. "That's really great to hear. I'll be sure to let everyone know. . . . So, Dad, there's this dance at school—"

"What's his name?" John realized he was going to need a second beer. He tried to stick with only one per day on school nights, but if there was going to be a discussion about a boy taking his daughter to a dance, he might need two to get through it, depending on who the boy was.

"It's not that kind of dance, Dad," Katie said with a laugh. "It's a dance performance. I'm giving it, with the Snappettes."

John relaxed. "Oh, your dance troupe. Oh, that's fine, Katie, fine. Congratulations. When is it? I'll make sure I'm there."

With his new position as county sheriff had come a lot of responsibilities John hadn't had as a detective. His social calendar was full, although not in the way he would have liked. He was constantly being called upon to attend fundraisers and political events that required him to wear his dress uniform, often outdoors in the blazing heat. It was a wonder to him that he had time to solve any crime, let alone ones as bewildering—and complicated—as the High School Thief and the Garbage Bag Baby.

His daughter's dance recital would be a welcome relief—he'd be sure to have Marguerite mark it down on the schedule as a priority. Katie really was a talented dancer, and the school auditorium was fortunately air-conditioned.

"Dad, you're not listening. It's a special dance." Katie sank into one of the dining room chairs beside him. Christina had insisted on ultrasuede because it'd been both stylish at the time and wouldn't show dirt with the baby—Katie. Christina had had all the chairs stain guarded. They looked as new as the day they'd arrived, much like Katie's eyes, as blue as his own, but of course years younger and filled with an innocence he'd lost long ago looking at burned-up corpses in dumpsters in Miami back when he'd worked homicide there. "It's a mother-daughter dance."

He nearly choked on his beer. "A what now?"

"A mother-daughter dance. Every year all of the Snappettes from previous classes get together and perform onstage with the current Snappettes. They do a really old number from like, the nineties, and then a number that the current class of Snappettes is working on. It's one of the biggest fundraisers of the year."

John shook his head in bewilderment. "Fund-raiser for what?"

"For the Snappettes, of course. You know we've been invited to perform at the Macy's Thanksgiving Day Parade next year. It's a huge honor, but we need to provide for airfare and housing, plus costumes, for thirty girls and eight chaperones. That's a lot of money."

John nodded as if he understood what she was talking about. It seemed like he was always doing this. Ever since his pretty, vivacious daughter had auditioned for and gotten into the high school's all-female dance troupe, she'd been happier than he could ever remember her being. This was good, since she'd been a little down, first over the divorce, then the move to Little Bridge, and then finally her best friend's acquisition of a boyfriend, Marquis Fairweather, a fine young man of whom John approved because he did well in school, played sports, and kept himself out of trouble.

Even though the Snappettes' name was absurd (literally, they were named after the fish most commonly found in the local waters, the red and yellowtail snapper) and seemed to rehearse an ungodly number of hours, Katie loved the camaraderie and creative outlet of her school dance troupe.

"Dance," she'd informed her father dreamily one day after another grueling four-hour rehearsal, "is my life, Dad."

So what was one more performance now?

"Well, honey," he said, taking another swig of his beer. "Sounds good to me. I will definitely be there. How long till we eat? That chicken smells good."

"No, Dad," Katie said. She was scowling. "I don't think you heard what I said. It's a *mother-daughter* dance."

He was still confused. "Well, no, I heard you. And you can invite your mother down for it. I'm sure if you give her the date in enough time, she'll be able to—"

"Dad, you don't understand." Katie's voice had gone hard as flint. "The mothers and the daughters perform in the dance *together*. Onstage. Rehearsals start now. And continue for the next twelve weeks. The performance is in June."

Now John realized what the problem was. And why he probably was going to need a second beer after all.

"Well, honey," he said, carefully. "I don't think that sounds real fair to the girls like you whose mothers don't live on the island. Or what about girls whose mothers are too busy with their jobs to spend twelve weeks rehearsing for a dance?"

He knew for a fact that several of the girls' mothers on Katie's dance team fell into this category. Like Molly Montgomery, for instance. Not that she had any children—he knew this, because, God help him, he'd found a little time to google her and discovered her social media page (she had only one). He'd learned from it that she was completely devoted to her job as a children's librarian. Or at least that's what he assumed since she only posted pictures of books and links related to books, libraries, and reading. There were no photos of herself—no selfies that some women seemed to love so much—and not a single photo of whoever had given her the ring that was now gone from her left hand.

This, he felt, was a good sign. Of what, he wasn't sure.

"And how about the girls who don't have mothers?" he asked. "Or who have two dads? Or whose mothers can't dance? What if there's a girl who has a mother like me, who has two left feet?" He did a fumbling step-ball-change, attempting to lighten the mood. "Are they gonna make those moms perform anyway?"

Katie did not crack a smile. "Of course they aren't. People like Leila's mom, who runs her own restaurant, or Sharmaine's mom, who's a surgeon, or Kayla's mom, who just had a baby—obviously no one expects their moms to participate. We have some of the old Snappettes alumni coming back to take their places. It's fine. We'll be fine. Except—"

He saw those blue eyes he loved so much fill with tears. It was exactly as he'd feared. Something was wrong.

"Except what, sweetheart?" He reached out to brush back a soft lock of her dark hair as she bent her head.

"Except I asked Mom if she would dance with us, and she said no. She'd just make a donation."

He'd known this was coming, of course. Of course she'd already asked Christina, and of course Christina had said no. What else could Christina say? She had a thriving design business back on the mainland. It took three hours—and that was in good traffic—to drive to Little Bridge, and another three hours to get back. She couldn't spend that much time driving back and forth for twelve weeks of rehearsals, several times a week.

And for what? A fundraiser? It was simpler to send a check. Which is what practical, level-headed Christina had very sensibly offered to do instead—especially considering how much they'd already paid for all of Katie's dance gear and choreography fees, which was nearing a thousand dollars for the year so far.

"But that isn't the point," Katie explained to John, who'd wrapped his arms around his daughter, pulling her in for a big bear hug as she sobbed. "It isn't about the m-money!"

"I know," he said into her hair as he patted and rocked her. "I know. But we've talked about this before. You're mother just isn't—"

"—that maternal." Katie pushed away from him and wiped her eyes. "I know. She's never been like other moms. She loves me, but in her own way."

John looked down at his daughter's wounded face and wished there was something he could say that would make the hurt go away, but he knew that there wasn't. Lord knows he'd spent enough time in marriage counseling with Christina to learn that she'd given all she could to the two of them, and that the offer to run for sheriff of Little Bridge had been the best thing ever to happen, as it had given them both the chance to make a clean break—from one another.

"But," Katie said, pulling her phone from her back pocket—it was never far from her—and studying her reflection in it to see how much damage the tears had done to her eyeliner, "Mom not wanting to be in it isn't a total loss. It kind of gave me an idea."

"Oh?" John examined his beer bottle. If he was careful, there was enough left in it to get him through dinner. "What's that?"

"Well, I think the whole mother-daughter dance thing is kind of sexist, anyway. I mean, it's so *done*, you know?"

"Yeah, I agree. What do they think, women don't have jobs?" His thoughts wandered, once again, to the pretty librarian he'd met earlier in the day. What would Molly Montgomery have to say about the idea of a mother-daughter dance? Plenty, he imagined. She certainly had plenty to say about every other subject, especially his job and how he performed it, which according to her was not very well.

The bell on the timer chimed in the kitchen, letting them know that the chicken was ready. Katie sprang to her feet to pull it from the oven, suddenly joyous again. John occasionally envied teenagers and their ability to swing from the pits of sorrow to the heights of happiness in mere seconds.

"Well, I started thinking: Why does it have to be a mother-daughter dance, anyway?" Katie asked from the kitchen. "Just because traditionally the Snappettes have always been female. But why can't there be a male Snappette? There's no rule that says there can't be."

John nodded at this, absently peeling away the label on his beer bottle. "Did you know that President George W. Bush was a cheerleader?" he asked. "And so was Eisenhower. And Samuel L. Jackson." He wondered if Molly Montgomery knew this. Probably she did, because she was a librarian. He wondered why he cared so much what Molly knew. He doubted she'd given him a second thought, except to curse him, maybe. She had definitely not looked up his social media. Not that he had any, except the departmental sheriff's account that Marguerite ran. "Many great men in our history have been male cheerleaders."

"I keep telling you, the Snappettes are dancers, not cheerleaders, Daddy." Katie came out of the kitchen with a large platter of delicious-smelling chicken in her oven-mitted hands. "So my idea is that, in cases where a mom can't, for whatever reason, be in the mother-daughter dance, then dads should be allowed to fill their place."

John eyed the gently steaming pile of chicken. Legs and thighs were his favorite, and there were plenty of these, each browned to perfection and oozing their juices on the platter before him.

"That's a great idea, honey," he said, inhaling the savory scent of the chicken. "You should totally do it. Now, why don't you sit down and eat with me before this chicken gets cold?"

"Really, Daddy?" Katie slid into her favorite chair, beaming. "You mean it?"

"Of course I mean it. You make the best chicken on this island."

"No, I mean, you'll be in the Snappettes mother-daughter dance in Mom's place? You know everyone would love it—you being the sheriff and all—and it would be a great thing, proving how sexist the whole thing is. And it would raise a ton of money—"

John spat out the swig of beer he'd taken, which was unfortunate, since it was the last of the beer from the bottle.

"Daddy?" Katie asked. "Is everything all right?"

"Everything's fine," he said, in a tone he hoped sounded convincing.

"So does that mean you'll do it?"

He gave her a wan smile as he rose from his chair. "Of course I'll do it. Anything for you, honey."

"Then where are you going?"

"Just to the fridge."

Molly Montgomery was going to see him onstage with the Snappettes. He might as well have another beer.

CHAPTER FIVE

Molly

If Molly felt like the morning after she'd found an abandoned baby in one of the old library's public bathrooms started out a little too well, it was because . . . well, it did.

Molly had stayed up even later than usual the night before—without having had to, as there were no late check-ins expected at the Lazy Parrot—and logged on to the Little Bridge Island Facebook community page, where she carefully corrected all the miscommunications about the baby who had been found.

As the person who'd discovered the baby, Molly felt she was the one most qualified to attest not only to the infant's correct sex, but also to the exact manner in which she had been found.

So she posted that it was most definitely a little girl, not a boy, who'd been found on the toilet—in a box, not a bag—and that she was a lovely little thing who deserved to be kept in everyone's thoughts, and *not* referred to as a trash-bag baby.

Furthermore, Molly wrote, rising to flights of fancy that might not have occurred to her had she not finished off the better part of the bottle of wine Joanne had opened, *it struck me as if this beautiful baby girl were rising from the waters of Little Bridge much in the way that the Roman goddess of love, Aphrodite, rose from the waves of the sea. Thus I believe that we should call this sweet little baby Aphrodite, because not only did she rise from the sea, but as residents of this island paradise, don't we all wish her nothing but love? Yours very sincerely, Molly Montgomery, Children's Library Specialist*

Sitting back after posting this, Molly watched in satisfaction as the *likes* began to pour in, slowly at first, then more and more quickly.

Perfect. Her job was done. The baby's new name—and a fine one it was; she'd have to thank Mr. Filmore later for the inspiration—was fixed. Aphrodite it would be from now on. A little highfalutin for a tiny baby, but much better than Trash Bag!

As she crawled wearily into her huge four-poster bed—all the beds at the Lazy Parrot were four-posters, just as all the rooms came with enormous Jacuzzi tubs and their own coffee makers and mini fridges—she hoped she hadn't done anything that might jeopardize the sheriff's case. He hadn't explicitly told her *not* to give out the details about how she'd found the baby (in a trash-bag box, etc.).

Then again, he clearly needed her help. He couldn't even crack the case of the High School Thief, which to her looked as if it might be one of the simplest crimes in the world to solve. Was Molly seriously supposed to believe that out of the six—or was it seven?—burglaries so far, there hadn't been a single image of the thief captured on home-security footage? Surely at least *one* of the homes possessed a video doorbell camera.

And what about fingerprints? Or footprints? Had no one thought of looking for these? Or for stray hairs (that did not, of course, belong to any of the homeowners or their friends) to run through the national criminal DNA database?

Oh, well, she thought tiredly, turning out her light and snuggling down with Fluffy, the large ginger cat that lived at the Larsons' hotel, yet did not belong to them. He had just shown up one day, begging for food, and so they'd begun feeding him, and now he slept every night with whichever of the hotel occupants allowed him inside their room first, which more often than not was Molly.

Everything would be all right if I were in charge, Molly thought to herself. *One day the sheriff will realize this and thank me.*

For the first time in as long as she could remember, she didn't check Ashley's Instagram, or switch on the television to watch her true crime shows, but instead fell fast asleep, Fluffy curled into a tight, contented ball beside her.

The next morning, it appeared as if she might have been

correct: everything seemed as if it were going to be all right. She was able to grab a quick breakfast from the buffet—without running into the Filmores, who'd slept in—before rushing off to the walk-through of the new library with its donor, Mrs. Tifton.

To Molly, Mrs. Tifton consulting her on nearly every decision having to do with the new library's children's wing was like a dream come true. According to Phyllis, Mrs. Tifton had always been a voracious reader, and had frequently mentioned to anyone who'd listen that she found Little Bridge's small public library lacking in adequate shelving space for romance, Mrs. Tifton's favorite choice of reading material.

So when Mrs. Tifton's husband of thirty-nine years passed away from a heart attack and turned out to have left her more than one hundred million dollars in cash, annuities, life insurance, and real estate holdings—a fortune no one in Little Bridge, least of all his wife, ever suspected he possessed—no one was too surprised when she donated a large portion of her sudden fortune to the construction of a new library.

The library board agreed to purchase the building—a beautiful though rundown example of classic revival architecture—which had once been the Little Bridge High School. A new, modern high school had been built years earlier after the discovery of asbestos in the halls of the old one, which had sat empty and decaying for more than fifty years until Mrs. Tifton and her fortune came along.

The new Norman J. Tifton Public Library, though not

quite finished, had already been restored to its former nineteenth-century glory, but with all the modern amenities: multiple media/movie rooms; plenty of free parking; *two* auditoriums; a children's *and* teens' wing; cheerfully lit reading rooms with large, comfortable chairs; a café; meeting rooms; study carrels; digital facilities; and of course enough shelving for all manner of genre fiction.

Sometimes Molly couldn't believe her good luck—especially now, going on a walk-through of the new building with Mrs. Tifton. They were accompanied by Richard Chang, the building's architect; the district's councilwoman, Janet Rivera; Meschelle Davies, a reporter from Little Bridge's local newspaper, *The Gazette*; and of course Mrs. Tifton's toy poodle, Daisy.

But Molly still felt special. It seemed too good to be true.

Which meant, of course, that it was.

It wasn't until they reached the second floor of the twelve-thousand-square-foot building that Molly realized something was wrong.

"What's that smell?" Janet asked.

"Oh, that," Mrs. Tifton said, waving a small hand dismissively. "I know, isn't it awful? All that drying paint."

"That isn't paint," Molly said. She loved eating and knew her food smells. "It's pizza."

"That's impossible." Richard Chang was looking down at his phone. Richard never went anywhere without his overly large phone in his hand and his overly small glasses on his face. "Nobody's been here since last week. All the work is done. We're just waiting on the final inspections and certificates."

Meschelle, the reporter, dutifully jotted this down.

"But." Molly realized the smell was coming from the new children's media room, the double doors to which were both closed. "It really smells like pizza."

"Oh, well," Mrs. Tifton said, brightly. "Maybe the crew had pizza last week."

"And didn't properly dispose of the leftovers?" Richard scowled behind his artistically framed eyeglasses. "That's not like them. They're normally very—"

He broke off as Molly pushed open the doors to the media room.

As soon as she stepped inside, she saw that she'd made a massive mistake. She ought never to have gone in there—at least, not while being followed by the donor and a reporter from the local paper. Quickly, she moved to shut the doors behind her, but it was too late. Daisy, Mrs. Tifton's little dog, darted between Molly's legs, making an eager beeline for the source of the odor.

"Daisy, no!"

There was nothing else Molly could do. She slammed the doors closed, shutting Daisy up inside the media room with all the boxes of leftover pizza someone—or more likely, quite a lot of someones—had left behind, then leaned against them, blocking Mrs. Tifton's—and Meschelle's—view into the room through the glass panes.

"Let's go back downstairs," she said, plastering a fake smile on her face. "I just remembered I forgot my bag."

"What?" Mrs. Tifton smiled up at her. The widow was quite small in stature but made up for it by being pleasantly curved, often reminding Molly of a bouncing ball because of her seemingly boundless energy. "No, you didn't, silly girl, it's on your shoulder. What's in there that you don't want us to see?"

"N-nothing," Molly said, quickly. "I just—I—"

Molly didn't normally stammer, but what was behind the media room doors wasn't something that a sweet woman like Mrs. Tifton—let alone a reporter, who would doubtlessly blast it all over the front page—ought to see. Molly wished she hadn't seen it herself.

Fortunately, Janet Rivera had also seen what Molly had seen, and hurried to help.

"Mrs. Tifton, I don't think the paint in that room is dry," Janet said. "Why don't we let Richard show us the meditation garden downstairs instead? We can check to see if they got that powderpuff tree you asked for."

"Oh, the powderpuff!" Mrs. Tifton's voice rose in delight as the councilwoman took her by the arm and steered her back toward the stairs. "I do hope they found a pink one. Let's go a take a look." She glanced back at Molly. "You'll follow along, won't you? And bring that naughty little dog of mine?"

"Of course, Mrs. T," Molly said. "I'll bring Daisy right down to you."

Mrs. Tifton nodded, smiling. "Thank you." As she followed an ashen-faced Richard to the stairs—because he, too, had seen what Molly and Janet had seen—Molly could hear the older woman murmuring, "I don't know what's gotten into that silly dog."

Molly knew exactly what had gotten into the dog. She also knew exactly who she was going to have to call about it.

And she wasn't looking forward to it.

CHAPTER SIX

John

John stood in the doorway taking in the wreck of what was apparently going to have been some kind of children's room in the new library.

The place was now being used as a teenagers' party den.

John knew it was teenagers because there were empty pizza boxes and mini bottles of cinnamon-flavored whiskey strewn across the room, in addition to dirty sleeping bags, piles of clothing, and—oddly enough—numerous books from the Little Bridge Public Library.

It was the empty bottles of syrupy-sweet flavored whisky—the preferred alcoholic beverage, John knew, of the young and inexperienced drinker—that gave away the age of the trespassers, but the phone chargers plugged into the wall outlets and the fact that most of the books appeared to be from the library's young adult section helped. John recognized them as some of the favorites from his youth—*Hatchet* by Gary Paulsen, *Into the Wild* by Jon Krakauer, and even Sternberg's *Wilderness Survival Handbook* (updated edition).

It was odd that the kids had checked out—or, more likely, stolen—so many books on wilderness survival, then chosen to camp out inside an unoccupied building that had air-conditioning, electricity, and working restrooms.

But that wasn't what bothered him the most. What really bothered him was the graffiti: red, black, and purple slashes across the once virginal white walls. This wasn't the ordinary, occasionally even beautiful, graffiti he found over by the new high school or under the bridges and viaducts—kids' names, lovers' initials entwined in hearts, goofy doodles, or other attempts at immortality by aspiring artists.

This was something different, something ugly, something someone—or several someones—had sprayed simply to desecrate and destroy.

It was the graffiti that gave it away and caused his heart to sink.

Sunshine Kids. The damned Sunshine Kids were back.

But the graffiti wasn't even the worst of it. The worst was the girl the kids had left behind, curled in a sleeping bag on the floor, for Molly Montgomery to find along with the rest of their mess.

"At first I thought she was dead," Molly explained to him when he returned to the neighboring room in which she'd been asked to wait until she could be questioned.

By him, of course. He wasn't going to allow any of the

nitwits who worked for him—except for Martinez, who was shaping up to be more than competent and would be due for a promotion to corporal soon, and Marguerite, who was excellent—anywhere near her.

"I see." John was careful not to look her in the eye. He didn't want her to see the rage he was having such a difficult time suppressing. Damned kids. "Well, I can't blame you. She looked awful rough."

"But Mrs. Tifton's dog kept licking her face," Molly went on. "And she kept pushing the dog away. So I knew she was alive."

John grunted. He didn't trust himself to say anything more. He couldn't believe that this had happened—*again*—in his own town, right under his very nose, and he'd been completely unaware of it. He must have driven by this building a hundred times in the past week, canvasing the neighborhood for the knucklehead who'd committed all those burglaries, and he hadn't noticed a thing. The kids had to have been keeping the lights on at night in order to have their pizza-and-cinnamon-flavored-whiskey-fueled graffiti parties.

How could he—or anyone—not have noticed?

"That's when I saw the blood," Molly went on.

The blood. There was blood, all right. Not a lot. Not like the crime scenes he used to see almost nightly in Miami.

But enough to have seeped through the sleeping bag in which the girl had been curled, and into the new gray industrial carpeting.

The stain would probably come out.

But John's anger over what those self-entitled little ass clowns had done wouldn't as easily be washed away.

"So I just sat by her until the EMTs got here, holding her hand, telling her everything was going to be okay . . . except, of course, I wasn't sure everything was going to be okay."

This was too much. He knew he was supposed to stay impartial. He knew he was supposed to stay detached. He wasn't supposed to refer to packs of privileged teenage vandals as "ass clowns," or to assure any citizen with whom he worked of any kind of outcome regarding a case, because no officer of the law could ever be sure what was going to happen.

But the Sunshine Kids were different. Molly Montgomery was different.

"Everything's going to be okay," he heard himself say, meeting Molly's gaze for the first time.

This was a mistake. Her dark eyes were as large as ever, and they met his with what felt, to him, like a shock from one of the Tasers he and his deputies carried.

Except that the shock from Molly Montgomery's eyes felt much, much more startling.

"How do you know that?" she asked.

"Because," he said, "Marina—that's one of the EMTs—said the girl's vitals were good. She's got a little bit of a fever, but that's only to be expected after—" He caught himself and went mum.

But it was too late.

"After giving birth?" She reached out and grasped his arm, her fingers even more of a shock than her gaze, her skin cool on his. He suddenly felt as if he'd burst into flame. But that was ridiculous, of course. "So you think it might be her—the baby's mother? She *has* to be, right? When the EMTs got here, I heard one of them say she wasn't shot or stabbed. All that blood *has* to be from giving birth."

He'd put his foot in it now. He'd been so careful, too, separating her from the crime scene as soon as he'd arrived. Molly was the one who'd been with the girl the whole time. The feverish teenager had been barely conscious, not saying much, asking only for water—which Molly had just happened to have with her, in a rose-gold reusable bottle, of course, because, like his daughter, the librarian was environmentally conscious and would probably never dream of using a disposable plastic container or single-use straw.

But no. John wasn't going to let what happened yesterday happen again. He wasn't going to allow the pretty librarian to suck him into another one of her conversations where she played amateur sleuth. No way. No matter how nice she looked in today's outfit, which happened to be a tight skirt paired with a white blouse under a cardigan.

A cardigan, on a tropical island!

No. He was a professional lawman. He would not stand for it. He was going to solve his own crimes. He'd already solved this one. He knew who was behind this gross atrocity, and he was going to make sure they were punished to the fullest extent of the law.

And quite possibly tased, if the opportunity arose.

"Well, I guess we'll just have to wait until she's in good enough shape for us to ask."

There. That sounded very professional. Exactly what a sheriff would say to someone in whom he had absolutely no romantic or sexual interest whatsoever.

"She's just so young, though." Molly had stopped touching him and was hugging herself instead. He guessed he understood what the cardigan was for. It was quite chilly inside the building, what with the air-conditioning. No wonder those ass clowns liked it there so much. "She can't be more than seventeen or eighteen. Surely, if she's the mother, you wouldn't press charges against her for what happened to the baby. She can't have been the one who left it at my library. I doubt she'd have had the strength to walk to the window, let alone two blocks away. Someone else must have done it. Whoever did *that*"—she nodded her head toward the wreck in the room next door—"probably."

He wasn't going to admit it—at least, not to her—but it was looking more and more as if she was right.

"Well," he said. "We'll just have to see." He began walking toward the door, indicating that the interview was over. He was relieved when she followed. At least he was going to get out of this without having made too big a fool of himself. "In the meantime, I'd appreciate it if you'd keep all this to yourself."

Molly gave him a look that he recognized. It was the same look his daughter gave him whenever he said something about a popular celebrity that was wrong—crushing disappointment.

"Of course! The privacy of my patrons is one of my highest priorities. And even though these people are not exactly my patrons—I'm fairly certain they stole all of those books—they were still in my library, so it's not in my best interest to go blabbing to the press about them."

John nodded, satisfied by this response—even though it seemed a little defensive—and opened the door just as members of his tech department were trudging down the hallway.

Molly saw them, too, and froze in her tracks.

"What are they doing?"

"That's a crime scene." He nodded toward the other room. "Trespassing and vandalism, at least." Who knew what other charges he'd come up with after the girl was well enough to start talking? If he had his way, he'd track down her friends, lock them up, and then throw away the key. Although he was sure their rich mommies and daddies up North would hire them expensive lawyers, and he'd never get the chance. "We've got to record and save the evidence."

"Am I going to get my books back?"

"Eventually, after they've been processed."

"Does 'processed' mean dusting them for fingerprints?" She sounded excited. She was craning her neck to look back at his techs, even as he was steering her toward the stairs.

"Uh . . . maybe."

That brought her head sharply back around. "What do

you mean, 'maybe'? Those books were stolen. And whoever stole them is probably the person who left Baby Aphrodite in my library. You should see if any of those prints match the ones left on that box we found her in."

That halted him in his tracks. "Baby Aphrodite?"

"Yes, didn't I tell you? I renamed the baby Aphrodite last night on Facebook. I had to. Do you know that people were calling her Baby Garbage Sacks?"

"Yes, well, I was made aware of that—"

Her hands went to her hips. "Then why didn't you do anything about it? It's unconscionable to call an innocent baby Garbage Sacks! And you're in the perfect position of authority to put a stop to such nonsense."

"Well," he said, taken aback. "It's not really the sheriff's job to—"

"Set an example for the people of your town? I think it is. Especially when they're doing things like that." She waved a hand in the direction of the vandalized media room. "That is simply amoral."

"Hey, now hold on a second." *Unconscionable? Amoral?* He wasn't going to let her stand there and bark SAT words at him like he was one of her patrons. "This wasn't done by locals."

Her dark eyes widened. "How do you know?"

"Because I don't recognize that graffiti. And I don't recognize that girl. So most likely what we've got here is nothing but a bunch of Sunshine Kids—"

"Sunshine kids? What are sunshine kids?"

Damn. So much for getting out of this without doing anything foolish.

"Never mind. Thanks for all your help. If we have any further questions, someone will be in touch. Let me walk you out."

He held out his hand to escort her down the stairs.

This was yet another mistake. She glanced at his hand, then at the stairs. She was wearing heels, but they were of a sensible height (of course). She didn't need his help and was miffed not only at the offer, but at his not sharing more information about the crime.

"Thanks, but I can see myself out," she said, before beginning to descend the steps on her own. "I'll let you know if I run across any more crimes I can help you solve."

Then she was gone.

Great. Just great. He'd blown it again. Of course.

CHAPTER SEVEN

Molly

Molly sat at her desk going over what she already knew.

Number one: No copies of *Into the Wild* were listed as checked out. And yet one was clearly missing. Same with *Hatchet* (only an audio copy was checked out) and Sternberg's *Wilderness Survival Handbook* (2016 edition).

Number two: There was no reference to anything called the "Sunshine Kids" on the Internet that made sense in the context that the sheriff had used it.

Oh, there were plenty of cancer societies for children called Sunshine Kids. There were church groups, choirs, and dance troupes with the name.

But she highly doubted any church groups, kids with cancer, choirs, or dance troupes had broken into the new library and had a beer-and-cinnamon-whiskey-fueled pizza party.

So who exactly were these Sunshine Kids, and why did the sheriff hate them so much?

Because he did hate them. She could see the hatred for them burning in his disturbingly blue eyes.

Really, she ought to have been working—there were several large piles of books on the trolley by her desk that needed reshelving.

But she was having trouble concentrating on work when there was such a big, juicy mystery to solve.

That's what she told herself, anyway: that it was the mystery of the baby she'd found, and her mother—because that poor girl she'd found in the new library *had* to be Baby Aphrodite's mother—that was distracting her, and not the tall, blue-eyed sheriff, and the extremely frustrating way he had of not meeting her gaze . . . and then suddenly looking her *straight* in the eye, and making her feel as if he could see directly into her soul and knew every single one of her secrets.

Except that Molly didn't have any secrets! Finding Baby Aphrodite had been the most interesting thing that had ever happened to her. She'd never broken the law in her life, with the exception of having smoked a little weed in college. But everyone did that—and marijuana was legal in Colorado, as well as plenty of other places now.

Maybe the sheriff's ability to make her feel this way was because he was a cop. Cops were supposed to be good at looking at you and making you blurt out your guilt.

But Molly had nothing to feel guilty about—except possibly how much time she spent on Facebook and Instagram spying on her ex and his new bride-to-be. But she'd really gotten much better at that lately. Now she only went on social media when she needed to. In fact, she decided that the best use of her time would be to go on Facebook right now and look for references to the Sunshine Kids.

But she could find none, save for a link on Meschelle Davies's page that led to a story from an online newspaper that was hidden behind a paywall. Molly would gladly have paid to see what it said, but the paper was now defunct, and none of the links worked.

Molly quickly realized she had no choice but to email Meschelle at *The Gazette* and ask her for the information.

She was surprised when her phone buzzed a few seconds later. It was a number she didn't recognize.

"I'll tell you what you want to know," Meschelle said when Molly picked up, "if you'll give me an exclusive interview about what happened at the new library this morning."

Molly smiled. She admired Meschelle's go-getter spirit, even if she didn't always approve of the mainstream media. It sensationalized violence and barraged children with hypersexualized images of young women (and men, too) just when they were beginning to develop and understand themselves as sexual beings.

"You know I can't do that," Molly said. "The sheriff asked me not to."

"Well, then, I guess you're never going to find out what you want to know."

"How about this," Molly said, glancing at her watch. "I'll take you to lunch anywhere you want to go, and give you an exclusive interview about finding Baby Aphrodite, in exchange for you telling me what I want to know."

"Hmmm." Meschelle seemed to consider this. "People do love an abandoned-baby story, so long as the kid's okay. Lunch today?"

"Today."

"Anywhere I want to go?"

"Anywhere you want to go."

"You got a deal. Meet me at Cracked in half an hour."

Molly swallowed. Cracked was one of the trendiest—and most expensive—restaurants on the island. It featured oysters and stone crab claws (when in season); thus the high prices.

"See you there," Molly said, and hung up.

It didn't take her long to wrangle coverage for her desk. Phyllis was at yoga—she never missed a Thursday—but Henry promised to watch over the children's section so long as Molly was back before two thirty, when school let out and the troublemakers—meaning Elijah Trujos—began showing up.

One of the many reasons Molly loved Little Bridge was that everything (except the airport) was within walking distance, and so she'd been able to sell her car. She biked or walked everywhere, and was looking forward to the day when this would result in a noticeable change to her fitness. So far, it hadn't, possibly because she'd gone from living at a mile above sea level to three feet above it, so she was actually exerting herself less on Little Bridge, despite exercising more. She still arrived at Cracked breathless and sweaty, most likely because of her stupid cardigan.

"Hi," she said, sliding into the posh leather booth in which Meschelle was already seated. "Sorry I'm late."

"No worries." Meschelle slid a wineglass filled with a golden beverage, its sides frosted with condensation, toward her. "I went ahead and ordered a bottle of sauvignon blanc. I assumed when you let me pick the restaurant that meant I also could order anything I wanted."

"Fine." Molly took a thirsty gulp. "Excellent choice."

"Yeah, I know my way around a wine menu." Meschelle played with the screen on her phone. "I already ordered a few appetizers for us as well. Is it okay if I record this?"

"Sure," Molly said, widening her eyes as a server approached with an amply filled basket of flatbreads. "So who or what are the Sunshine Kids?"

"Whoa, slow down, sister. Me first. Why do you want to know so badly? Does it have anything to do with what happened today at the new library?"

Molly broke off a piece of one of the flatbreads. It was still warm from the oven and lightly covered in cheese and slivers of olive. *Hmmmm.* "I already said I can't talk about what happened today. I promised the—"

"—sheriff, right." Meschelle rolled her expressive dark eyes. Molly knew that Meschelle was of West African descent because she'd written about it before in the paper. Her skin was as smooth as silk and she wore her hair braided and piled on top of her head out of deference to the heat. She chose a piece of tomato-smeared flatbread from the basket. "Fine. Tell me about the baby."

Molly gave what she considered a highly detailed but also touching account of how she'd found Baby Aphrodite. By the time she'd finished, the dozen oysters that Meschelle had ordered had arrived, and Meschelle had eaten four of them. She didn't look very impressed by Molly's story.

"What's going on between you and the sheriff?" she asked.

"What?" Molly nearly choked on the oyster she was swallowing. "Nothing. What do you mean?"

"I mean you talk about him a lot. And then you agreed to pay for this lunch, all because you want to know about the Sunshine Kids."

"What does my interest in the Sunshine Kids have to do with the sheriff?" Molly felt her cheeks beginning to warm. But that was probably because of the wine, and of course the cardigan.

Meschelle reached into her purse, which was a stylish rattan basket, from which hung dozens of brightly colored tassels. "Here, you can read the story I wrote about them last year for the alternative paper we used to have here. It went under due to people on this island having no interest in reading dissident viewpoints. The *Gazette* wouldn't let me write about the Sunshine Kids because they didn't want the tourists getting wind of them."

Molly took the sheaf of papers Meschelle handed to her. "Why?" she asked breathlessly. "Are they dangerous?"

Meschelle shrugged. "Not particularly. Just annoying. Your sheriff sure seemed to think so. I interviewed him about them, and he called them, and I quote, 'The most frustrating group of individuals I've ever dealt with in my entire career in law enforcement.'"

Molly flipped excitedly through the pages Meschelle had handed her, noting that there were several full-color photos of Sheriff John Hartwell in uniform squinting off into the distance. He looked handsome, but generally disapproving. It was an expression Molly recognized.

"Who *are* the Sunshine Kids, exactly?" she asked.

"What they sound like. A bunch of kids." Meschelle dug into the bowl of mussels in white wine sauce that the server had just slid in front of them. "High school and college dropouts, mostly, from up north who come down for the winter to enjoy our warm weather here in Florida, the Sunshine State. They've fought with their family or gotten kicked out of school for whatever reason, and now they're living on the road, usually in a big group."

"Safety in numbers," Molly murmured.

Meschelle gave her a stern look over the garlicky mussel she was lifting to her lips. "Now don't go feeling sorry for them, Molly. That's another reason the sheriff can't stand them—none of them are suffering from mental illness or drug addiction, like so many of the homeless you see in your library."

"Displaced persons," Molly corrected her.

"What?"

"At the library we don't call them homeless. We call them displaced persons."

Meschelle rolled her eyes. "Whatever. These kids aren't 'displaced persons.' I interviewed a bunch of them for my article, and they all had plenty of cash—including credit cards. They live the way they do by choice. They're kids, remember. They think it's romantic—like Jack Kerouac in *On the Road*. They think they're sticking it to the man by not paying rent—only they're not camping. Instead, they sponge off someone else's electricity and Wi-Fi . . . and mortgage. Read my article, it's all in there, especially about how much they worship their unofficial leader, Dylan someone."

Molly flipped to another page and saw the photo of a handsome, dark-haired boy with a well-groomed goatee, a smattering of tattoos, and extremely large ear gauges. "Dylan Dakota?"

"That's him. He thinks everyone should go back to living off the land, like the Native Americans. Only the Native Americans have disavowed him and the entire group for cultural misappropriation and implying that land is anyone's for the taking, and presumably for always managing to crash in a place that has AC and running water, and then leaving it trashed." Meschelle dipped a piece of flatbread into the broth of the mussels. "Last year Sheriff Hartwell caught Dakota and a bunch of other kids living in the old MTV house on Stork Key."

"Where they filmed *Spring Break-A-Thon?*" Not that Molly would ever watch such a show—well, not more than a few episodes. But the teens in her old library had talked about the hit reality sensation nonstop.

"Yeah. Since the show moved on to filming elsewhere, the owners have been renting it out to tourists, but when it's not booked, it just sits empty. So Dylan and his gang reasoned they were doing society a favor somehow by breaking in and living there themselves, and of course completely wrecking it. I could never quite understand the logic, but they basically did the same thing to that house that they did to your library."

Molly shook her head. "Why weren't they arrested?"

"They were. That's what I'm trying to tell you. But because they're wealthy, their parents hired fancy out-of-town lawyers, and they got off with fines—especially since they're juveniles, except for Dakota. He's a little older, but from some kind of superrich family up north. His lawyer managed to get the charges against him dropped entirely. I thought the sheriff was going to have a stroke." Meschelle reached toward the silver ice bucket sitting in a stand at the end of their booth, pulled the wine bottle from it, and refilled Molly's glass. "Girl, you are the easiest interview. You've basically confirmed that the sheriff thinks the Sunshine Kids are back, and that they're the ones who trashed the new library."

Molly nearly choked again, midgulp. "I didn't!"

Meschelle laughed. "You did. But don't worry, I'm gonna make out like I didn't hear it from you. I have other sources I can squeeze. Some of those deputies on the sheriff's staff are so dumb, they can be bought for a single beer over at the Mermaid. But because I feel bad about what a pushover you are, I'm not going to make you pay for this lunch. We'll split it."

This was a relief, because even though Molly was saving a lot by not having to pay rent, her salary did not stretch to cover two-hundred-dollar lunches. Still, she didn't like being thought of as a pushover. She preferred to think of herself as curious. Isn't that what led most librarians into the profession in the first place—their love of books and thirst for knowledge?

It was only as the two women were signing their checks that Molly heard someone call her name and looked up to see merry little Mrs. Tifton standing at the end of their booth, her dog, Daisy, in her arms.

"Molly! Meschelle! Oh, you don't know how happy I am to see you two girls!"

Daisy gave an excited little bark. Only service dogs were allowed in Little Bridge restaurants, except when it came to Daisy. This was not because Mrs. Tifton was so rich or Daisy so well-behaved, but because her owner was so generous and well-liked.

"Hello, Mrs. Tifton," Molly cried, a little perturbed that her *missus* came out sounding like *mishuss*. Perhaps she should not have split an entire bottle of wine with only one other person at lunch on a workday. "How are you?"

"Well, I'm fine, but it's you two I'm worried about. How could you not have told me about that poor girl in the media room?" Mrs. Tifton was wearing a light warm-up jacket and leggings. It was clear she'd just come from yoga class. "I had to find out from the sheriff!"

Molly exchanged a guilty look with Meschelle.

"We're so sorry, Mrs. Tifton," Meschelle said. "We just thought it was better you didn't know."

"But Daisy was so great," Molly volunteered, because she couldn't think of anything else to say. "She stayed by that girl's side and licked her back into consciousness."

After she said it, Molly wished again that she hadn't had quite so much wine, or had at least drunk more water. Was this something a dog owner wanted to hear?

Apparently it was, as Mrs. Tifton looked delighted, as did her dining partner—whom Molly only then recognized as her mentor and (now retired) boss, Phyllis. Phyllis was also dressed in yoga wear.

Inwardly, Molly wanted to die. Naturally her (ex-)boss was in the same yoga class, and apparently, she lunched regularly with the library's most generous donor.

Mrs. Tifton gave the panting Daisy a squeeze and said, "Oh, Daisy! I always knew you were a very smart dog!" To Molly and Meschelle she said, "She is, you know. She's very perceptive. When I'm feeling down, she crawls onto my lap and licks my face. So I'm not surprised she did the same to that girl. You're just as brave, you know." This was to Molly. "I understand you sat with her until the ambulance came. You simply must let me make it up to you."

"Oh," Molly said, laughing nervously. What was the delightfully eccentric widow going to do, offer her a cash reward? Not that Molly would mind, but as a public servant, she couldn't possibly accept. "That's quite all right, Mrs. Tifton, it's part of my—"

"I know," Mrs. Tifton interrupted, snapping her fingers. "You must come with me this weekend as my date to the Red Cross Ball."

To Molly this was nearly as mortifying as being offered a cash reward. Not that she didn't want to go to the ball—she did. She'd heard all about it from Joanne, who had never been ("It's three hundred and fifty dollars a ticket!") but knew people who had, and described it as "the most glamorous party on Little Bridge, black tie with an all-you-can-eat buffet that includes locally caught stone crab claws, champagne, and of course a chocolate fountain."

It wasn't that Molly wasn't grateful. She simply didn't want the widow to pay for her ticket. It wouldn't be ethical.

"Oh, Molly," Meschelle said, cutting Molly off before she could even draw breath to protest. "You *have* to go. It's the best party of the year. I'm going, to cover it for the paper."

Molly felt her resolve wavering.

"I already bought twelve tickets," Mrs. Tifton said. "I'm taking the entire yoga class, aren't I, Phyl?"

Phyllis—whom Molly would never in a thousand years consider calling Phyl—said, in her calm, throaty voice, "She is. We're all going."

"See?" Mrs. Tifton threw Molly a triumphant look. "You have to come. Especially since we have so much to celebrate."

Molly was puzzled. "We do?" She didn't see what there was to feel happy about. Their library had been vandalized, apparently by kids who were, according to Meschelle, unstoppable. What was so good about that?

"The girl!" Mrs. Tifton cried. "She's in the ICU, but she should do just fine. I called the hospital, and they told me so."

"Really?" Meschelle's eyebrows were raised to their limits. "They usually only give information about patients to family members."

"Oh," Mrs. Tifton said, with a dismissive wave of her hand. "They know me there."

Of course they do, Molly thought, wryly.

"And do you know what else they said?" Mrs. Tifton asked, and went on without waiting for a reply. "They said that she's Baby Aphrodite's mother!"

Molly wasn't a bit surprised, given what she'd seen in the media room, but Meschelle snatched up her phone and quickly hit record.

"Really, Mrs. Tifton?" she asked. "May I quote you on that for an article I'm writing about the abandoned baby for the *Gazette*?"

"Why, yes, you may!" Mrs. Tifton cried. "You can say that Dorothy Tifton has it on good authority that the poor girl found in the children's media room of the new library today is the mother of Baby Aphrodite."

Molly was beginning to get a very bad feeling about all of this.

"Oh, Mrs. Tifton," she said, sliding from her booth. "I don't think that's the kind of news we should be sharing right now. It might hamper the sheriff's investigation."

Mrs. Tifton instantly looked stricken. "Oh, dear! I wouldn't want to do that."

"It's fine," Meschelle said, giving Molly a dirty look. "It's just the local paper, not the *New York Times*. I'll tie it in to the story I interviewed you for, Molly—which, by the way, I'm going to need photos for."

Molly froze. "Photos?"

"Yes. You know, of you by the bathroom stall where you found the baby, and all of that."

Molly thought, fleetingly, of both how unflattering the florescent light in the girls' bathroom was and how disapproving the sheriff was going to be when he found out about the story.

"Don't worry, we'll make you look good," Meschelle said, only partly reading her mind. "I'll send one of the staff photographers over to the library this afternoon. Okay?"

Molly knew she'd dug her own grave. There was nothing for her to do now but lie in it.

CHAPTER EIGHT

John

The day was turning into a debacle. It had started out badly enough, with the discovery of the girl and the vandalism in the library, and it had gone downhill from there. His deputies weren't too happy with his request that they canvass the entire neighborhood around the old high school for possible CCTV footage of the Sunshine Kids, since they'd "done that already" during previous break-ins and found nothing.

His tech crew was even less happy with his order that they swab and fingerprint everything they'd found in the media room where the librarian had discovered the unconscious girl.

"Everything?" Murray had balked.

"Yes, everything. And don't forget to match them against that box from yesterday, the one they found the baby in."

Murray had looked around at the mess in dismay. "Sheriff, most of this stuff is garbage. You want us to fingerprint *garbage?*"

"Yes, I do." John didn't see why he had to explain himself to his own tech crew, most of whom, it was true, had been hired by Rich Wagner, the previous sheriff, and were still loyal to him, even though he'd turned out to be a douche of the first order.

If John wanted garbage swabbed for DNA and also fingerprinted, it was his right to ask for it to be swabbed for DNA and fingerprinted. That's what these guys got paid for.

Things didn't improve when John returned to his office to find a five-foot-long plush dolphin sitting in his desk chair.

"Marguerite," he yelled when he saw it.

Marguerite sauntered slowly down the hall from her office, a cup of coffee in her hand.

"It's for Baby Aphrodite," she said, when she saw what he was upset about. "On account of her rising from the ocean waves."

John thought his head might explode. "I don't care who it's for. Get it out of my office."

"There's nowhere else to put it. There're baby toys and boxes of diapers and formula all up and down the—"

"I don't care. Just get it out."

Marguerite sighed. "Sure, Chief. What do you want me to do about the bachelor party riding a goat down Truman Avenue?"

"The *what*?"

"A bunch of guys down here to celebrate their pal getting

married found a goat somewhere—unless they brought it themselves—and are now taking turns riding it around downtown."

"For Christ's sake." Was the entire country going insane? "Send Martinez down there to arrest them for drunk and disorderly."

"Can't, Chief. He's over at the bus station checking a suspicious passenger. Could be Dakota. You sent a Be On The Lookout for him, remember?"

"Well, send Reynolds, then. And tell him to get that goat over to the petting zoo, and have the vet come over to check it out for injuries."

"Got it, Chief."

"And stop calling me Chief. I'm the sheriff, not the chief of police."

"Right, Chief. I mean, Sheriff."

John glared at his computer screen. Sometimes he wondered how he'd managed to become not only a sheriff but also a zookeeper. The population of Little Bridge was so small that it could sustain only a minuscule animal shelter, so overflow abandoned or abused animals tended to end up in the care of law enforcement. It had been John's decision early on in his tenure as sheriff to begin using an outdoor area of the jail as part animal hospital, part permanent petting zoo. Studies showed that recidivism decreased in individuals who spent time during their incarceration working with animals, so John saw to it that whatever nonviolent inmates he deemed worthy of the privilege were allowed to care for the numerous sloths, snakes, tortoises, alligators, parrots, rabbits, chinchillas, pigs, chickens, ducks, miniature horses, and now, apparently, goats that were housed there.

Did it bother John that the hard-bitten homicide detectives with whom he used to work back in Miami occasionally sent him teasing gifs of himself in overalls and a sun hat, shoveling manure?

Not as much as it bothered him that law enforcement agencies from across the country contacted him almost daily, begging him to take on injured animals they'd found in drug raids or other busts, and that he usually had to say no because his "jail zoo" was already at capacity.

He didn't think things could get any worse until he went to try on his dress uniform to make sure it fit before the Red Cross Ball.

"Marguerite!" he shouted, staring down at himself in dismay.

Marguerite came strolling in, this time holding a turquoise reusable water bottle in her hand. "Something else wrong, Chief?"

He showed her. "My dress pants don't fit."

She was unimpressed. "It's called aging. It happens to the best of us. Try squeezing three kids out of your ying-yang, like I did. It happens even quicker."

"Well, these fit last week," he said, tugging on the waistband of his trousers. "What am I supposed to do?"

"Stop drinking beer," Marguerite suggested. "My husband stops drinking beer and he drops ten pounds overnight. It's God's joke on women."

"I only drink one beer a night." John looked mournfully

at his reflection in the full-length mirror attached to his office's closet door.

"Actually," Marguerite said, taking mercy on him, "you don't look so bad for your age, Sheriff." For all she liked to razz him, he noticed she'd been softening toward him, often bringing him an extra café con leche when she stopped at the Coffee Cubano on the way to work (which was probably not helping with his waistline). "Maybe the cleaners made a mistake and delivered the wrong pants. They do it all the time. I'll look into it for you."

He relaxed—as much as the tight pants would allow. "Thanks, Sergeant."

"Don't mention it. I'll get that dolphin off your hands now, too, if you want."

"No." John glanced at the stuffed animal grinning so maniacally from behind his desk. "I'm starting to like it. Maybe I'll take it over to the hospital later myself."

She shrugged. "Suit yourself."

After he'd changed back into his regular uniform, John moved the dolphin to a corner and sat down at his desk, then brought up the file on Dylan Dakota. Everything about the kid, including his name, was fake—everything except the very real harm he'd caused to people and property, including the young girl who was currently in the Little Bridge ICU.

Her condition was stable, but if she hadn't been found when she had, and gotten help, she could have died. Thank God for Molly Montgomery—and no thanks to Lawrence "Larry" Beckwith III, aka Dylan Dakota.

Of course, John didn't have proof that Larry was behind any of this. That's why he needed the DNA swabs and fingerprints. If Larry turned out to have anything to do with what had been done to the new library or to the girl, John was going to find some way to nail him this time, fancy lawyer or no fancy lawyer. And when Larry landed in his jail, John would make sure he'd get zero privileges. That kid wasn't going to set one foot in the Little Bridge jail petting zoo.

John was poring over his notes on Beckwith and getting hot under the collar all over again when there was a tap on his office door.

"What?" he bellowed, thinking it was Murray with another complaint about the task he'd been assigned.

Only it wasn't.

"God, Daddy, it's only me." His daughter, Katie, came in, then closed the door behind her. "If you yell at everyone like that, it's no wonder no one here likes you."

He stared at her. She was wearing her Snappettes uniform, nothing more than a red bodysuit with a tiny pleated skirt and matching red tennis shoes. "I've asked you before to change out of that thing before you get here," he groused. "And who says no one here doesn't like me?"

"It's obvious none of them like you." Katie leaned over his desk to give him a peck on the cheek. "Except maybe Sergeant Ruiz. The rest of them are still devoted to that gross old Sheriff Wagner. But they all like me, and it's *because* I wear this thing. Everyone loves the Snappettes. We represent everything that is good and wholesome in the world.

Did you forget you were supposed to meet me after school today for dance practice?"

Startled, he glanced at his watch. "Is school out already? Sorry, honey, it's been a crazy day."

"I heard." Katie turned toward the stuffed dolphin. "Everyone's talking about how they found Baby Aphrodite's mother bleeding to death at the new library. Hey, who dropped this off? Is this for Baby Aphrodite? It's supercute."

Could his deputies keep nothing confidential? "Who told you that the girl in the library is the baby's mother? And stop calling her Baby Aphrodite. That's not her name. The baby doesn't have a name yet."

Katie flopped into his office visitor's chair, draping her long legs over one of the arms and swinging her red-sneakered feet. "Aw, come on, Dad, it's all over town that the new librarian found her, just like she found the baby. And what's wrong with Baby Aphrodite? I like it. Can I have the dolphin if no one else wants it?"

"No, you may not. Whoever left it meant for the baby to have it, not you. Listen, honey, I don't have time for dance practice today, I have an actual crime to solve."

Katie snorted. "Oh, as opposed to a fake crime like all those burglaries that keep happening around town?"

He glared at her, not finding the joke funny. "Exactly. In fact, the two might be connected. So if you could just scoot on home—" Then something dawned on him. "Hey, wait a minute. How did you even get here?"

She rolled her eyes. "Duh, Dad. Uber."

"You Ubered?"

"Yes, Dad, Mom set up an Uber account for me. She said it was the least she could do, considering how busy you are and the fact that she isn't around and you're the one who has to drive me everywhere. Remember?"

He did dimly remember discussing something along those lines with Christina, and even agreeing to it.

But now, seeing the plan in action, he did not like it one bit.

"I don't want you alone in cars with strange men you don't know, especially dressed like that."

"God, Dad." She rolled her eyes, as she did at nearly everything he said these days. "Could you be more nineteenth century? All of the drivers are superprofessional because they want a good rating and tip. And besides, you've been teaching me self-defense since I was five. Can we just drop it and get to what's important? How am I going to teach you to dance if you don't even show up to practice?"

He thought about this, and how woefully underqualified he was to raise a teenage daughter. He wondered if the parents of the girl Molly Montgomery had found in the new library had felt the same way, and if that's how she'd ended up in her current predicament. Had she gotten pregnant and run away (or been kicked out of the house), or become pregnant while on the road? Was Larry Beckwith III aka Dylan Dakota the father of her baby? Was he the one who'd put that newborn in an empty trash-bag box and left her in a toilet stall for Molly Montgomery to find?

If he was, John would find a way to make his existence here on earth a living hell. Once he was in jail, John would assign him to beachcombing duty, making sure he was out there in his bright orange coveralls raking up seaweed in the blinding sun every day from sunrise to sunset.

Molly, he thought, would know all the right things to say to Katie. Molly was a children's specialist. It said so, right on the signature line of that Facebook entry she'd written, instructing the entire town to call the infant Baby Aphrodite.

"I have an idea," John said, smiling suddenly at his daughter, who'd gone sulky at the implication that she wasn't old enough to handle Uber on her own and was now picking black polish off her nails and letting the flakes fall onto his floor, a habit he found irritating.

She did not look up from her nails. "What."

"Let's go to the library."

This made her lift her head in astonishment. "Why would we do *that*?"

"They have books to teach you how to dance, don't they?" He was already getting up from his chair. "And videos."

Katie did not stir from her seat. "Dad. They have videos online. For free."

"Everything is free at the library, too. You just have to apply for a card. It's my fault, really, I should have gotten you one a long time ago. Let's go."

Katie unfolded herself reluctantly from the visitor's chair. "This isn't about you wanting to check out books on how to dance. This is about the Baby Aphrodite case, isn't it?"

He glanced at his reflection in the mirror, just to make sure his hair was all right. He'd had it cut recently over at the barbershop—regulation length—but you could never be too sure. It was streaked with gray here and there—depressing, but only to be expected with a teenage daughter and a job like his—but otherwise, he thought he looked okay.

"No, no," he said, tightening his tie. "I really want to learn, Katie. And you know books are the best way to learn anything."

She was unimpressed. "If you need to do something for the case, Dad, all you have to do is say so. Especially if it's for Baby Aphrodite. You know the whole town is backing you on this one. Not like the High School Thief, who some people are thinking of as a kind of Robin Hood."

He threw her a startled glance. "They are?"

She picked up her backpack and shrugged. "Well, yeah. He robs from the rich—the people who live in that area—and the naive—who else would keep their doors unlocked? I heard some of them keep the back doors by their pools wide open to let in the night air. They're practically *asking* to get robbed, if you ask me. And the thief only takes little things, like sunglasses and wallets and laptops and stuff. He never takes things that hold sentimental value, like jewelry."

John frowned at her. "Some people feel quite sentimental about their wallets, Katie, and their laptops, too, especially if they have financial information on them and haven't backed them up."

She rolled her eyes—again—and gave another shrug. "Well, what kind of idiot doesn't back up their computer?

I'm just saying, kids at school think the thief is kind of cool."

On this disheartening note, they left the sheriff's department, but only after John issued a firm warning that no one was to touch the stuffed dolphin in his office, to which Marguerite replied with a weary "Whatever you say, Chief."

The ride to the old library was unpleasant, since the middle and elementary schools in the area were also just letting out, so John and Katie were caught in what counted in Little Bridge as a traffic jam—an extra two minutes sitting at the stoplight, waiting for people to make their turns. Everyone was on their best behavior, however, because they saw the sheriff's vehicle behind them, and John didn't catch a single one of them failing to use their turn signal, something he knew would not have happened had he been back in their old neighborhood in Miami.

Even Katie grudgingly remarked, as they pulled up in front of the library and easily found a parking space, "At least it's easier getting around here than it was back home."

This warmed his heart, though it pained him that she still referred to Miami as home.

"But," he said, as they walked the neatly swept path toward the library door, "here they have the Snappettes."

"That's true," Katie said, looking thoughtful. Then she paused. "Oh, look, how cute." She raised her phone to snap a photo of a mother hen that ran by, a dozen fluffy brown chicks scurrying closely behind her. The library grounds were a nesting area for the native chickens that had freely roamed the streets of Little Bridge since Bahamians had brought them there in the 1800s. The chickens were popular with tourists, tolerated by locals, and lived long and happy lives since they were protected by city law.

John, too, was pleased. So far, everything was going well. Katie already found the library as charming as he did. Perhaps she'd like Molly Montgomery, too—providing that he, for once, could avoid offending her, and she, for once, could avoid trying to do his job for him.

They'd only taken a few steps inside before he saw that, unfortunately, neither of these things was going to happen.

CHAPTER NINE

Molly

Molly was minding her own business, reshelving the books she'd neglected earlier that day and keeping Elijah away from Story Time—she'd secured a copy of *It* for him, and he seemed engrossed enough—when Meschelle Davies came bursting in, as breathless and sweaty as Molly had been at lunch.

"Great news," Meschelle said, not even bothering to whisper, despite Story Time. No one bothered to whisper in the children's section or anywhere, really, in the Little Bridge Public Library, but some respect might have been given to the volunteer story reader, Lady Patricia, a kindly drag queen who generously gave up an afternoon a week to read to toddlers.

"What?" Molly asked. "Is the photographer here?"

"Not just a photographer. Molly, I wrote the story and filed it—I always write best with a little white wine in me—

and it went live online and already got picked up by the *Miami Herald*. I told you, people love an abandoned baby story. And now Miami Channel Seven News has choppered a film crew down to interview you!"

Molly stared at her. "Meschelle," she said. "That isn't what we agreed. You said you were just—"

"I know what I said. But isn't this better? Think of the publicity this is going to get your library! Donations are going to roll in."

Molly chewed the inside of her lip. This was bad. Really bad. She'd promised the sheriff she wouldn't talk about the investigation with anyone. Being interviewed by a Miami news crew would definitely be breaking that promise.

On the other hand, she'd only promised not to talk about the baby's mother. Surely she was free to discuss Baby Aphrodite.

"Do it!" Henry had appeared from nowhere—as he was wont to do—and was hissing from behind the junior nonfiction section. "Come on, do it, Molly!"

"See?" Meschelle turned her bright eyes back upon her. "You have to do it, even your colleagues say so. And besides, the film crew is already here. They're in a taxi coming from the airport as we speak."

Which is how Molly found herself, a half hour later, standing beneath a very bright light being interviewed on camera by a handsome young man named Trevan Wilkinson.

"And how did you feel when you realized what was inside the box?" Trevan asked her.

"Scared," Molly said into the microphone, exactly the way he'd coached her. "I was really scared."

Trevan, smiling handsomely, brought the microphone back to his own lips. "Because you were worried for Baby Aphrodite's life?"

"Exactly," Molly said. "She was so little, and so cold."

"Is it true," Trevan asked, "that you used your own body heat to warm Baby Aphrodite until the paramedics arrived?"

"Yes," Molly said. "She was freezing."

Trevan turned to face the camera. "So there you have it, folks. A librarian giving warmth from her own body to save the life of one of her most vulnerable—and tiniest—patrons. Now that's what I call a true hero. I'm Trevan Wilkerson, Miami Channel Seven News."

"Cut," said the producer, whose name was Naomi. "That was perfect. Let's get some more shots of Molly in the toilet stall, and then we can head over to the hospital for some exteriors."

"What's going on here?" thundered a new, particularly deep, male voice, and Molly turned, her heart sinking, to see Sheriff John Hartwell and a young girl in a cheerleading uniform standing in the doorway.

"Cheese it!" cried Elijah, who'd long since put down his copy of *It*, apparently finding the filming of the newscast a little more exciting. "It's the po-po!"

The cheerleader looked at him and, her cheeks reddening, asked, "What are *you* doing here?"

Molly was surprised to notice that Elijah's own cheeks had darkened a shade or two, and that he suddenly appeared flustered. The two teens obviously knew each other. "I—I could ask the same thing of you."

The girl pointed at the sheriff. "He's my dad. He made me come."

"Well." Elijah couldn't seem to meet the pretty girl's gaze. It was the first time Molly had ever seen him at a loss for words. "That . . . that sounds unlikely."

The girl's jaw dropped. "What? What are you even—"

"The two of you knock it off." John Hartwell didn't look or sound as if he was in the mood to put up with any kind of shenanigans, teen or otherwise.

So Molly felt a little bit for Naomi when she stepped up to him, her right hand extended, and said, "Sheriff, great to see you, Naomi Hernandez, Miami Channel Seven News. You might remember me from when I was down here with my crew covering Hurricane Marilyn. I wonder if we could have a word with you about that baby you helped save yesterday."

"I'm unable to comment at this time." The words seemed to tumble as automatically from the sheriff's lips as if he'd been saying them all day—and perhaps he had.

Molly knew she had nothing to feel guilty for—she hadn't uttered a word about the girl she'd found in the new library, and fortunately, Meschelle hadn't mentioned her in her story, so no one had asked.

But she still felt as if she'd betrayed the sheriff somehow.

"But, Sheriff," Trevan said, putting on the charm, which was easy for him since he had as much of it as he had good looks. "It's a real heartwarming story, and our viewers could use good news like that right now. Just a few quick words on camera, like maybe about how the baby's doing now, and your search for the mother—"

"Absolutely not." The sheriff looked as if he was longing to throw the news crew off the property, but he couldn't, because the property belonged to the people. "When I have something to say on the record concerning the matter, I will let you know. Now, if you'll excuse me, my daughter and I were just leaving. Come on, Katie."

He took his daughter by the arm and began to drag her from the premises, but she pulled back, reluctant to leave. "Da-aad," she said.

"Katie." The sheriff looked sterner than ever.

Molly watched in consternation. This was a disaster.

"Excuse me," she said to Trevan and Naomi, as well as the cameraman and boom operator, whose names she'd forgotten. Then she darted after the sheriff and his daughter.

"I'm so sorry," Molly said when she reached them. By that time they were by the reception desk, where Henry was busy pretending he wasn't eavesdropping on their conversation. "But I swear to you, Sheriff, none of this was my idea. It was Meschelle—I mean, Ms. Davies. And I didn't tell them a thing about the girl from this morning."

He looked down at her with those hypnotically blue eyes. "I sure hope not."

"I didn't. I only want to help."

Now his face creased with irritation. "Miss Montgomery, I've told you, I don't—"

"—need my help, I know. And it's Molly, please. And

even though it may not look like it at the moment, I'm staying out of it." She wasn't going to mention how the only reason she'd ended up in this mess was that she'd been pumping a journalist for information about the case. "But there must be some reason you brought your daughter here." She smiled at the girl in the cheerleading uniform to whom Elijah had been so rude. But then, Elijah was rude to everyone. "Hi, I'm Miss Molly. Is there something I can help you with?"

It was a relief when the sheriff's daughter, keeping her gaze on Molly and well averted from Elijah, replied by reaching out her right hand and saying, "Hi, I'm Katie Hartwell, I don't have a library card. My dad wanted me to get one. Also, he seems to think you have books or videos or something that teach dancing? Because he needs to learn how."

As Molly shook Katie's hand, she felt a rush of warm feelings toward the girl, but also toward her father—especially when she saw his face reddening at his daughter's words, and he began to stammer, "That's . . . that's not . . . I mean, yes, about the library card, but not—"

Molly was used to patrons, particularly male patrons, expressing embarrassment over their reading requests, so she hurried to quell his anxiety, even though, internally, she was bursting with curiosity. Why did he need to learn how to dance? Was there a special occasion coming up? Could it be the Red Cross Ball?

But there wasn't dancing at the Red Cross Ball. Both Joanne and Meschelle had already assured her of this. It was more of a dinner party, although there was a silent auction and games of chance to raise additional money for the charity. It was only called a ball because of the formal attire.

"I can help you with both those things," Molly said, swallowing down her inquisitiveness, even as the voices inside her clamored, *Is there a special lady in his life who is asking him to learn to dance? If so, who is this lady, and why isn't she simply taking dance lessons with him? And why do I care?* "We can set you up with a library card, Katie, and also help you find some nice books and videos—I think you mean DVDs?—on how to dance. What kind of dancing do you want to learn, Sheriff? Is this for a wedding or some other event you'll be attending?"

There, that didn't sound too nosy.

It was his daughter who answered.

"It's for the Snappettes," Katie said proudly. "I'm a Snappette, and my dad's agreed to dance with us at the next mother-daughter performance because he and my mom are divorced and she lives in Miami. It's sexist, anyway, not to let men perform. But first he needs to learn to dance, so that's why we're here."

Molly wasn't certain she'd heard all this correctly, because it sounded so incredible, so she glanced up at the sheriff for confirmation and knew the second her eyes met his, and she saw the sheepish look on his face, that it was all true.

"Yeah," he said with a shrug. "I'm gonna be an honorary Snappette."

Molly was just as astonished as she'd been when she'd learned that Carolyn Keene, the author of her favorite book series from childhood, Nancy Drew, was not one person, but a whole team of authors, all writing under a single pen name.

Only that discovery had been disappointing. The one she'd just made about Sheriff John Hartwell was pleasant. So pleasant that she was too stunned to speak. It was as if every preconceived notion and prejudice she'd had against the sheriff had been blown away in a second, and she was seeing him in an entirely new light.

As she just stood there, staring, Henry came popping up from where he'd been hiding behind the reception desk, having heard every word. He said, matter-of-factly, "Okay, then, you need one library card and some how-to books and videos on dancing. I can help you with that."

Later, when Katie and the sheriff were gone, Henry allowed himself to guffaw.

"Oh my God. Your face. Your face, Molly, when he said he was going to be a Snappette!"

"Stop it." Molly took a sip from her water bottle. She'd been carefully hydrating ever since lunch, but now she felt as if she needed more water than ever. "It isn't funny. Men can dance, too, you know."

"Um, I think I know that more than you. I'm the gay man with season tickets to the Little Bridge Theater, where they routinely put on *Naked Boys Singing!* What I'm saying is, our sheriff is going to dance onstage with a bunch of teenage girls and yoga moms. I'm going to post this all over the Little Bridge Facebook community page tonight and love every minute of peoples' reactions."

Molly banged her water bottle onto the desk. "Henry, no. Don't."

"Why not? It's going to be public knowledge soon enough."

"The man has a hard enough job. Let him have his dignity."

"He already dressed in an evening gown on a float in last year's pride parade, Molly. I don't think his dignity is something he worries about too much—unless . . ." Henry grinned at her. "It's not his 'dignity' you're interested in."

She felt herself blushing. "Stop it."

"I knew it! Librarian's got a crush on the sheriff."

"Which librarian's got a crush on the sheriff?" Elijah demanded, appearing at the end of the desk, his copy of *It* in his hands.

"No one," Molly said quickly. "It was a joke."

"Phew." Elijah wiped his brow in mock relief. "Because if it was you, Miss Molly, I'd be real disappointed, you fraternizing with the enemy and all."

"Law enforcement officers are not our enemies, Elijah."

"The po-po? Are you kidding me?"

"No, I'm not kidding you. Not all of them are—"

"Wrong. Plenty of them'll pull a brown brother like me over and shoot him, especially when they find out I'm the guy who's been robbing all those houses down by the new library. They'll fry my brown—"

"Elijah," Henry interrupted. "There is no way you are the High School Thief."

Elijah rolled his eyes. "How do you know? Imagine how dumb you're gonna feel when you find out it's me, and all those girls back in school like Katie Hartwell, who won't even give me the time of day, realize that the great High School Thief they can't stop talking about was me all along."

Molly was starting to feel annoyed. In the brief time she'd lived in Little Bridge, she'd come to love Elijah, despite how irritating he could be at times—and how much cologne he doused himself in—much in the way she'd come to love Fluffy the Cat, who constantly hung out at the hotel, even though he clearly belonged to someone else. Both Elijah and Fluffy were equally exasperating and yet adorably vulnerable, each in their own way.

"Elijah," Molly said, in her best strict librarian voice. "You spend all of your time when you're not in school here. And you spend the rest of the time playing video games or sleeping. When would you possibly have time to go around robbing houses?"

Elijah opened his mouth to protest, but Molly cut him off. "Look, I get that you want to be famous, and you're going to be. I believe that in my heart. You're smart, funny, and very, very intelligent. But give it some time. You don't have to be famous at sixteen. And you should never want to be famous for doing something that hurts other people—especially something I know you're not doing."

Elijah looked a little sulky, lowering his head toward his copy of *It*, but didn't seem quite ready to give up yet. "Okay, fine, Miss Molly, you might have a point. Touché. I get it. So how about if it turns out I'm not really the High

School Thief, but I help the po-po catch him, like the kids in this book you gave me are helping to catch this evil guy? Then I could be on the news, like you were for finding Baby Aphrodite. That'd get me some cred with the popular kids for sure, right?"

Now Molly felt a different kind of emotion toward Elijah: anxiety.

Was this why the sheriff kept asking her not to get involved in his cases—because he worried for her safety?

No, certainly not. He hardly knew her.

He simply didn't want his hard work compromised by an amateur sleuth, a literary know-it-all who was new to the island but still full of ideas about how she could do his job—the job he'd been doing for years—better than he could.

Now she understood how idiotic she must seem to him. As idiotic as Elijah—Lord love him—seemed to her now, declaring that he was going to help catch the High School Thief.

Of course, Elijah was only a child, and Molly was a full-grown woman with a master's degree. And of course she had seen every single episode of *Forensic Files* and read just about every mystery that existed, both children's and adult, except the truly gory ones, because who needed that in their life?

But still.

She'd never stopped to consider that the sheriff might actually be concerned about her stepping into danger, as she was for Elijah. Was that why he had stopped by on the flimsy pretext of getting his daughter a library card (and some how-to-dance books and DVDs, which he hadn't really needed)? To check up on her?

If so, how cringeworthy. A part of her wanted to go home and never show her face in town again.

Another part of her, of course, wanted to solve the crime and show the sheriff just how wrong he was about her.

"Elijah," she said in her most serious tone, "leave the crime solving to the professionals. You work on what you're best at."

Elijah was still sulking. The encounter with Katie Hartwell seemed to have really thrown him. Molly had never seen him like this. "Oh, yeah? And what's that?"

Henry laid a friendly hand upon his shoulder. "Comedy, man. You're the funniest guy I know."

Elijah lifted his head, looking slightly less disconsolate. "You mean that?"

"Yeah, man," Henry said. "That cookie porn you did the other day was comedy gold."

Elijah cracked a smile. "It *was* pretty good. I should do it again, only, you know, at home, and film it, and put it up on YouTube."

"Totally," Henry said. "Get some subscribers."

"And advertisers," Elijah said. "What I need is a brand."

Satisfied that her favorite patron had been warned off any attempts at amateur crime solving, Molly went back to her own desk, telling herself that she would do the same. No more looking into the Sunshine Kids, no more combing social media for possible updates on the case. She was going to be a good, law-abiding citizen from now on and stay out of the sheriff's business. In fact, she was going to avoid him completely. The sheriff was dead to her. She was never even going to glance his way again.

This resolve lasted until Saturday night when she attended the Red Cross Ball and saw how mouthwateringly good Sheriff John Hartwell looked in his dress uniform.

CHAPTER TEN

John

As John dressed for the Red Cross Ball—an annual Little Bridge tradition that had gone on for as long as he could remember—he was surprised to realize that things were looking up.

His dress uniform fit, for one thing. The dry cleaner really had delivered the wrong trousers, an error he'd been too preoccupied to notice himself.

Even better, the tech crew had found the fingerprints of Lawrence Beckwith III, aka Dylan Dakota, all over one of the pizza boxes and several of the beer bottles found in the media room of the new library. Nothing had been discovered yet on any of the CCTV footage—Beckwith and his crew somehow always managed to figure out where any security cameras were hidden and stay far away from them—or from the DNA swabs, but that, at least, would show up eventually. On television crime shows, of course,

DNA results always came back within hours. In reality, it took weeks or often months before they got answers.

John always sent swabs anyway, hoping for a miracle.

That wasn't all, though. Murray, showing unusual initiative, had combed through the garbage he'd been tasked with testing and found a driver's license that someone—John was willing to bet it was Larry—had thrown in one of the construction dumpsters outside the new library. The photo on the driver's license looked identical to the girl Molly Montgomery had found on the library floor—the girl whom the hospital was able to confirm was the mother of the baby Molly Montgomery had found as well.

Her physician would not allow him to interview her, though, as the girl—Tabitha Brighton, of New Canaan, Connecticut—was still in the ICU, recovering from having given birth in a construction zone.

"And those party kids hardly lifted a finger to help her!" Dr. Nguyen, the island's ob-gyn, was outraged. "Aside from cutting the cord, and who knows what they used to do that."

John knew better than to argue with Dr. Nguyen, who'd delivered Katie.

But John didn't need to interview Tabitha—not yet, anyway—to proceed on her case. He had most of the information he needed about her from her driver's license, including her name, age—eighteen, so *not* a minor—and home address. He spent most of the morning before the ball on the phone, attempting to gather the rest.

Ever mindful of what Molly had said to him the first time they'd met—that it was possible the baby's mother hadn't abandoned her child, that someone else was responsible for placing it in the restroom (something he thought even more likely now that he knew Beckwith was involved)—John called the girl's parents.

It was true that she was no longer a minor and, because of the HIPAA Security Rule, neither the hospital nor law enforcement could contact her next of kin without her consent (unless, of course, she died, and then the coroner or police—if it was homicide—would make that notification).

So what he was doing wasn't entirely by the book.

However, it was also true that she was only two years older than his own daughter, and if someone had found Katie in the condition in which Tabitha had been found, he'd want to know.

But when he called the number listed at Tabitha's home address, his good luck ran out. The Brightons were not there, and according to the woman who answered the phone, they were not expected back any time soon.

"Mr. and Mrs. Brighton are on a cruise," the woman—who identified herself as Luisa, the Brightons' housekeeper—explained.

"A cruise," John repeated, in order to make absolutely certain he'd heard her correctly.

"*Si.* A cruise to Alaska."

John had some difficulty processing this information, as he himself had never considered taking a vacation on a cruise ship, and didn't understand why anyone would.

"Is this the same Daniel and Elizabeth Brighton who have a daughter named Tabitha?" he asked.

Luisa gasped. "*Si!* Do you have news of Tabby? Where is she? Is she all right? It has been so long!"

"Really? How long?"

"A year," the housekeeper responded eagerly. "One morning, the Brightons wake up, and she is just gone. Is she all right? She is a nice girl. Just a little mixed up."

"I'm afraid I can only share that information with an immediate relative." John's response was automatic. But the kind concern in the woman's voice caused him to add, "But if you can give me a number where I can reach her parents, I promise I'll have some good news to share with them."

He hoped they'd consider hearing that they were now grandparents good news, anyway. He had his doubts, considering the fact that they were vacationing on a cruise ship while their daughter was missing.

Luisa gasped. "Good news? Oh, *gracias, señor, gracias*! Hold on one moment."

The housekeeper gave him the parents' cell phone numbers, but advised him that she'd been told service would be sketchy on the ship, and not to expect to be able to reach them right away. Cell towers were apparently few and far between along the Bering Sea.

It was possible she was right. His calls to both Daniel and Elizabeth Brighton went straight to voice mail. He left messages explaining who he was but didn't give details, asking only that they called him back regarding information he had about their daughter. He tried to feel glad that at least one person in the Brighton household—the housekeeper,

Luisa—seemed to care enough about Tabitha to answer the phone.

Then he sat at his desk performing some swift arithmetic in his head.

If the girl had run away a year ago, it seemed likely she'd gotten pregnant while on the road.

That made it possible that Beckwith was the baby's father.

If this was true, that meant John would not only have the pleasure of locking Larry up, but of finding some way to make sure the wealthy Beckwith family—not Larry, because of course he was going to be incarcerated—paid for Baby Aphrodite's care and education for the next eighteen years. Possibly a college fund, too.

This thought gave John a great deal of satisfaction.

Now, after making sure his cell phone ringer was on high in case the Brightons called him back or one of his deputies actually found Beckwith in a bar or any of his other known haunts, John was driving to the hotel where the Red Cross Ball was being held.

Of course no mere hotel ballroom was grand enough to hold such an extravaganza, so once guests parked, signs encouraged them to stroll across the hotel grounds to a small boat dock where a dozen little launches waited to ferry them to their final destination—Jasmine Key, a small private island belonging to the hotel, about a five-minute ride away.

John had been there many times before, not only for previous years' balls but because there were also tiki-thatched bungalows on the island available for hotel guests to rent. Occasionally these guests overimbibed on sun, surf, and spirits, and needed professional law enforcement and/or medical aid.

Still, John never tired of the sight of the Victorian rooftops of downtown Little Bridge fading away in the distance as the launch approached Jasmine Key, or the sight of the sun slowly sinking into the sea ahead of them, casting the sky into pink, orange, and lavender streaks.

And then there was the sight of Jasmine Key's dock. Brightly burning torches lined a path along the beach to a Caribbean-style resort, complete with high-backed leather chairs and gently swinging ceiling fans. By the time John arrived—slightly late because of his phone calls—the buffet was already open and crowded, a decadent and glittering display of excess. He looked upon it with approval—all of the stone crab was local, harvested and donated by friends of his from high school who'd taken over their fathers' fishing boats. This made him feel good about his decision to move back with Katie to his hometown. It was the circle of life, like in that movie she used to enjoy so much, with the talking animals.

"Beer, please," he said to the bartender, when he finally made it through the crowd to the bar.

"What kind?" the bartender asked.

John frowned. "I don't know. The liquid kind."

"He'll take whatever you have on tap," said a voice from behind him, and John turned to see the state's attorney, Peter Abramowitz, dressed in some kind of strange tuxedo, complete with a silk scarf and carnation, slip a few dollars into the bartender's tip jar. "Hey, John."

"What are you supposed to be?" John asked, staring in disbelief at his friend—one of the few he had on the island, since it was hard to be the chief law enforcement officer and have friends.

But Pete wasn't a local. A native New Yorker who also happened to be an avid windsurfer, he'd come to Little Bridge on vacation a dozen years earlier, surfed the reef once, and decided to cash in his return ticket.

To say that he was eccentric would be an understatement, but he'd never lost a case . . . except against Beckwith.

"I'm a gangster." Pete handed John his beer.

"I didn't know this was a dress-up party."

"It's not." Pete was drinking a bottled craft beer. John wondered, as he often did, what was wrong with regular beer. "My admin told me it was, though, and that everyone was supposed to dress like it was the Roaring Twenties. Turns out she got some bad intel."

"Oh," John said, and sipped his beer. It wasn't that bad. "It's good to see you here, Pete, even if you do look sort of stupid in that outfit."

"Same to you, John. What's the latest with your mortal enemy, that Beckwith kid?"

"The latest is that we can't find him. But we will."

Pete sipped his own beer. "You know he has to be long gone by now."

"I don't think so. Those Sunshine snots don't believe in wasting fossil fuels traveling by car. They only ever travel by bus and I already sent all the bus companies Be On The Lookouts for him, so he's not getting out of here that way. Same with TSA and the ferry companies."

"Oh, come on, John. That kid could easily, at any time, slip onto a private boat and sail right out of here, and none of us would know."

"Fine." John drank some more of his beer. "You're probably right. Boat's the way he's going to go. But what good is it going to do him? I've got his prints all over that media room. I sent the mug shot from his previous arrest, for the MTV house thing, to every law enforcement agency in the state. Wherever he goes, someone's going to nab him for something, and eventually he'll end up back with me."

Pete shook his head. "For what? All you've got on him is vandalism. You'll need more than that if you intend to keep him."

"He took that girl's baby, Pete," John said, staring ahead at nothing. "He took it, and he left the mother to die."

"Well, prove it. Prove it, or—"

"Sheriff!" John was pounded hard on his back by someone and nearly spilled his beer. "You gonna beat everyone again this year in cornhole?"

John turned to see several city commissioners, a former mayor, and Randy Jamison, the city planner.

"I'm gonna try," John said, in a falsely jovial tone.

He disliked all of them, because as far as city safety went, they were corrupt and also incompetent.

But for Jamison, the city planner, who turned down every request he received that might lead to low-income housing being built, John reserved special contempt. The island had been overcrowded before last year's hurricane, but now it was even worse.

Jamison seemed interested only in allowing projects to move forward that might line his own pockets (Jamison's son-in-law owned one of the island's only plumbing businesses), not ones that could help reduce overcrowding and therefore crime.

"Ha-ha," cried Jamison, who was smoking a cigar—Cuban, John could tell. "Last year I damned near kicked John's butt in cornhole, didn't I, Pete?"

But John was no longer listening. That's because, over the city planner's shoulder, he'd seen something. Not just something, but someone. It was Molly Montgomery, standing in the buffet line, looking magical in a black dress that shimmered when she moved.

What was she doing here? He hadn't expected to see her. Now his heart was unaccountably racing at the sight of her. The last time he'd seen her, he'd made a fool of himself, getting so upset over her talking to that film crew from Miami, and then admitting that he'd come to the library in search of how-to-dance books and DVDs.

But why did he care what she thought of him? She was only a citizen. A very attractive citizen, it was true, especially in that dress, which wasn't formfitting at all, but still clung to her body in such a way—

"Hartwell!"

John turned to look at Jamison, who had evidently asked a question to which he hadn't replied.

"What?"

"I asked how it's going with the search for Baby Aphrodite's mother."

"Oh," John said, noticing that Molly Montgomery had reached the end of the buffet line and was moving with Mrs. Tifton toward one of the outdoor tables overlooking the sunset and the beach. "Fine. Just fine."

"Fine? Well, does that mean you found her? Because you know my daughter might be interested in adopting that baby if you don't have any other—"

"It doesn't work like that," Pete said.

John watched Molly sit down. Of course Mrs. Tifton had brought her dog. It played around both women's feet.

Jamison coughed blue cigar smoke. "I beg your pardon?"

"It doesn't work like that, Jamison," Pete repeated. "There're people who've been on a wait list to adopt from foster care for years. If the baby goes up for adoption, they'll get first crack at her, not your daughter, not unless her name comes up on the wait list."

"Well, now, Pete, I don't think you've met my daughter. She's a real go-getter. If there's some kind of list she needs to get on, can't you get her on it?"

Pete finished his beer. "No."

Maybe, John thought, he should take Molly and Mrs. Tifton drinks. They didn't have any. Yes, that's what he would do. He would get a glass of champagne for each of them from one of the servers and go up to their table and give them the champagne and say hello.

"Why doesn't your daughter just get one of those Asian

babies?" the former mayor asked the city planner. "Then her kid will be guaranteed to be good at math."

"It doesn't work like that, either," John said, snagging two glasses of champagne from a passing server. "Also, that's racist."

"Why?" Jamison asked, looking offended on the mayor's behalf. "It's a compliment!"

"Still racist." John started toward Molly's table. "And still doesn't work like that."

The city planner shouted after him, "Well, I'm still gonna beat your butt in cornhole tonight!"

John winced as he walked away, hoping no one, particularly Molly Montgomery, had overheard.

As he approached, he saw that she most definitely had not. She was deeply engaged in conversation with Mrs. Robinette—the librarian from his childhood!—and the reporter Meschelle Davies, who'd just stopped by her table with—what else—a whole bottle of champagne and several glasses.

John simply could not win with this woman.

CHAPTER ELEVEN

Molly

Molly had never been to such a glamorous party in her life.

She was sitting on a soft black leather chair within yards of the beach, listening to the rhythmic pulse of the waves while a gentle tropical breeze stroked her cheek, and champagne—not the cheap stuff she was used to drinking, but the kind in the green bottle with the orange label—flowed like water into her glass every time she drained it. There were open bars scattered all around the island serving anything you could think of, from martinis with blue-cheese stuffed olives to salt-rimmed margaritas.

Then there were the piles—*piles*—of fresh stone crab claw. This was a delicacy that Molly had rarely tasted in her past life, partly because stone crab claws were only available in season, October through May, and partly because they were so costly to ship to Colorado. Even in Little

Bridge, where the crabs were plentiful (they were caught in traps right off the beach and then released again), the claws could cost up to forty dollars a pound. On a librarian's salary, this put them out of Molly's budget.

But at the Red Cross Ball the claws were free (well, discounting the cost of her three-hundred-and-fifty-dollar ticket that Mrs. Tifton had paid for), and already broken up for her, and came accompanied by the most delicious honey-mustard sauce Molly had ever tasted. She'd already eaten six large ones and was on her seventh when she looked up and saw a group of party guests headed toward the far side of the beach, the women barefoot, their high heels abandoned, champagne flutes held delicately in their manicured fingers, the men wearing determined expressions and clutching beers.

"What's going on?" Molly asked, wiping her mouth and hands on a napkin in the hopes that no one would notice her gluttony.

"Oh, God." Meschelle had eaten a fair amount of crab, as well. The broken shells lay all over her plate. "The games have begun."

"Every year the ball holds a game of skill to raise money for local charities, as well," Phyllis Robinette explained, "so that we can share the love, so to speak."

As Phyllis spoke, Molly noticed a tall man in military uniform moving swiftly across the room and toward the beach. It took a second for her to realize that the man was Sheriff John Hartwell, and that he wasn't in military uniform but dress uniform.

Her heart skipped a beat. Her heart *actually* skipped a beat, because he looked so good. She was used to seeing him in the beige uniform he wore daily, in which he didn't look bad—he was an attractive man, tall and broad-shouldered, with a strong jaw and of course those disconcertingly blue eyes.

But there was something about seeing him in his dress uniform—dark gray trousers with a perfectly tailored black long-sleeved jacket, beneath which he wore a white shirt and black tie—that made her suddenly aware that he wasn't only attractive—he was *extremely* attractive. He looked as good as the crab she'd just eaten, succulent and sweet but with a sharp tang, the kind that made you keep eating even after you knew you'd had way too much, because you wanted more and more.

Good Lord, what was wrong with her? It must be all that champagne.

He didn't notice her, because he was so intent on getting to the games on the beach.

That's when Molly knew that she, too, had to get over there. Not to join the games. Molly had always been miserable at games. No, Molly needed to keep an eye on the sheriff in his dress uniform. She simply didn't have any other choice.

"Excuse me," she said, quickly abandoning her napkin and chair. "I'll be right back."

Then she hurried as quickly as she could after the sheriff, slipping off her heels so they wouldn't sink into the sand,

and bringing her champagne flute along—it was still more than half-full, after all, and it would be a shame to abandon such good champagne.

Lit by tiki torches—though there was still plenty of light in the lavender sky—were several raised wooden platforms sitting well away from the reach of the waves. Cut into each platform was a small hole. Beside the boards were piles of what appeared to be little beanbags. The sheriff was standing near these with a group of men who were smoking cigars.

Molly wasn't sure what game this was, but she didn't particularly care, either. Her gaze was glued to John Hartwell, who apparently planned to play . . . at least if the fact that he was peeling off his well-fitting jacket was any indication.

Molly's knees suddenly felt weak. She looked around for somewhere to sit, but as they were out on the beach, there was nowhere to sit except on the ground, and she didn't want to get sand in Joanne's beautiful sequined dress (which had been too loose on Joanne and was subsequently a little too tight on Molly, especially now that she'd had so many crab claws).

"May I?" asked a voice to her right, and Molly turned to see Patrick—also known as Lady Patricia, the drag queen who volunteered at the library to read at Story Time—offering to lay his tuxedo jacket down upon the sand for her to sit on.

"Oh, I couldn't!" Molly was mortified.

"Please do." Patrick took a seat on the sand beside the folded jacket. "I was broiling in that thing, anyway. And I'd hate for you to ruin that lovely frock."

"Well . . ." Molly looked down at the tempting folded jacket. In front of her, the sheriff was loosening his tie and undoing the first few buttons of his shirt. It was a white button-down short-sleeved shirt. She could see how closely the darkly tanned curves of his biceps filled those short sleeves.

Molly sat with a thump, spilling a little of her champagne.

Patrick glanced at her with amusement. "See something over there—or should I say some*one*—that interests you?"

"Not at all," Molly replied, more firmly than she meant to. She took a restorative sip of her champagne and then asked, hoping to change the subject, "What game is it exactly that they're about to play?"

Patrick had been taking a sip of the martini he'd brought along with him, which he now nearly spat out in surprise. "Don't tell me you've never heard of cornhole."

"Of course I have." Had she? It was hard for her to remember anything when John Hartwell was standing just a few yards away, looking so tall and attractive in the waning light of the sun. "It's, uh . . ."

"I can see that you've led a very sheltered life, tucked away behind all those books, Molly Montgomery."

Molly didn't feel like correcting him. People always thought this about librarians—that they were introverts who only wanted to stay indoors and read. Of course, this was true of some of them.

But Molly had always had a very active social life. Even when she'd been studying for her degrees, then working, she'd still made time for fun. That's how she'd met her ex, Eric, a dark-eyed radiologist with whom she'd been teamed up at a local brewery's trivia night, and with whom she'd always trounced the competition. He'd known everything about sports and science, and she'd known everything about pop culture and literature. All their friends had been sure they were made for each other.

It was only after they'd gotten engaged and begun discussing their future that she'd realized a talent for trivia was the only thing they had in common.

"Of course, this is *charity* cornhole," Patrick was saying, "not *regular* cornhole. The object of this particular version of the game is to toss as many beanbags as you can into the hole. Whoever gets the kitty wins the pot, which our generous donor—in this case, the Little Bridge State Bank—then matches. The winner traditionally then donates their winnings back to the Red Cross, or some other charity of their choice. But on one or two occasions"—he sent a dark look in the direction of the men to whom the sheriff was talking—"players have been known to keep it."

Shocked, Molly raised her eyebrows. "Really? Someone's kept money meant to be donated for charity? Who would do such a thing?"

"Well, you didn't hear it from me, but our city planner."

He pointed at one of the men to whom the sheriff was speaking, and Molly realized she recognized him because of the frequency with which his name and photo appeared in *The Gazette's* "Cheers and Jeers" section—Randy Jamison, who was well known for delaying or even denying building permits for no good reason, including many the new library had needed. For this he often received "jeers."

"Hmmm," she said. "That doesn't sound very sporting."

"No, but there isn't much we can do about it, except get in there and beat him. And I've never had much of a pitching arm—have you?"

"Oh, God, no."

"I didn't think so. No offense. I feel like this sort of thing is best left to the athletes, like our good sheriff there. Did you know he was all-state in baseball when he was in high school?"

Molly shook her head, though she wasn't surprised, given how strong and sinewy his arms looked. She wondered idly what arms like that would feel like around her. . . .

She had *definitely* had too much champagne.

"Oh, yes," Patrick went on. "Right here in Little Bridge. From what I understand, he would have gone to the pros if he hadn't gotten his high school sweetheart pregnant and chosen instead to marry her, stay here on the island, help raise his daughter, and become a police officer. He was a good one, too, until he got a criminal justice degree at the local community college and eventually applied for and made detective up in Miami."

Molly dug her free hand into the sand and found a pretty

seashell with which she pretended to be fascinated. "Why did he move back?"

"The sheriff? Oh, well, the island needed him, after what happened with the last sheriff. And I think he missed it here and wanted a change. He was working homicide in Miami, which I can't imagine would be very pleasant."

She sipped her champagne, silently agreeing. She'd seen a few news broadcasts from Miami. Some of the murders there had been horrifyingly violent, even from a crime junkie viewpoint. "But his wife . . . ?"

"Oh, his wife—now ex-wife—has quite a flourishing home-design business up there. So when he came back to Little Bridge to take the sheriff's position, she stayed up north. I heard the split was perfectly amicable—no hard feelings."

Molly considered this delicately put answer while pretending not to watch the sheriff's every move. He was stuffing a wad of bills into the kitty, a large crystal vase being passed around by one of the Red Cross volunteers, whom Molly recognized as the nurse Daniella—she'd done multiple blood drives at the library. Bubbly and outgoing, Nurse Dani had also been appointed the game referee, if the shiny silver whistle around her neck was any indication. It complemented the short silver cocktail dress she wore.

Abruptly, Molly turned and handed Patrick two twenty-dollar bills she'd drawn from her clutch. "Here."

He looked down at the bills with puzzled surprise. "Don't tell me you're going to play?"

"Oh, no. But I want to contribute. Would you mind

slipping those into the kitty for me, please? They can be from both of us. I'm much too comfortable here on the sand to get up."

He gave her a knowing look as he rose to his feet. "Oh, of course. *That's* why you don't want to get up. You're too *comfortable.* Not that you're too shy to speak to a certain someone."

"I'm simply enjoying this lovely moment on the beach," she said, and after delicately placing her champagne glass on the sand, drew her cell phone from her clutch to snap a photo of the sun as it sank behind a mangrove in the distance—and also to hide her face and the fact that she was blushing.

While Patrick smirked and strode through the sand toward Nurse Dani with Molly's offering, she willed herself not to look in his direction, in case he exchanged words with the sheriff and the latter ended up glancing her way. She told herself she was still recovering from all the champagne and crab claws and that it was wiser for her not to speak to handsome men in uniform.

Instead, she concentrated on how nearly all of the guests from inside the dining room had come out onto the beach to observe the game alongside her, most with drinks in their hand. Quite a few more people had lined up to play, many of whom Molly knew, not necessarily from their library usage but from around town. There was the pink-haired waitress, Bree, and her boyfriend, Drew, whom Molly often saw at the Mermaid Café when she popped in to grab a quick lunch. Several of Mrs. Tifton's guests—Robbie and her fiancé, Ryan—were also in line to play, as was Patrick's husband, Bill, and even Meschelle. The competition was starting to look a bit fierce.

Which Molly told herself was good. So long as Randy Jamison didn't win and keep all the money to himself. That's all that mattered.

That's what Molly thought, anyway, until the game finally started. Then, as she watched the sheriff play and saw just how truly good he was—how gentlemanly and sportsmanlike, giving others friendly advice on their throws that could help them beat him—she realized how badly she was rooting for him, and him alone, to win, especially as player after player except the sheriff and the insufferable Mr. Jamison failed to propel their beanbag even remotely close to the nearest hole. Most throws landed in the sand. Those players were immediately disqualified by Nurse Dani, who turned out to be quite the tyrannical referee. (Not that anyone seemed to mind. It was a good-natured game, with quite a lot of joking and laughter.)

As the sky turned from pale lavender to dark blue, and they actually needed the light from the tiki flames to see by, the sheriff's and the city planner's beanbags were the only ones seeming to go into the holes.

By this time Molly was on her feet, having hurried closer so that she could watch what appeared to be an old-fashioned—and epic—showdown. She didn't want the sheriff to *see* her watching, of course—not because she was shy, but because it would be embarrassing if he caught her staring at him.

So she hung behind Patrick as he narrated the game like a sports announcer to anyone who would listen, which turned out to be basically everyone.

"The score is now seventeen to fifteen in favor of Sheriff Hartwell. The game is close, but I believe the sheriff's killer cornhole technique will, in the end, make him victorious."

Molly didn't know about that, but she did know that the sheriff's dress pants fit him in just such a way that when he leaned forward to make a toss, her pulse stuttered. She'd also finished her champagne and developed a very powerful thirst. She wanted to go inside and order another drink—perhaps a water, to cool off—but she also didn't want to tear herself away from the game in case she missed something, like a crucial shot or the sheriff bending over to lift something.

What on earth was wrong with her tonight?

Just then Randy Jamison's fourth bag of the round swept clean past his hole and skidded into the sand. A cry went up, the loudest of which was Molly's own. Everyone turned to look at her except, fortunately, the sheriff. He was so wrapped up in his game that no one else appeared to exist to him. This was true sportsmanship.

"Why," Molly clutched Patrick's arm and asked, "isn't there an Olympic category for cornhole? If there was, the sheriff would definitely win the gold!"

Patrick looked down at her with an odd expression on his face, possibly because she'd caused him to slosh a little of his martini into the sand. "My dear girl," he said, "I'm sure you're right. You should—"

But then the sheriff's final toss sailed cleanly into the hole, and Molly screamed loudly enough that Patrick wasn't the only one who spilled his drink in alarm.

She didn't care, though. She jumped up and down in the sand, thrilled that John had beaten the dreadful city planner.

"Oh my God," murmured Meschelle, who'd ended up standing beside her. "Someone's taking their cornhole a little personally, aren't they?"

But Molly couldn't help it, especially when Nurse Dani presented the sheriff with the crystal vase stuffed with bills and announced, "We've collected over *four thousand dollars* from the generous people here tonight, which the Little Bridge State Bank has graciously agreed to match, dollar for dollar."

This was greeted with hoots and cheers, the loudest of which came, again, from Molly. Dani had to raise her voice to be heard over the applause.

"That makes over eight thousand dollars, which I'm now handing off to our new cornhole champion, Sheriff John Hartwell, to either keep or donate to the charity of his choice."

Nurse Dani passed the vase to the sheriff, who accepted it with a lopsided smile of sheepish embarrassment, made all the more adorable—in Molly's opinion, anyway—by the fact that his shirt had become untucked in places by the vigor of the game, and his already too-short hair was sexily mussed.

"Uh," the sheriff began. "Thanks, Dani. I—"

"Keep!" shouted some of the more inebriated men in the crowd. "Keep it!"

"Shut up," roared Nurse Dani, in the same voice that Molly imagined she used on drunks in her ER, of which there were many, Little Bridge being known as a party town. "Let him talk."

"I'd just like to say thanks to everyone for coming out again this year to support this important cause." The sheriff's voice was gruff, as if he were unused to speaking much, which was ridiculous as Molly knew for a fact that he used his voice quite a lot, especially when he was disagreeing with her about something. "I'm sure many of you remember all the help the Red Cross gave those of us who were in need last year when we were hit by Hurricane Marilyn, and they continue to do vital work not just in the United States but all around the world. They save lives, and they absolutely need the money we've all donated here tonight."

Oh, Molly thought, a warm feeling growing in her heart. *He's going to donate the money to the Red Cross. That is very sweet.*

"And of course there's a nonprofit very close to my heart, our own city jail petting zoo, where we could certainly use the money," John went on. "But there's an individual here in our community who needs our financial help even more, someone who is just getting started in life. I'd like to donate this money you've all so generously donated to Little Bridge's newest resident, Baby Aphrodite."

Molly was so shocked by this that her mouth fell open wordlessly. Then her knees gave out completely, and she sank down onto the powder-soft sand.

It was only then that the sheriff's gaze finally met hers.

CHAPTER TWELVE

John

John wasn't sure what the proper etiquette was anymore when it came to approaching attractive single women in whom he had a romantic interest, particularly at charity fundraisers. They had not covered this topic at the four-hour sexual harassment–awareness training program.

And the Red Cross Ball was still technically a work function, since he had not paid for his ticket himself—it had been comped, as his tickets were to most such functions.

So after his failed attempt at offering her a drink, he'd stayed assiduously away from the librarian, even though he'd been highly aware of her presence, especially during the cornhole tournament, where she'd made a very pretty—and enthusiastic—spectator.

It was gratifying to have anyone appreciate what a challenging and ultimately tricky game cornhole could be. Most people considered it a children's game, or something to be played only at birthday parties or outside of bars. In Little Bridge, it was generally considered that the more intoxicated the participants, the better.

But if anyone really gave it a moment's thought, the way Molly Montgomery obviously had, they could see how difficult a sport it was, and how much hand-eye coordination it required. John liked that Molly respected that, and also how closely she'd observed his technique.

But even that didn't seem like enough of a reason to approach her at what was, technically, a work event . . . until she tripped in the sand in front of him and fell over. As a first responder, it was his responsibility—his *duty*, really—to go over to her, and make sure she wasn't in need of first aid.

"Are you all right?" John asked, reaching down with a supportive hand.

"I'm fine." Her small hand felt warm in his, vibrant and alive as a little yellow finch Katie had once found in the backyard, stunned from a tropical-storm-force wind.

It was only when Molly lifted her head and saw who it was who'd offered her help that her large, dark eyes flared even wider than usual, and she quickly slipped her hand from his, almost as startled as the finch had been.

"Oh," she cried. "You!"

"Yes," he said, still concerned. "It's me. John. Are you hurt?"

"No." Quickly brushing sand from her knees and strands of her fine dark hair from her damp cheeks, she said, in a shaky voice, "I just feel stupid."

"You shouldn't," he said. "Everyone trips sometimes."

"Oh, yes. I tripped," she said. "That's exactly what happened. *So.* Baby Aphrodite. That was so nice of you!"

"Well." Obviously he hadn't chosen to donate the money to Baby Aphrodite to be nice. He'd done it to get Molly to like him. He didn't actually believe the kid was going to need the money. The grandparents would call him soon for the good news—it was a bit odd they hadn't called already, but he'd never been to Alaska, who knew what their cell service was like—and reconcile with their daughter, and in no time, mother and daughter would be back in the Brightons' mansion in New Canaan, Connecticut (he'd looked up the Brightons' address on Google Earth—they had a four-car garage), enrolled in some fancy Mommy and Me class that cost more than his monthly mortgage payment, and living happily ever after.

And, of course, if Beckwith really was the father, John would get him—or his family—to pay up as well.

But he couldn't let Molly Montgomery know that this was something he thought. He had a pretty strong feeling that somehow she wouldn't approve of his having interfered in the girl's affairs in this way.

"It seemed like the right thing to do," he said, instead.

He hadn't been the only one to hurry over to help the librarian. Patrick O'Brian, owner of Little Bridge's Seam and Fabric Shoppe and the island's most popular drag queen (who, John had to admit, was pretty damned entertaining), had also rushed over to make sure she was all right.

Upon seeing John already at her side, Patrick took a quick

step back and said, "Miss Molly, I told you, you need to *hydrate.* In this heat, you have to drink one glass of water for every glass of alcohol." He looked at the sheriff and rolled his eyes. "Mainlanders. Am I right? Maybe you should take her inside, Sheriff, and get her some water."

John could not have agreed more. He slipped his fingers around one of Molly's bare arms (how could her skin be so satiny?) and said, "Yes, that's probably a good idea."

"Oh," Molly murmured weakly. "No, it's fine. I'm all right—"

"You're not all right, honey." Meschelle Davies, whose articles in *The Gazette* rarely treated law enforcement fairly, gave the librarian a little push. "You go on with the sheriff. You look a little flushed."

"Oh, well," Molly said. "Okay, then, I guess."

John swore he would never grouse about his treatment in one of Ms. Davies's articles again.

The librarian allowed him to lead her along the beach path back to the hotel's open-air dining room, with its tropical plantation décor and large, gently swinging ceiling fans. She held her high-heeled shoes and sparkling evening bag in her hands, and seemed much less chatty than at any other time he'd ever encountered her. She must, he told himself, truly be dehydrated. This happened often to those who were new to the Florida Keys. A combination of the heat and humidity, coupled with alcohol consumption, occasionally caused them to become ill. It was a very good thing he'd come along and rescued her.

Her silence, however, lasted only until they reached a

booth inside the hotel restaurant and he guided her onto its soft black leather, then slid in beside her and ordered two large ice waters from a conscientious server. That's when she lifted her face and asked, her dark eyes seemingly even larger than ever in the mysterious flame of the hurricane lamp on their tabletop, "Did you really mean what you said out there? You're going to donate all that money you won to the baby?"

"Well, of course," he said, surprised that she'd doubt him. "And to her mother, as well. I'd make a pretty sorry public officer if I said it in front of all those people and didn't mean it."

"It's just . . ." She drew a circle in the condensation on the side of the water glass that had been placed in front of her. "I thought you were going to arrest her. The baby's mother, I mean. You said the other day—"

John stirred uncomfortably in his seat, remembering their initial meeting, when he'd sat in that tiny chair beside her desk. "I know. And it's still a criminal offense to abandon a newborn, unless it's in a state-appointed safe haven. But my investigation so far has given me reason to believe that the mother of Baby Aphrodite was probably not the person who did the actual abandoning—"

"I *knew* it!" Molly leaned forward to wrap her ruby red lips around the paper straw inside her water glass. Damned if he couldn't stop thinking about other things he'd like to see those red lips wrapped around. What was wrong with him? He was an elected official and here he was, with a member of the public—a librarian, no less!—and all he could think about was sex. "The leader of the Sunshine Kids, right? Dylan Dakota? Fingerprint analysis proved it?"

All thoughts of those red lips around any body part of his evaporated. John felt a not-unfamiliar spurt of irritation. Dylan Dakota? How on earth did she know about him? What was it with this woman? Librarian or not, had she been faking dehydration the entire time?

Because suddenly she looked not only perfectly alert, even cool, in what should have been a very romantic setting, but extremely curious, even feline. Dylan Dakota? How was he ever going to make love to this woman if all she ever wanted to talk about was his mortal enemy?

Not that he wanted to make love to her! Not at all. Because he was a professional and so was she and they were at a professional function and he was in uniform and he'd just rescued her (maybe) and he'd given up on romantic relationships because they never worked out.

Or had he?

But damn! Suddenly she did not seem at all flustered or faint. She seemed to be in perfect possession of her faculties.

"I mean, this Dylan Dakota person sounds like a very bad guy," she said, in a deceptively innocent tone, after swallowing some more water.

Deceptively innocent to some people. But not to Sheriff John Hartwell.

"Are you even dehydrated?" he demanded.

"I don't know," Molly said. "Why? Do I not seem dehydrated to you?"

"No."

She shrugged, her smooth bare shoulders luminous in the candlelight. "I don't think I am, either. But you know what I do think?"

This, he said to himself, *is a very dangerous conversation.* "What?"

"I think you're an excellent cornhole player."

John frowned. "Now you're only sucking up to me, probably because you want to hear more inside information about the case, which I can assure you I am not going to give you."

She removed her lips from the straw to make a soft noise of indignant protest, which a part of him found incredibly sexy, but another part of him worried was only an act to gain more information. "Where did you even hear that stuff about Dylan Dakota? Wait, let me guess. Meschelle Davies."

She had the grace to look affronted. "I'm sorry, but did you miss the fact that I am a librarian? I have access to a vast network of resources. *Vast*. But I feel that as the person who found Baby Aphrodite and saved her life, I have the right to know everything involving her case."

"You do not," he said irritably, aware that he felt irritable only because she looked extremely attractive in the candlelight, and was also morally, although not legally, correct, "You do not."

"I do. How are your dance lessons going?"

"What?"

"Dance lessons. With Katie, your daughter?"

Belatedly, he remembered another demoralizing moment in their relationship, which so far seemed to consist of almost nothing but demoralizing moments.

"Not so great," he said. "It turns out I only need to know a very specific dance for the performance. A very specific dance that goes to a very specific song by a very specific performer you might have heard of—Beyoncé?"

Molly's red lips pressed inward, as if she was trying to keep herself from smiling. "I've heard of her. What very specific song of hers are you dancing to?"

"'Single Ladies.'" He tried not to show how uncomfortable the dance made him, although he enjoyed the song. "I'd never heard of it."

Molly's lips curled into a smile. "You're not exactly the target demographic. Do you want me to help you learn it?"

He was surprised. "You know the dance to 'Single Ladies'?"

"Oh, you wouldn't believe the things I've had people ask me to teach them in my capacity as a librarian. The 'Single Ladies' dance is the least of it. Come here."

The next thing he knew, she'd slid from the booth and taken hold of both his hands. Then she was gently pulling him from his own seat and toward the center of the room. He let her, because the feel of her skin on his was so magical, and also because there was no one else in the room except a few servers, and they were paying no attention to the librarian teaching the bumble-footed sheriff to dance. They were bustling around, putting glassware away. All of the party guests were outside on the now night-darkened beach, drinking and laughing in the red-orange glow of the tiki torches.

"Stand up tall like this," Molly commanded, and put her hands on his shoulders to straighten them. When she stood close to him, he could smell the fresh flowery shampoo she used on her shiny dark hair, and something else—something fruity. It took him a minute to recognize it. It was the key lime–coconut signature scent the Lazy Parrot inn housekeepers sprayed everywhere. It must have sunk deep into all of Molly Montgomery's belongings by now.

He'd never smelled anything as intoxicating.

"Now put your feet about shoulders' width apart," she said, inserting her foot, still bare, between his feet and giving them both a dainty little kick until he widened his stance. "That's it. Now put this hand on your hip—no, this hand—"

He did as she asked, looking down at her bent head, her narrow brows furrowed with concentration, and wondered how they ever could have argued when she was so adorable.

"Perfect. Now put your other hand in the air, like this—" She manipulated his left arm so it bent at the elbow. "Remember when you sang 'I'm a Little Teapot' with Katie? You two sang that together, right?"

"I did." He couldn't take his eyes off her.

"Well, your arm should look a little like that."

She stepped back to observe her handiwork, and John didn't even care how ridiculous he might appear to whoever might happen to come strolling in from the beach. Randy Jamison or even Pete could walk by and laugh all they wanted. John had Molly Montgomery all to himself, and right now, he couldn't think of anything he wanted more.

"Good," she said, after giving him a critical once over. "That looks good. Though it might help if you could maybe . . . loosen up a little."

"Loosen up?" He glanced down at himself. He felt plenty loose. "How do you mean?"

"Well, you just look kind of . . . tight. The whole point of this dance is to have fun, and you look like you're on the way to the guillotine."

He gave her a sarcastic look. "That's just my face. I'm a cop. I have to be ever vigilant for would-be miscreants."

"No." She shook her head, still studying him critically. "It's not your face. It's your body language. You need to loosen up in here." She stepped forward, her gaze on his face, but her hands in the air. "May I?"

"Um . . . sure." What was she going to do with her hands?

He supposed he shouldn't have been surprised when she placed them on his hips. This was a dance lesson, after all.

"You need to loosen up *here,*" she said, pressing firmly on his hips, and then swaying her own in front of him to illustrate what she meant—while not releasing her hold. "Do you see what I mean? You've got to feel the music. If they were playing Beyoncé, I mean, and not this—"

What they were actually playing was jazz. Coltrane, to be exact. John liked Coltrane and listened to him quite a lot in his car on the streaming channel that Katie had set up for him. The combination of the Coltrane and Molly Montgomery's hands on his hips, plus her own hips swaying so suggestively in such close proximity to his own, plus the sweet scent of her hair and coconutty smell of her clothes in this darkened room, with the ocean breeze blowing in from the beach, was doing something to him. Something he hadn't felt in a long time.

Something he liked a lot.

Still, he wasn't sure what he should do about it. He hadn't dated in so long. And this was the librarian. Up until this very moment, he'd been fairly sure she hated him.

But would a woman who hated a man be holding him by the hips and encouraging him to loosen up while also smiling up at him with such enticingly red lips?

He didn't think so.

Still, his heart pounding as nervously as it had the time he'd asked his first-ever girlfriend—Lori MacNamara, seventh grade—to couples skate at the long-since-demolished Little Bridge Skateland, he lowered both hands to her hips.

"Molly," he said, in a voice that had gone suddenly hoarse.

Her body instantly stilled, and she brought her questioning gaze up to his. Those red lips were still smiling, invitingly to his mind. "Yes?"

Should he ask first or just kiss her? What did people do these days? He knew what they'd said in the sexual harassment seminar, but that had been about work, and this wasn't work . . . or was it? Why did everything have to be so confusing? Why couldn't—

To his utter shock, Molly pulled him toward her, raising up on tiptoe in her bare feet to bring her mouth toward his. He wasn't even aware of what was going on at first, it all happened so fast. One minute they weren't kissing, and the next, they were, her arms slipping around his neck so that her soft, round breasts pressed up against his chest, her scent enveloping him in a heady cloud.

He might have considered himself the luckiest man alive

if his cell phone hadn't chosen that moment to let out a shrill blare from the pocket of his dress uniform.

She pulled away immediately, startled. For him, the sudden break in contact was as if he were an astronaut traversing a bleak and airless planet and she was his only connection to home and oxygen.

"Goddammit," he swore, and clawed at his uniform trousers in an attempt to find the phone, which was continuing to ring loudly.

Fortunately Molly seemed to find the situation funny. She stood a few feet away, her arms folded across her chest, laughing at him. "Does this happen to you often?" she asked.

"Too damn much." He managed to extract the phone and glared down at the screen. For a second or two he'd been worried it was Tabitha's parents—he'd left them his personal number. How was he going to explain to the librarian that he'd violated what he'd expected were the personal wishes of Baby Aphrodite's mother by contacting the family from whom she'd run away?

But it was only Marguerite, who'd volunteered to skip the party and work late, since so many of his deputies were still out looking for Beckwith and John had wanted someone competent at the office (and Marguerite professed to hate parties, anyway).

"What is it?" he barked into the phone. He couldn't help it. He'd been kissing Molly Montgomery. What were the chances of that ever happening again?

"Well, and good evening to you, too, Chief," Marguerite said with cheerful sarcasm. "Sorry to bother you, but I just thought you might want to know that while you and everyone else was over there on Jasmine Key, partying it up, the High School Thief has been busy."

John threw a glance at Molly. She'd turned away from him because Mrs. Tifton and a number of her friends had come into the bar, all chattering at once. Mrs. Tifton was waving her cell phone and looking alarmed.

"Oh, yeah? Busy doing what?" But John was pretty sure he already knew the answer.

"Robbing Dorothy Tifton's house," Marguerite said, confirming his suspicion, "while she was there with you."

CHAPTER THIRTEEN

Molly

Molly had never been to a crime scene before. Well, aside from the one at the library the other day.

She'd had no intention of ending up at another one, except that Mrs. Tifton insisted that if *all* of her friends didn't come along with her on the boat back to Little Bridge Island in order to help her inspect whatever damage had been done to her home by the High School Thief, she wasn't certain how she was going to make it through the night emotionally.

The sheriff didn't look too happy about that, given how firmly he kept his lips pressed together throughout the ride . . . those lips that mere minutes before had been so tantalizingly pressed to hers.

But Molly refused to think about that. This was a serious situation, and she intended to keep her mind focused on the matter at hand, and not at all on the fact that a little while earlier, the sheriff had been holding her so tightly in his strong arms, she could hardly breathe, and kissing her as if his life depended on it.

John had decided that Mrs. Tifton could have *one* friend with her inside the house during "this difficult time." The rest had to wait for her outside, so as "not to disrupt the crime scene."

"And I," he'd added, "will be the one picking which friend gets to come inside."

That's how Molly found herself sitting on one of the pure-white couches in Mrs. Tifton's living room, taking in the scene around her and trying very hard not to think about the sheriff's lips.

"I just don't see how he did it." Mrs. Tifton was crying, and not for the first time. She'd been wailing this same statement, or something along similar lines, since they'd left Jasmine Key. "I always keep all my doors locked. And I have an alarm!"

It was true. Mrs. Tifton, unlike the thief's previous victims, had kept all the French doors leading from her beautiful, high-ceilinged living room to her backyard pool locked.

But neither this nor the security alarm appeared to have troubled the thief, who'd merely broken the pane of glass closest to the gilt door handle, reached inside to unlock it, then snatched up whatever he could carry between the time it took for the alarm to begin to blare and the arrival of the first sheriff's deputies on the scene—which turned out to be seven minutes, John explained.

"Seven minutes?" Molly repeated, throwing an incredulous glance in John's direction.

But he ignored her. He was busy staring at his deputies—not the crime scene techs, who were busy dusting the door handle for prints, or taking photos of what they believed to be the thief's footprints in the pile of Mrs. Tifton's recently vacuumed carpet—a thin young blond woman and an equally thin young man, who'd apparently been first to arrive.

"There were a couple of youths throwing down in the parking lot over at the Coffee Cubano, Chief," whined the male deputy, whose badge had the name Swanson printed on it. "It took us a little while to get it under control and get over here."

"Youths throwing down at the Coffee Cubano?" The sheriff raised a single dark eyebrow. "Or was Carmelita giving away free con leches again?"

The young deputies stared down at their shoes, their humiliation so complete that Molly almost felt a little sorry for them.

She also realized why John had allowed none of Mrs. Tifton's friends but herself into the house. Imagine what Meschelle Davies might do with this piece of information. "*Deputies Too Busy Accepting Bribes to Catch High School Thief*" was only one of the many headlines Molly could imagine in tomorrow's *Gazette*.

"There were no youths throwing down, sir," the female deputy had the courage to pipe up and say. "But no one was offering free coffee, either. It's the house alarms, sir. They tend to go off for no reason. Sometimes if the wind blows too strong, they go off. Then we haul ass to get over there, and it's a false alarm."

"And was the wind blowing too strong this evening, Deputy Juarez?" John asked in a tone that made Molly thankful she wasn't Deputy Juarez.

"Well, no, sir," the deputy responded meekly. "It was a fairly calm evening, weather-wise."

"Right. Just like I imagine it was fairly calm in the parking lot of the Coffee Cubano. You both wanted to finish your coffees before driving over here to check out what I'm assuming you thought would be another false alarm. But it wasn't a false alarm, was it?"

Both Swanson and Juarez kept their gaze on the carpet, which, like the couch Molly was sitting on, was pure white, except for several dirty gray footprints that the crime scene techs were measuring, photographing, and tweezing for what Molly assumed were soil samples, though it seemed obvious to her that the dirt had come from Mrs. Tifton's backyard pool area.

"No, Chief, it wasn't." Only Juarez had the courage to reply. "Sorry, Chief."

"Go write up your reports," the sheriff said in a stern voice. "And quit calling me Chief."

Dismissed, the two young deputies hurried away, their heads hanging in shame. John turned his attention back to Mrs. Tifton, who was huddled on the couch beside Molly, sipping a cup of tea, her poodle, Daisy, on her lap. Mrs. Tifton had insisted on making everyone tea, a special herbal blend she'd brought back with her from a yoga trip to India. So far everyone had declined except for Molly, who hadn't wanted to be impolite.

"So what exactly are we missing here, Mrs. Tifton?" John asked.

"Well, like I told the other officers, I'm not really entirely sure. I know I left my iPad right there." She touched the low glass coffee table in front of her and Molly, where the tea service sat and where there were several large glossy art books. "And of course now it's gone. And Norman's camera—it was a very expensive Leica—it's gone from the bookshelf over there. And I don't see my sunglasses. But perhaps I was wearing my sunglasses. Molly, was I wearing my sunglasses? Perhaps they're in my bag—"

"You were wearing your sunglasses." Molly laid a gentle hand on the widow's shoulder. "Remember? You put them on at our table when the sun was in our eyes."

"Oh, right!" Mrs. Tifton set down her teacup and opened her evening bag, which was on the couch beside her. "Yes, here they are. So he didn't take my sunglasses. But my iPad and Norman's Leica are definitely gone. Oh, that's so upsetting. Norman loved that Leica. You can't get them like that anymore. It was one of the first digital kind, but pocket-sized. It still worked quite well."

John nodded and wrote something down in the weatherproof notepad he always seemed to carry, even on nights he was attending a charity ball. Molly tried not to notice how strong his hands looked, or imagine how those hands might feel on various parts of her body.

Fortunately she was spared from these very unprofessional thoughts by another officer she didn't recognize—this one an older woman with thick dark hair coiled in a tight bun at the nape of her neck and a different-colored uniform than the others—entering the living room from one of the open French doors. She was carrying a paper bag.

"Chief," she said. "We might have found something."

The sheriff snapped his notebook shut. "Now that's what I like to hear. What have you got, Marguerite?"

John stepped across the room to speak with the officer, whose nametag read *Sergeant Ruiz*. Molly didn't want to look as if she was eavesdropping, but she also didn't want to miss a single part of the first criminal investigation in which she'd ever taken part (obviously the search for Baby Aphrodite's mother didn't count because she'd already been found and she was clearly not a criminal).

So she asked Mrs. Tifton brightly, "More tea?" and before the old woman could respond, she leaped up to refill her cup, putting herself in a perfect place on the far side of the coffee table to listen to the officers.

"Found it out back," Sergeant Ruiz was saying in a low voice, opening the paper bag and showing whatever was inside to the sheriff. "It was hanging from some of the bougainvillea along the homeowner's fence."

John nodded. "Maybe when he was making a run for it, it got snagged."

"Would make sense that he'd leave it behind, rather than risk getting caught."

"But it could be hers." John nodded at Mrs. Tifton, who'd answered her cell phone (it had been ringing nonstop as news of the break-in spread across the island, and the widow couldn't be persuaded not to answer it). She was twittering once more about how fortunate it was that she'd taken Daisy with her to the ball, since who knew what that nasty thief might have done to the poor animal if he'd found her there, all alone and defenseless (although Molly had once seen Daisy lunge at a chicken at the library, so she wasn't entirely sure how defenseless the dog actually was).

Sergeant Ruiz shook her head. "And what, it blew off a wash line? Didn't see a wash line, and this isn't really her style. My boy's got one just like it. This is menswear."

"One way to find out," the sheriff said with a shrug, and took the paper bag from her, turning just as Molly was lowering the teapot back onto the coffee table. They almost collided.

She thought she recovered nicely by smiling, hoisting the teapot high, and asking, "Tea, Sheriff?"

He looked at her with a comical expression—comical to her, anyway. His mouth was twisted as if he were trying not to smile—this was a serious situation, after all—but his blue eyes were alight with humor.

"Thank you for the offer, Miss Montgomery, but not right now." He turned toward the homeowner. "Mrs. Tifton, this was found just now in your backyard. Does it look familiar to you?"

From the paper sack, he withdrew something black, using the pen with which he'd been scribbling in his notepad so as not to taint it with his DNA (or so Molly assumed). It took her a moment to realize that the object was a hoodie.

A black hoodie, exactly like the one Elijah wore nearly every day, despite Little Bridge Island's heat.

Her heart seemed to skip a beat.

No. No, it wasn't possible.

"What is it?" Mrs. Tifton asked curiously. "Is it a shirt?"

"It's a hoodie," Sergeant Ruiz said. "A men's hoodie, size small."

Mrs. Tifton shook her head in bewilderment. "No, that doesn't belong to me. Or Norman, either. He wore a large. And he'd never have worn such a thing. He liked big, baggy, short-sleeved shirts. And he never wore black. And of course I donated all of his things to the Salvation Army a while back. They were so grateful. They really do need men's clothing, you know."

John allowed himself to smile this time. It was a kind and patient smile.

"That's nice to know, Mrs. Tifton," he said. "Do you know anyone else who might wear a shirt like this?"

Elijah, Molly thought to herself, feeling a little sick. *Elijah wears a shirt like that. But it can't be his. He'd never do a thing like this.*

Except that he'd bragged that he was the High School Thief.

"Not really," said Mrs. Tifton. "But I suppose I could. I do have an awful lot of friends, especially now that Norman has passed. He didn't like to socialize much, but now that he's gone, people have been so nice to me, and I get so many invitations—"

Molly wondered if John was sharing her same thought: that Mrs. Tifton was receiving so many invitations because she was the wealthiest widow in Little Bridge, and everyone wanted her to donate to their cause. But this seemed an ungenerous sentiment and would probably never occur to the sheriff. Mrs. Tifton was also unfailingly bubbly and sweet, which was also why she was so popular.

"—it seems rude not to accept them, so I've met so many people, especially young people who might wear a shirt like that. All those young men with the Little Bridge Theater Company, for instance. But you don't think one of them—?"

"Not at all," John said mildly. "It was just a thought."

"Let's try this," Sergeant Ruiz said, and, taking the pen from John's hand, brought the hoodie closer to Mrs. Tifton. "Would you mind taking a sniff, please, Mrs. T?"

Mrs. Tifton looked surprised . . . but she couldn't have felt half as surprised as Molly, who never in all her crime viewing or reading had heard of a victim being asked to sniff a suspect's garment. What on earth was wrong with the Little Bridge Sheriff's Department?

"Smell it?" Mrs. Tifton's surprise had turned to bewilderment.

"Yes." Both Sergeant Ruiz and Sheriff Hartwell wore expressions of perfect seriousness. "The olfactory sense is one of the strongest," Sergeant Ruiz said, "and sometimes scent can trigger memories that we might otherwise have forgotten or have even suppressed."

Mrs. Tifton glanced uncertainly at Molly, who could only shrug. "It couldn't hurt," she said. Except that inside, of course, she was quaking. What if it smelled like Elijah? Mrs. Tifton had never met Elijah—that Molly knew of—but his scent was very distinctive. He doused—*doused*—himself in body wash and cheap cologne every morning, believing the constant barrage of media advertising that told him and other young males that this would make him more appealing to females. So far, it hadn't worked. In fact, it seemed to have had the opposite effect.

So her heart was hammering when Mrs. Tifton gave a little laugh and said, "Oh, well, fine," leaned forward, and sniffed the hoodie.

Molly thought her heart would explode when the widow instantly reared back, wrinkled her nose, and cried, "Ew!" then said, "Oh, my," and fanned her face.

This was exactly how Molly felt whenever she got too close to Elijah.

Sergeant Ruiz nodded as if she'd expected this response. "That bad, huh? Remind you of anyone?"

"Well, it's bad. But I can't say it *reminds* me of anyone."

"What?" Molly asked, her heart now in her throat. "What does it smell like?"

"Very cheap men's cologne," Mrs. Tifton said.

Molly had to sit down again. How was she going to handle this? She couldn't turn Elijah in, of course. He was her patron and she cared about him.

But she couldn't let him get away with this kind of behavior, either. It was possible he was breaking the law, and hurting people, too. Obviously his parents' divorce was affecting him much more than his mother had ever suspected and causing him to act out in a completely unacceptable way.

Still, he'd have to be held responsible for his crimes.

But he was only sixteen. Maybe the court would show a little leniency, due to his young age.

"And cigarette smoke," Mrs. Tifton added.

"What?" Molly looked up sharply.

"I suppose the cologne is to cover up the smell of the cigarette smoke," Mrs. Tifton went on. "Norman used to smoke Cuban cigars whenever someone gave him one, and that's a trick he'd use, thinking I wouldn't catch him. But I always did!"

Cigarette smoke? Not Elijah! He'd never smoke. He was always railing against the kids at his school who vaped in the bathroom—the "vaperoom," he called it. He scoffed at them for spending all their money on vaping when they could be using it for more useful things, such as video games and pizza.

It wasn't Elijah. It couldn't be Elijah.

Unless . . .

Unless he'd finally made some friends, and those friends smoked.

Oh, God.

Sergeant Ruiz dropped the hoodie back into the paper bag and sealed it up again. "Thanks," she said. "That's very helpful."

Molly didn't see how any of what had just transpired was helpful . . . unless they already had a suspect in mind and knew he smoked and used an excessive amount of cologne. She needed to find out, if only to set her mind at ease.

The problem was, she was fairly certain the sheriff wasn't going to tell her, any more than she'd violate the privacy of a patron by sharing information about them with him—unless he had a court order, of course.

"I can leave a couple of my deputies to sit outside your house tonight, Mrs. Tifton," John was saying, "if that would make you feel more comfortable. Or I could stay myself. It's the least I can do until you can get that window fixed—"

"Oh, no!" Mrs. Tifton, who never liked to be a bother, pooh-poohed this offer immediately. "I'll be all right."

"I'm happy to stay the night with you," Molly offered. Joanne wouldn't need her until tomorrow, when the hotel would have its usual flurry of Sunday-morning checkouts. And though Sunday was one of the busiest days in the library due to the number of fathers who had child visitation that day, she hadn't scheduled any difficult programming, such as cookie decorating. She'd learned her lesson after what had happened with Elijah, and of course all the sprinkles she'd found spilled all over the floor afterward. "We could watch a movie together to settle your nerves."

"Well." Mrs. Tifton looked tempted. "I have been wishing for a quiet moment together to work a bit more on the invitation list for the library's grand opening. I keep having this terrible feeling there are people I've forgotten."

"We could do that, certainly." Molly glanced at John and

felt a blush of pleasure when she saw that he was gazing at her with approval.

"That's settled, then," he said. "Let me take Miss Montgomery to her place so she can get an overnight bag, and then I'll bring her right back. And in the meantime, my people will clean up this mess for you."

Molly blushed even more deeply as she realized John was angling for them to spend a few moments alone together in his car—a huge, gas-guzzling SUV. Not that she'd have expected him to drive anything else.

"Oh, how kind of you," Mrs. Tifton said, looking delighted. "I must say, the Little Bridge Island Sheriff's Department certainly provides quality service!"

John, his gaze glued to Molly's, said, "We aim to please, ma'am."

CHAPTER FOURTEEN

John

The evening might not end up being a total disaster after all. He had Molly Montgomery alone in his car, didn't he?

Still, there was every chance he could screw it up. It had been such a long time since he dated. He had hardly even tried since he and Christina split, since the local sheriff couldn't very well be seen on dating apps or hanging around in bars.

Everything had been going so well back on Jasmine Key until Larry Beckwith III, aka Dylan Dakota, had come along and ruined it.

And it had to have been Beckwith who'd broken into Mrs. Tifton's house. Beckwith was slim enough to fit into a size small hoodie and also smoked. It wouldn't surprise John if he'd taken to wearing cologne, too, probably from a bottle he'd stolen.

John had known the mope was still in town. He'd known

it. He'd sensed it. His only question was, Why? *Why* was Beckwith still hanging around on the island instead of fleeing? He had to know John was gunning for him.

Oh, well. There was no accounting for the stupidity of the common criminal.

Although the Larry Beckwith John knew wasn't stupid—he was cunning. Too cunning to stick around somewhere after committing the kind of crimes he had this time in Little Bridge.

Something was different. If only John could figure out what it was.

Molly was sitting very upright and proper in the passenger seat beside him as he drove her to the hotel where she lived (and worked), her gaze glued to the road. Her profile looked very delicate and feminine against the dark car window beside her. She was being unusually silent, but he could understand that. What had happened back at the widow's house had probably frightened her.

He cleared his throat.

"It's very nice of you to offer to stay the night with Mrs. Tifton."

She turned those huge dark eyes to look at him. "It's nice of you to offer to sit outside her home, as well. We couldn't very well let her stay there alone after what happened."

"Of course." They were getting very close to the hotel, which was really only a couple of blocks away from the widow's house. That was one of the few problems with Little Bridge: Everything was only a couple of blocks away. This was an advantage most of the time, but not during situations like this: their ride wasn't going to last very long. But then he had the ride back to Mrs. Tifton's to look forward to. "But you really don't have to worry about him coming back. The High School Thief, I mean."

The dark eyes seemed to grow even larger, but that might have been a trick of the streetlights beneath which they were passing.

"So you think it was him? The High School Thief?"

"Well, it's the same M.O."

"Except for the break-in. I thought the High School Thief only sneaked in through unlocked doors."

"That's true." John didn't want to say what he really thought—that it was Beckwith, and that he'd done it as a huge "eff you" entirely to John, to ruin his evening at the Red Cross Ball, his attendance at which was known islandwide, because that would sound conceited. What kind of law officer went around thinking that criminals committed crimes for the sole purpose of annoying them?

But it could not be denied that some criminals did, in particular sociopaths like Beckwith.

"We'll have to wait until my tech crew has finished processing the scene, and see what they come up with," he said instead.

This made Molly swallow hard and look away.

"But I am really certain it's him," John hurried to assure her, sure now that he'd been right: she'd been frightened back at the house. "And he never hits the same place twice—certainly not in the same night. So you and Mrs. Tifton will be totally safe. Besides, I'll be right outside—"

"Oh, I'm not worried about that." She gave him a tight little smile. "Here we are."

He hadn't even noticed that they'd reached the Lazy Parrot, a large Victorian mansion not unlike Mrs. Tifton's home, only this one had been converted into an inn. He pulled into the single parking space outside the hotel, marked with a hand-painted sign that read "*For Lazy Parrot Guest Drop-Off/Pickup Only.*" Parking spots were at a premium on the island. Many of the fights John and his deputies broke up were over parking spaces.

Molly was already undoing her seat belt. "Would you like to come in and wait while I get my things?"

Was this an invitation to her room? He had no idea. But he wasn't about to turn it down.

"Sure," he said, and put the car into park and followed her.

Like many houses in Little Bridge, the Lazy Parrot was much larger on the inside than it appeared from the outside. Once they'd gone through the lobby—an old-fashioned foyer, complete with an (unmanned, at this hour) front desk—and sitting room, they reached the gigantic backyard, lush with subtropical foliage, in the center of which sat a large, sparkling swimming pool, lit up turquoise blue. The air was heavy with the scent of chlorine and night-blooming jasmine. All of the guests, as well as the hotel owners, appeared to have retired for the evening. He and Molly seemed to be the only two souls alive, save for some frogs he could hear croaking near the hot tub.

It was one of the most romantic places he'd ever seen.

He turned to Molly to tell her so—or tell her something,

anyway—only to see her hurrying toward a set of outdoor steps leading to the Victorian's second floor, the doors of which could be reached only by a long balcony.

"I'll just get my things and be right back," she said. "You can wait right here. I'll only be a second."

She indicated a wrought-iron lawn chair beside the pool.

"Oh," he said. "Okay. Great."

"Can I get you anything?" she asked. "A drink or something while you wait? The bar is right over there—"

"No, no. I'm fine."

"Are you sure? It wouldn't be any trouble."

"Miss Montgomery," he said, with mock severity, "I'm the sheriff. I can't be drinking and driving."

"Ha." She laughed weakly. "Yes, of course. But, you know, a Coke or something."

"Molly, I'm fine."

"Okay. I'll just be a second."

She turned and fled.

So. Evidently not an invitation to her room.

Well, that was fine. Better not to take things too quickly, right? Wasn't that what was wrong with the world these days? Everyone was always rushing around, not paying attention to what they were doing, failing to savor the moment.

That's what he told himself, anyway, in his disappointment.

He sank down into the lawn chair and pulled out his cell phone to check his messages. Still nothing from Tabitha Brighton's parents. If he had received a message from a law enforcement agency regarding information about his missing daughter, he'd have called back right away. No, he'd have gotten on a plane and flown to that law enforcement agency immediately.

Maybe that's what the Brightons were doing. Maybe that's why he hadn't heard from them: they were on a red-eye flight from Alaska to Little Bridge.

Except that John suspected the Brightons were doing no such thing.

It was as he was texting Marguerite to have the deputies begin a search of every vacant house, boat, and outbuilding on Little Bridge for Larry Beckwith III that an extremely fat, fluffy orange cat emerged from the shadows and sauntered toward him, meowing plaintively.

John didn't dislike cats, but he had no particular love of them, either.

This cat, however, did not seem to care about John's feelings on the matter. It butted its head against his shinbone, getting orange fur all over his dress pants, and meowed up at him some more.

Then, before he could move away, the animal leaped up onto his lap and began to knead its claws into his belly, all while purring very loudly.

"What the—" John began, extremely startled, but before he could pull the cat from him, Molly appeared at the top of the stairs, a small overnight bag in her hand.

"Oh," she cried in a loud whisper. "I see you've met Fluffy the Cat. Isn't he the sweetest?"

Suddenly it occurred to John that he liked cats—or at least this cat—very, very much.

"He really is," he said, stroking the cat's head and causing him to purr with even more intensity and volume—and also to sink his claws more deeply through John's shirt and into his skin. "Is he yours?"

"Oh, no." Molly came tripping down the stairs a lot more lightly than she'd gone up them, most likely because she'd changed out of her heels and into a pair of canvas sneakers. She'd also exchanged her sparkly dress for a large button-down shirt over a pair of leggings. "No one knows who he belongs to. He just shows up here, so we feed him. He sleeps with me most nights, but sometimes with the guests. They love him. He's just the best."

"He seems that way," he lied, as the cat mauled him.

Molly came over and stroked the feline in his lap. How was it that even in an oversized shirt and leggings, she looked just as sexy to him as she'd been in a tight-fitting dress?

"Do you and Katie have pets?" she asked.

"No." It was all he could do to keep from flinging the cat off his lap and snatching Molly up in his arms and kissing her again. "Too busy. One day, maybe."

"Me, too, when I get my own place."

"Did you, uh, used to have pets?"

"When I was growing up, of course. But I've never lived in a place on my own that allowed them."

"I see."

This was unbearable. Her proximity—the sweet, clean scent of her—was going to drive him insane. She'd made it clear there was to be no more hanky-panky by making him wait out here, so he was going to abide by her wishes, but it was hard. John managed to pry the cat's claws from his shirt and deposit him gently onto the ground, trying not to feel too dismayed about the amount of orange fur all over his newly laundered dress pants. Then he stood up. "Well, do you think you have everything you need?"

She looked surprised by his abrupt shift in mood. "Yes, I'm ready. But—"

He paused. "But—?"

"Well, there was something I wanted to ask you."

Hallelujah. *Would you like to come upstairs after all?* That's what he was hoping she'd ask, anyway. "What is it?"

"There isn't any chance—I mean, you don't think, do you, that the High School Thief could actually *be* in high school, do you?"

What? That was not what he'd been expecting—or hoping—she would ask. "Excuse me?"

"I know it sounds nuts, but one of my patrons was bragging the other day about being the High School Thief. The crazy part of it is, he's in high school himself. I think he was only saying it to get attention—"

"He was," John said shortly.

"Do you think so?" Her expression was worried. "It's just that tonight, at Mrs. Tifton's—well, he wears a hoodie just like that and nearly drowns himself every day in cologne—"

"It's not him," John said. He was beginning to realize why she'd seemed so worried in the car. She hadn't felt frightened at all about what had happened at Mrs. Tifton's. She was scared of who he was going to arrest for it. "I'm fairly certain after tonight that I know who it is, and it isn't a high school kid. And it certainly isn't a high school kid who goes to the library and tries to impress you by bragging that he's the High School Thief."

Even in the wavy blue light of the pool, he could see that she was blushing. "Oh, I don't think he's trying to impress me. I think he's just going through a hard time. His parents are divorcing, and he doesn't have many friends, and—"

"Can we go back?" he asked abruptly.

She stared up at him, confused. "Go back to what?"

"To earlier this evening, when you were teaching me to dance."

Now she looked even more confused. "You want to dance? Now?"

"No," he said, and took her in his arms. "I want to kiss you."

"Oh." She smiled up at him, the confusion gone, and dropped her overnight bag. "Well, that would be fine with me."

The next thing he knew, her arms were around his neck, her body melded against his, and she was kissing him. It took less than a second for him to realize she'd shed her bra upstairs when she'd gone to pack and change. He could feel her firm nipples pressing against his heart.

A heart that was slamming hard against the inside of his rib cage.

The night was taking a sudden turn for the better.

He forgot all about his troubles with Katie and the mother-daughter dance, the abandoned baby and Tabitha, and even the High School Thief and Larry Beckwith III (who seemed likely to be one and the same) as he held Molly close. Her body, so warm and alive, felt like heaven in his arms, her lips like paradise. For a few seconds, he lost his head, forgetting that they were standing by the pool in the courtyard of the Lazy Parrot where anyone could look out from their room and see them at any moment, and feeling instead that they were somehow in their own private utopia.

Maybe that's why he did what he did next—something he'd never have done under other circumstances, but he was simply too swept away by the feel of her lips on his and the smell of the night-blooming jasmine and the tiny sounds she was making, little gasps of desire—

It was no wonder, really, that one of his hands slipped beneath the soft material of her shirt, then cupped the even softer skin of one of her breasts. She reared her head back to look up at him in surprise—then a slow, sly smile spread across her lips, and she pulled him even closer by his shirt-front.

It all would have been perfect if a cell phone—hers, this time—hadn't gone off.

"Darn it," she said, and released him with such abruptness that he felt wind rush to cool all the places where her body had been pressed to his—and the temperature outside was in the seventies. They'd really been heating up the place. "That has to be someone in my family," she said as she reached inside her bag for her phone. "Only they'd call so late. They all live in a different time zone. I'm so sorry—"

But it wasn't anyone in her family.

"Oh, Mrs. Tifton," Molly said, giving John a comical look of mock horror as she answered the call. "No, I'm sorry, we're on our way back now. It just took me a little longer than I—yes, I can certainly pick that up on my way. No, it's no trouble at all. Of course, I understand. No, we'll be happy to. We'll be right there. Okay. Bye."

She hung up and gave John an owl-eyed look. "Mrs. Tifton wants to know if we can bring her some whiskey. She's all out and she thinks a little of it in her tea will help calm her nerves after what's happened."

John took a steadying breath. He felt as if he could use a little whiskey himself. "We can certainly accommodate her."

"Yes." Molly tucked a wayward strand of dark hair behind one ear. "We have plenty of whiskey here at the bar, as a matter of fact. I can borrow a bottle and replace it in the morning. I doubt there's any place open where I can buy some now."

"No." John didn't want to correct her, because he most certainly didn't think it appropriate to take the town's children's librarian to Ron's Place, a bar that was open twenty-two hours a day and also sold liquor, and at which he had broken up more than a few fights and even several attempted murders.

"I'll just go grab a bottle," Molly said. She was looking flushed in the light from the kidney-shaped pool—flushed, and more beautiful than any woman he'd ever seen. "Then we should probably—"

"Go," he finished for her, though the thought of having to say good-bye to this woman was killing him.

She smiled—a little ruefully, it seemed to him. Was she thinking the same thing? "Yes. But maybe—"

"We could do this again sometime? Another . . . dance lesson?"

The smile widened. "Yes. That would be lovely."

He felt as if his heart might burst with joy.

Unfortunately, the feeling didn't last.

CHAPTER FIFTEEN

Molly

Molly had a hard time sleeping that night. It wasn't because she was in a strange bed—Mrs. Tifton's guest room was one of the most luxurious Molly had ever stayed in, with its own en suite bathroom, wide-screen television, and sheets the widow said she'd picked up on a trip to Egypt, the thread count dizzyingly high and soft as cashmere.

Molly wasn't worried about the High School Thief's return, either. She knew the alarm was on and that it was unlikely the thief would come back, especially while there was a law enforcement officer sitting in a sheriff's cruiser right outside the house.

It was that law enforcement officer who was keeping her awake, and the memory of his lips on hers—not to mention those lean, hard hands on her body.

Her attraction to him surprised her. She wasn't even sure she liked him. Except . . . well, she liked the way he'd donated the money he'd won to Baby Aphrodite. And she liked how willing he was to learn that dance for his daughter. And of course she liked how good he looked in his uniform. And how very, very good his body felt against hers in that uniform.

Okay. She liked him. A lot.

She thought about slipping out of bed and creeping downstairs to visit him in the cruiser. When she peeked through the curtains of her guest-room windows, she could see him sitting behind the wheel of the parked car, bathed in the streetlight, sipping coffee, and evidently listening to something on the radio, since he was tapping his fingers on the steering wheel. *What was he listening to?* she wondered. She of course listened to true crime podcasts, but she highly doubted that's what law enforcement officers listened to. You didn't tap your fingers to a podcast.

She was dying to find out—and not just about what he was listening to, either. She could come up with some excuse about why she had go down and see him—bring him a refill, maybe, or a book to read from Mrs. Tifton's vast romance library—and get an answer to all her many questions, most of which were about what lay beneath that dress uniform.

But that felt wrong. He'd know she was only coming out there for one thing, and he'd be exactly right. She didn't want to seem thirsty, as Elijah would call it, even though she was.

Besides, creeping out of the house to quench her thirst wouldn't be right, especially with Mrs. Tifton sleeping down the hall, depending on her for protection (not to mention the fact that she might wake Daisy, Mrs. Tifton's dog, who was alert to the slightest movement). Molly was an adult, not one of the teenagers in the books she loaned out every day. She decided she wasn't going to act like one.

And John had assured her during the ride back to Mrs. Tifton's that they were going to get together for a proper date—for some reason he seemed fixated on taking her for a "steak dinner"—soon. Just as soon as they could coordinate their schedules. Which, John had kept saying, wasn't going to be that difficult.

"Unless you have a lot on your plate right now." He'd looked—and sounded—sweetly nervous as he gripped the steering wheel. "I just have to get through Boat Safety Day. But then I'm free."

"And learning 'Single Ladies' for the Snappettes," Molly hadn't been able to resist gently teasing him. "And solving a few crimes."

"Well, uh, sure, those things, too." He'd thrown her a surprisingly shy smile. "But then it's the two of us at Island Steak House. They make the best rib eye you've ever tasted. You like steak, don't you? You're not vegan or anything, are you?"

"I am not. I like steak." She didn't want to point out to

him that she came from a state that was known for having some of the best beef in the country. She thought it was cute that he seemed to have forgotten that. "I try not to eat it every day, but—"

"No, no. Same here. I mean, they say it's not that great for you, or the environment. But a little every now and then for a special occasion is okay."

Molly hadn't been able to keep from smiling at the fact that he considered the two of them going out for a meal together a special occasion. In fact, she felt as if she'd been doing nothing but smiling since they'd kissed. Her cheek muscles were beginning to feel a little sore.

But he was just so sweet, in a gruff, manly sort of way. So she agreed to join him for a steak dinner at some as-yet-to-be determined date in the future.

And instead of sneaking out to visit him in his cruiser, she climbed into her soft-as-feathers bed, leaving it only once to peek out at him, wondering if he was thinking about her, too. She finally managed to fall asleep by watching a baking show on Mrs. Tifton's giant guest-room television.

She didn't wake until close to eight, when she heard Daisy's excited barking, and Mrs. Tifton shushing her—she was taking the dog out for her first walk of the day and didn't want to disturb Molly.

But Molly was already up and rushing to the window, only to find that John had disappeared, probably to return to his own home and get some sleep. Or at least that's where she hoped he'd gone. When did sheriffs sleep, when crimes were committed twenty-four hours a day? This wasn't something she'd ever bothered asking herself, but now she couldn't help wondering. It didn't seem fair. Poor John. No wonder he was so grumpy most of the time.

Of course, the fact that she was at the library a few hours later, as she'd been nearly every day since she'd arrived on Little Bridge, was different. The library was closed at night. She wasn't there because people were committing crimes, but because they needed her to help find books or information they were looking for.

And, of course, in the case of Sunday Story Time, they needed her to set up the puppet theater and train table, and make sure none of the dads spilled the coffee they'd brought into the building. Food and drink as well as pets were allowed in the Little Bridge Public Library (mainly because it was impossible to stop people from bringing them in), but that didn't mean they didn't make messes, which Molly and her colleagues then had to clean up.

It was as Molly was busy sopping up one such spill by a particularly incompetent dad (who seemed to have added bourbon to his coffee and was lamely murmuring, "I'm sorry, Miss Molly") that Elijah appeared and said, "Hey. Miss Molly, look what I've got."

Molly wasn't exactly in the mood for any of Elijah's shenanigans, especially since she herself hadn't gotten much sleep, the guests at checkout at the hotel that morning had been particularly unruly, and the volunteer puppeteer was late.

But she still had a bit of a flutter in her heart because of what had happened the night before with the sheriff. Nothing could really be all that bad when a man who was that kind and that good-looking and that talented with his hands—and lips—was interested in her. The world had a slightly rosier tinge to it this morning, so even Elijah's antics and the coffee and bourbon spilled all over *Six-Dinner Sid* couldn't bother her too much.

Until she turned to see what Elijah had in his hands.

"It's a Leica," Elijah said, proudly showing off his new camera. "Now I can start filming my acts. I mean, I could do that before, on my phone, but this is classier. I thought I could pick up some photography assignments, you know, with the school paper. Maybe shoot headshots for the Snappettes, or whatever."

Molly felt as if her blood had run cold. She forgot not only her tiredness but also the warm, happy feeling that she'd been hugging to herself all morning. She certainly wasn't smiling anymore.

"Where did you get that?" she heard herself asking Elijah, through suddenly numb lips.

He looked down at the camera. "What, this? My dad left it in a box of stuff when he moved out. I know it's kind of old, but you're the one who's always telling me I need to get more involved in stuff. One of those kids in *It* turned into like the town historian or something. I know you loaned *It* to me because of the comedian character, but that other guy was kind of cool and I was thinking maybe I could—"

"Give me that," Molly said, and snatched the camera from him.

"Hey!" Elijah looked shocked. "What are you doing?"

Molly examined the camera. Just like the one that had been stolen from Mrs. Tifton's house the night before, it was pocket-sized and also digital. It looked very old—and very expensive.

Molly reached out, seized Elijah by the arm—noting he was wearing a black hoodie, but that meant nothing, didn't it? Tons of kids his age wore them, even on a tropical island—and steered him toward her desk, even though rule number one of being a librarian was that you never, ever touched a patron unless they were in immediate danger or in need of medical assistance.

But Elijah was in danger, and also in need of immediate assistance . . . just not the medical kind.

"Hey, Miss Molly," Elijah said, allowing himself to be dragged. He looked more amused than indignant. "What gives?"

Molly pushed him into the child-sized chair beside her desk. "Where did you get this camera?" she asked him again, perhaps a little too intensely.

"Whoa," he said. "I told you. It was my—"

"Your dad's, I know, you said that. Does he still have the receipt? Can you *prove* he bought it?"

"How should I know? Probably not. He bought it, like, a million years ago. What's wrong with you, Miss Molly?"

Molly wondered herself. John had assured her last night

that there was no way the High School Thief was in high school. He'd all but sworn he knew who the culprit was and that an arrest was imminent.

But here was Elijah, carrying a used, older Leica like the one stolen from Mrs. Tifton's home, and smelling—there was no way around it—like the men's fragrance section of a department store. He reeked.

He did not, however, smell of cigarettes. So that was one small mercy.

"Where were you last night around eleven o'clock?" she demanded.

"Where was I? Where I always am when I'm not here or at school—at home, playing *Call of Duty*."

"Can you prove it?"

"What's all this with having to prove it?" he asked. "What's going on, Miss Molly?"

Molly sat down behind her desk, feeling suddenly tired and defeated. Not even the memory of the sheriff's kiss or the hopeful promise of their steak dinner could buoy her spirits.

"The High School Thief struck again last night, Elijah," she said. She probably wasn't supposed to be sharing this information, but it would be public soon enough. Meschelle Davies would see to that. "He robbed Mrs. Tifton—you know, the lady who donated the money to build the new library? And one of the things he took was her dead husband's old Leica camera. It was one just like this."

Elijah looked down at the camera in Molly's hand, not understanding. "So? What does that have to do with me?"

"Elijah, you were literally in here the other day bragging that you were the High School Thief."

"Oh my God, Miss Molly." He started to laugh. "Don't tell me that you believed all that!"

Molly glared at him as he clutched his stomach, doubled over in laughter. "It isn't funny, Elijah," she said. "There are people in this town—people who work in law enforcement—who might, given the preponderance of evidence, come to think of you as a suspect."

"Preponderance of evidence!" Elijah was laughing so hard that he had tears in his eyes. "Oh, Miss Molly!"

Now Molly was genuinely irritated. Some of the mothers—and even some of the fathers—were beginning to glance over at them in curiosity. Even worse, Phyllis Robinette—the woman responsible for Molly's good fortune in finding this job in the first place—was volunteering over at the main desk (as she did most days, when she didn't have yoga) and had noticed the commotion. She frowned at them.

"Cut it out, Elijah," Molly whispered urgently. "It isn't that funny."

"But it is," he said, wiping away his tears. "The fact that you'd believe I was the High School Thief. Oh, Miss Molly. You really are one of my favorite people ever."

Molly had had about all that she could take. She set down the camera and reached for her telephone. Elijah continued to laugh. "Wait," he said, chuckling. "Who are you calling? I know it's not the po-po. Not Henry again. Please don't say Henry."

"No." Molly didn't have to consult her directory to dial. She knew the number by heart. "I'm calling your mother."

All the humor drained from Elijah's face. Most of the color did, as well. "Oh, Miss Molly," he whispered. *"No."*

CHAPTER SIXTEEN

John

John couldn't remember the last time he'd felt this happy. He whistled "My Favorite Things"—the Coltrane version, not the one from the movie his daughter had liked so much as a kid—as he fried up bacon and eggs for breakfast.

He didn't have to worry about anyone nagging him for eating such fatty foods, because Katie had spent the night with a friend from her dance team and wasn't due to return home until noon. He had the house to himself to do whatever he wanted.

And what he wanted to do was eat breakfast and think about Molly Montgomery, at least in the short amount of time he had before he had to get back to the office and figure out how to catch Larry Beckwith III.

It was as he was thinking about Molly Montgomery and the impossible softness of her skin that his cell phone rang. He glanced down at the screen, irritated by the interruption, then saw that it was Peter Abramowitz, the state's attorney. He picked up before the second ring.

"Pete," he said. "What's up?"

"You tell me what's up." Pete sounded as casual and good-humored as always. Like any true surfer, he didn't get wound up about things that didn't matter, which was one of the reasons John liked him. "What happened last night?"

"Beckwith hit the Tifton house." John chewed on a piece of bacon. "Least, I'm pretty certain it was Beckwith. I'm still waiting for Murray to get back to me with prints. But I'm sure they'll match. I've got every officer on staff out combing the island for that little twit. We'll find him, and when we do, I need you to nail him to the wall this time. I don't care what kind of big-deal lawyers his father brings down from the mainland, I want you to put the screws to—"

"I'm not talking about that." Pete was laughing. "I already know about that. I'm talking about you and the librarian."

John stopped chewing. He felt suddenly cold, even though Katie kept the air-conditioning at a meticulous seventy-five degrees, far too warm for him. But his daughter, like many in her generation, was ever conscious of wasting precious resources, frightened for the planet and its imminent demise. "What do you mean, me and the librarian?"

"The new children's librarian. The one you were macking on last night at the bar on Jasmine Key."

Macking? John had to take a hasty swig of coffee in order to wash down the bacon, on which he'd nearly choked.

"Don't think I didn't see you." Pete was practically crowing. "Everyone did. You couldn't have been more obvious."

"We were not *macking*," John said, when he could finally speak. "Miss Montgomery—Molly—is a very kind, intelligent woman, and we were merely—"

"Jesus Christ!" Now Pete was hooting with laughter. "I'm messing with you. Not that we didn't all see you two kissing. But I think it's great. How long has it been since you've been on a date? Not since you and Christina split, right? And before that, what was it, high school? Hasn't Christina basically been the only woman you've ever—"

"All right." John was on his feet, his breakfast and Coltrane forgotten. "We don't need to go into the details about that. Especially since nothing happened last night. I got the call about the Tifton place and took Molly home." He didn't feel it was necessary to fill his talkative friend in on the details about what had happened after he'd taken Molly home. "End of story."

"But you're gonna see her again, right?" Besides being an excellent attorney—the Beckwith case aside—Pete Abramowitz was a good and supportive friend. He'd never missed a Snappettes performance since Katie joined the team, and had brought every single one of his relatives—including his elderly mother—to the jailhouse zoo when they visited Little Bridge for the holidays. *Why, yes, that is a convicted felon holding a lop-eared rabbit on his lap. Go ahead, you can pet it.* "You like her, she likes you, yadda yadda yadda?"

John's mind went back to the night before. The softness of Molly's body as she wrapped her arms around his neck and pressed up against him. The little sounds she'd made in her throat as he'd kissed her. The eagerness with which her nipple had hardened beneath the palm of his hand as he'd cupped her breast.

"I think so," he said, and then had to clear his throat. "Yes, I like her, and I think she likes me. I asked her out for dinner sometime later in the week, and she said yes."

Pete hooted so loudly that John had to hold the phone away from his ear. "That's what I like to hear," he said. "Now don't mess it up."

"How am I going to mess it up?"

"Well, like we just discussed, it's been a while since you dated, buddy. The rules have changed. Don't think you can take this little librarian out to dinner and then jump her bones."

John was horrified. "I wasn't planning on doing that."

"Good. Because it takes three dates, bud."

"Before you can jump someone's bones?"

"That's what I'm telling you. Unless she jumps yours first."

"How very enlightening. Thank you for this information, Mr. State's Attorney."

"Oh, and none of that, either," Pete said. "None of this acting like a grumpy dad instead of your actual age. She won't like it any more than I do."

John was offended. "I don't act like a grumpy dad."

"Are you kidding me? May I introduce you to Sheriff John Hartwell? I can't have more than one beer on a weekday. My pants are too tight. The music these kids today listen to has too many bad words. Get off my lawn."

Although some of these sounded slightly familiar, John

still felt annoyed. "I've never said that last one. And if you drink too much beer, your pants *are* going to get tight, unless you work out. That's a fact."

"Just try to play it cool with the librarian, okay? Don't do anything stupid."

"Such as jump her bones before the third date?"

"Such as text her right away. Or bring her flowers when you haven't even—"

Fortunately, another call came through. When John glanced at the screen of his phone, he saw that it was Dr. Nguyen.

"Pete," he said. "I gotta go. It's the ob-gyn. She's probably calling about the abandoned baby or her mom."

"Talk to you later, buddy." Pete sounded as cheerful as ever. "And keep me posted about—"

John clicked over to the other call. As was her habit, Dr. Nguyen wasted no time on social niceties. What she lacked in bedside manner, she made up for with competence.

"You can come interview the mother now if you want to, John. She's out of the ICU."

John was sure he knew who she was talking about, but since it seemed too good to be true, he checked to be certain. "Tabitha Brighton?"

"Correct. We got her temperature back to normal, but she's still a little weak from blood loss. So please go easy."

"But she's going to be okay?"

"She's going to be fine," the doctor said. "Physically. Mentally? It could take a while. She's been through a lot."

Out of habit, he reached for his notebook. "She tell you anything? Who took the baby? Who the father is?"

"No, nothing like that. Giving birth to a baby under conditions like she did is trauma enough. Still, she asked to see the baby, and as you know, our goal, as well as Child Services', is always to reunite mothers with their babies if we possibly can. Tabitha's been holding her baby, and even took a stab at nursing. I consider both hugely positive steps forward."

John grunted. "And the baby is okay?"

"Baby's fine. Tox screens were completely clean. The mother's were, too."

"So she wasn't partying while pregnant."

"Not at all. But I'm still worried about her. She's barely eating. And she hasn't asked to make a single phone call, which I find unusual. You'd think someone who's been through what she has would call someone. No one has called her room, either, or come to visit her. Part of that is because you've been so careful not to release any news about her to the press—but doesn't she have any family? Or friends?"

"Yeah." John tapped his pen against the page he had open. No cell phone had been found among Tabitha's belongings. Beckwith had probably taken it, the way he'd taken the baby, and stashed it somewhere. "She does, but they don't seem too anxious to get in touch. Something's not right. Thanks, Doctor. I'll be over there soon."

And he was, twenty minutes later. Standing in what

served as the maternity ward for the small island—four private rooms and a desk—he stood with his arms crossed in front of Nurse Dani, who seemed to have made a remarkable recovery from her inebriated state at the ball last night and was looking professional and alert in pink scrubs covered in purple teddy bears.

"Don't you normally work in the ER?" he asked.

She smiled. "I do! Thanks for remembering. Couple of the nurses up here were out sick with that cold that's going around, so I volunteered to fill in. What a week to be short-staffed! Ever since that news station showed us on TV, we've been getting calls around the clock from people begging us to let them adopt Baby Aphrodite. As if we have any say in the matter."

John shook his head grimly. The same thing had been happening down at the station house, and probably, he suspected, at the library, too. He wondered if Molly regretted her well-intentioned but enormously ill-considered decision to go on TV with her story about finding the infant.

"Has Tabitha Brighton said anything to you?" he asked the nurse. "Anything at all about how she ended up here, who put the baby in the library, who the father might be?"

He'd noticed that women opened up more to other women than they did to men—and certainly to members of law enforcement—and Nurse Dani was the chatty type. If anyone could get a kid to talk, it would be her.

But she disappointed him by shaking her head.

"Sorry, no, nothing. She just lies there and cries and

watches TV. Food Network, mostly, which is weird, because she won't eat. We've got her on an IV for hydration, of course, but Dr. Nguyen says if she doesn't eat soon, we might have to resort to a feeding tube. Which is terrible, but what else can we do?"

He shrugged. "If someone won't help themselves, how can you help them?"

"Exactly. Honestly, I know what she did is awful, but I feel bad for her. You're not going to charge her, are you? She's just a kid."

John was getting a little tired of everyone—mainly women, mainly Molly Montgomery—asking him this. Luckily, Marguerite chose that moment to come strolling up.

"What took you so long?" he asked. He didn't want to do the interview without a female officer present, and he preferred Marguerite over his younger female deputies because the sergeant was both more experienced and possessed a mother's radar for lying.

"Incentive." She held up a white paper bag with a couple of golden arches on them. "I heard the kid wasn't eating."

John shook his head. "But fast food? I thought these eco-friendly hippie types stayed away from it . . . except for pizza, of course."

"Trust me, when she gets a whiff of these fries, she'll go to town on them. I remember not wanting to touch a thing they were serving in this place after I gave birth to my kids. It all looked like congealed mush. But this stuff? Manna from heaven. She'll eat every speck." Marguerite wasted no time throwing open the door to the girl's room. "Hi, honey. Hope we aren't disturbing you."

They weren't. At least John didn't think they were. The pale, slightly doughy-faced girl was doing exactly what Dani had said she'd been doing—watching the Food Network, with tears streaming down her face.

"Oh," she said when she saw them, looking startled but not wildly so. "Are you the police?"

"Sheriff's office, honey," Marguerite said, swinging the girl's food tray around so it sat in front of her, and unpacking the white paper bag. "This is Sheriff John Hartwell, and I'm Sergeant Marguerite Ruiz. We brought you a little something to eat, just some fries and a couple of cheeseburgers. I already checked with your doctor, and she said it was okay."

John knew this was a complete lie, but he didn't imagine it could matter much. The girl's nose was twitching like a hungry rabbit's at the aromas coming out of the paper sack. "Are there any chicken nuggets?" she asked faintly.

"There are," Marguerite said. "I didn't know which dipping sauce you liked, so I brought them all. And a soda and a vanilla milkshake, too. You've been through a lot, so you really need to eat. I know, I've had three kids myself, right in this very hospital. I also know how bad the food is here. So try this instead."

The girl, her gaze darting nervously between John and his sergeant, murmured a polite "Thank you so much," even as she began discreetly shoveling fries into her mouth.

Score one for Marguerite: the hospital food was why she hadn't been eating. Though she probably had plenty of deeper trauma, too.

"So, Tabitha," John said, lowering himself into the visitor's chair by the window, which had a very stunning and healing view of the island's garbage dump. "Your name is Tabitha, isn't it? Tabitha Brighton of New Canaan, Connecticut, and you're eighteen years old? Because that's what it says here."

The girl, who'd been taking a large slurp of her milkshake, stopped midswallow and stared owlishly at the driver's license he'd pulled from his shirtfront pocket. She had mouse-brown hair that was currently parted in the middle and hung like curtains on either side of her face. It gave her an innocent and rather nunlike appearance.

And like a nun, she didn't lie. Slowly, she nodded. "Yes," she said in a tiny voice. "That's me." Then she burst into tears, this time noisily, with large, gulping sobs. "Are you going to arrest me?"

"Oh, sweetheart," Marguerite said, moving to wrap the girl in her arms. "Shhhh."

John was more glad than ever that Marguerite had come along. He also wondered if Tabitha had noticed Marguerite had not said no.

"Well," he said. "Why don't you tell me what happened first, starting with how you ended up here in Little Bridge to begin with."

The girl gave a tiny shrug—all she could manage with

Marguerite sitting beside her in the bed, her arms still around her. "I . . . I don't know. I'd always heard Little Bridge Island was a nice place."

"Right," John said. He'd heard this a thousand times—maybe a hundred thousand times—in his lifetime. "Everyone thinks Little Bridge Island is a nice place. It's one of America's top tourist destinations. But usually when people come here they rent an Airbnb or a hotel room. They don't break into a public building, squat in it, and then vandalize it with trash and graffiti."

Tabitha's eyes overflowed again. She looked as sorrowful as any human being John had ever seen. . . .

And yet he thought he saw a spark of indignation in her hazel eyes, as well.

"Just because some people reject societal norms and resist total assimilation to the dominant culture doesn't mean our values don't have worth," she said in a shaky voice.

It was obviously something she'd learned by rote.

John didn't have to ask where she'd learned it, either. He'd heard it—like he'd heard the thing about Little Bridge being nice—a thousand times.

But he'd only heard what Tabitha was spewing from one person . . . and that person's followers.

He closed his notebook with a *snap*.

"Okay, Tabitha," he said. "Where is he?"

She blinked several times. "What—who do you mean?"

"Dylan."

"I—I don't know any Dylan."

"Oh, you don't? Dylan Dakota?"

She shook her head. "N-no."

"Never heard of him?"

"I t-told you. No."

She was a very bad liar. Not only did she not make eye contact when she lied, but she did the same thing that Katie did when she lied, which was to glance up at the ceiling and far to the right, as if the way out of the difficult situation she suddenly found herself in might be found there.

This made John feel slightly more sorry for her, but he still had to do his job.

"Don't give me that, Tabitha," he said, sternly. "Only one person in this town goes around spewing that nonsense about societal norms and resisting total assimilation, and that's Dylan Dakota—whose real name, in case he failed to mention it, is Lawrence Beckwith III. I know he probably told you some fanciful tale about being raised in an orphanage in Morocco, but guess what? Larry is from Cleveland Heights, Ohio, where his father owns a very popular chain of tire stores, and his mother is a homemaker. Larry himself graduated from Ohio State—although I'm sure he wishes it was Brown or Dartmouth or some other Ivy League school so he could brag about how he dropped out because he was rejecting our society's dominant norms. Maybe that's where this sense of entitlement he has comes from—that he never got the fancy art degree that he feels he deserves from a top-tier school. Anyway, I don't know about any of that, and I don't care. I just want to know where I can find him so I can arrest him for what he did to you and your baby and Miss Montgomery's library. Do you have any thoughts about that?"

She swallowed, her stare still glued to the ceiling. "I . . . I don't know Dylan Dakota or this Larry Beckwith person. And I don't know what happened to me. I gave birth, and it was beautiful, and then I fell asleep." She finally brought her gaze back toward his. Now she was telling the truth. "When I woke up, the baby was gone, and some lady was there."

Marguerite had drawn her arms away from the girl and slipped off the bed. "Is that what you're going to tell your daughter about her birth when she's older? How beautiful it was, giving birth to her on the dirty floor of an unfinished building surrounded by empty liquor bottles and pizza boxes and without an epidural or any medical aid?"

"And you didn't fall asleep," John added. "You passed out from blood loss. Your so-called friends abandoned you. Not one of them has come here to visit you or even called to see how you're doing. And that lady was the children's librarian, Miss Molly Montgomery. If she hadn't found you, you'd be dead. Same with your daughter. Someone—I'm guessing it was your good friend Dylan—put her in an empty box of trash bags and dumped her in a bathroom at the library. She'd have frozen to death if Miss Montgomery hadn't found her."

"I—I don't believe you." Tabitha reached up to wipe her tears with one of the napkins Marguerite had given her. "This is what he said you people would do. Try to demonize us for rejecting the materialism and technology of today's world."

"No one's demonizing you, sweetheart," Marguerite said

in a kind voice. "We're trying to make you see common sense. Eat a chicken nugget."

"Who's *he*?" John asked. "Dakota?"

"You fear us, you know," Tabitha said, her eyes still bright with tears, but also now with defiance. Nevertheless, she listened to Marguerite and nibbled on a nugget. "That's what he says. He says you fear us because we reject your definition of happiness, finding fulfillment in a life without money, mortgages, material goods—"

"We found cell phone and laptop chargers all over that room." John felt more sad than angry. "For a group that rejects material goods, you sure seem to enjoy going on Facebook."

"Only so we can spread our message of peace and love."

"You know, Tabitha, we're on the side of peace and love as well," he said. "Your side, and the baby's. We know what happened to you was traumatic . . . probably so traumatic that you haven't even been able to face it. At likely the most vulnerable moment of your life, you were left for dead by people you thought you could trust. Let us help you by finding these people and stopping them from ever doing this to anyone else. Because next time, there may not be a Miss Montgomery around to save them."

Tabitha's eyes went right back to the ceiling. "There isn't going to be a next time."

"What are you talking about?" He shook his head. "Are you telling me that Dylan Dakota isn't going to take advantage of some other naive girl like you, get her pregnant, and then leave her and her newborn baby for dead somewhere?"

For the first time, she smiled at him. It was a wan and sickly-looking smile. But it was a smile just the same.

"Yes," she said, looking him dead in the eye. "That's what I'm telling you. Because Dylan loves me. He loves me and the baby. And he's going to come back for us. Just you wait and see."

CHAPTER SEVENTEEN

Molly

"*No*, Miss Molly."

Elijah leaned across Molly's desk and pressed the receiver, ending her call to his mother before it had even connected. "Please. *Please* do not call my mom."

Molly looked into his suddenly pale face and felt that she had no choice but to relent. He was her patron. More than that, he was a child.

"Fine, Elijah," she said, slowly lowering her handset. "Then tell me the truth about where you got this camera . . . and why you don't want your mother knowing about it."

Elijah let out an exaggeratedly large sigh and slumped in the child-sized chair, which for him was not entirely too small. Like a puppy, his hands and feet were large, but the rest of him hadn't quite caught up.

"Okay, look. I didn't *just* find my dad's camera. I found it a few days ago, and I got this idea: a lot of the girls in school—the Snappettes, especially—want headshots. Not selfies, but, like, real professional headshots. They have this cheer camp they all go to every summer, and there's this parade in New York City. It happens around Thanksgiving—"

Molly tried to keep the impatience out of her tone. "The Macy's Thanksgiving Day Parade?"

"Yeah, yeah, that's it. It's this real big deal. They have to send in a headshot for it and also for the camp, or something. I don't know. So when I found my dad's camera, I thought, why not start my own business, offering to do headshots for the girls? I mean, I can do it way more cheaply than the regular guy they use. Plus, like, they know me. I'm not some creep—"

"Elijah. Is this story going anywhere?"

"Oh, yeah." He reached into the pocket of his skinny jeans and pulled something from it. "Sorry. So, anyway, I started my own business. See?"

He passed Molly a stiff black business card that had the words ELIJAH TRUJOS, FREELANCE PHOTOGRAPHER embossed on it in elegant silver print. Beneath the words was his cell phone number.

"I handed those out at school, and you wouldn't believe the number of Snappettes who started texting me, asking if I could do their headshots for the application thingie. So that's where I was last night."

"Where?" Molly was confused.

"At one of their houses," he said, reaching for the Leica—but not to take it from her, only so that he could show her the photos he'd taken. There was a small display screen on the back of the camera. "Doing their headshots for the application. See?"

He switched some buttons, and photos began to appear on the tiny screen. Molly realized she was looking at the inside of a Little Bridge Island living room—she recognized the shiplap walls and nautical-themed décor—in which several girls wearing Snappette uniforms were posing for the camera, sometimes together, sometimes alone. She recognized John's daughter, Katie Hartwell, right away. The other two girls were unfamiliar.

"See," Elijah said, as he flicked through the photos. "It was hard to get the light right, because it was so dark in there."

Molly could see that behind each girl was a bank of sliding glass doors—not unlike Mrs. Tifton's French doors—leading to the backyard. Since the photos were taken at night (there was a digital date stamp on the top right-hand corner of the screen, indicating that the photos had been taken the evening before), the glass was dark, except for the girls' reflection. Elijah had apparently realized this at some point and tried to get around it by having the girls pose in front of a white wall on the other side of the room.

"I really feel like I captured the essence of each girl's personality," he said as he showed Molly the photos of which he was most proud. "Like Katie, for instance? She's really extroverted, so having her do that handstand was just a last-minute thing that I came up with, but I think works great."

"Fine, Elijah," Molly said. "But if this is all you were doing last night, why didn't you want me calling your mom?"

"Oh, er, well, because I sort of lied about finding this

camera in a box of junk my dad left behind." Elijah had the grace to look embarrassed. "I mean, he *did* leave it behind—just like he left me, my mom, and everything else he *should* care about. But it turns out he wants the camera back. My mom's been looking for it to send to him because he keeps asking for it. But I stole it and hid it in my room. I don't feel like he deserves to have it back after leaving us like that."

Molly frowned at him. "Elijah," she said, in mock disapproval.

"I know. I know! But he doesn't even send child-support payments. The guy's a loser. I should get *something* from him. And, anyway, if my mom found out I had his camera *and* I was using it to take pictures of girls, she'd kill me."

Molly actually thought that Mrs. Trujos would be relieved—at least about the girls—because it showed that Elijah was finally coming out of his shell and spending face time with people his own age.

But she didn't say so because she sensed Elijah was getting a little bit of a thrill out of his disobedience. Instead, she kept looking at his photos, which weren't bad—it would be difficult to take a bad photo with such a high-quality camera—until she saw something curious and cried, "Elijah! Stop!"

He stopped scrolling through the photos. "What? Why? What's wrong?"

"Go back a photo or two. I thought I saw something—there!"

Molly took the camera from his hands. At first she thought she'd imagined it.

But as she looked more closely at one of his photos of the girls standing in front of the sliding doors, she saw precisely what she thought she'd seen.

And what she saw gave her goose bumps, even though she was wearing a cardigan, as usual, to guard against the chill of the library's strong air-conditioning.

"Elijah, who is that man?" she asked, showing him the photo.

Elijah squinted at the screen. "What man?"

"The man standing outside in the yard, looking in from behind the sliding glass doors."

Elijah squinted some more. "Oh, wow. I never noticed that before. You're right, there is a man out there." He scrolled through a couple more photos as Molly looked on. "He's in a few of them. Ugh, what a creeper. He's just standing out there looking at us."

"So you don't know that man?" Molly asked carefully. "He wasn't a guest last night?"

"What?" Elijah's eyes were still glued to the camera's display screen. "No! It was just me and the girls. Sharmaine's parents weren't even home. They were at some party, or something. Ew, look at him here. He must have known we couldn't see him because of how dark it was outside and how bright it was inside. But he's giving us the peace sign anyway!"

Elijah showed her the photo. It was true. The man—a

white man about Elijah's same size, but ten or so years older, and with a well-groomed goatee—stood in the darkened glass behind the three Snappettes mugging for the camera, two fingers of one hand raised to give the peace sign, a smirk on his face.

He was dressed in dark jeans and a black sweatshirt—a black hooded sweatshirt, the hoodie pulled up just enough to cover his hair but not his large ear gauges or vine neck tattoos.

And certainly not enough to keep Molly's chills from increasing tenfold. She knew they were looking at a photo of the High School Thief . . . and also that the High School Thief was Dylan Dakota. There'd been a picture of him in one of the articles Meschelle Davies had shown her.

"Elijah," she said, hoping he wouldn't notice her wildly beating heart. "Where does Sharmaine live?"

Elijah told her an address she knew well. It was only a block or two from Mrs. Tifton's house. While she and John had been kissing on Jasmine Key, Dylan Dakota—aka the High School Thief—had been creeping through the backyard of the house in which sweet, cheerful Katie had been having a sleepover, spying on her as she playfully posed for photos with her friends.

"Could you text me copies of these photos?" Molly asked, trying to keep calm. If she felt this freaked out, she could only imagine how John was going to feel when he saw how close his daughter had come to the most wanted man in Little Bridge without even being aware of it. "I need to send them to someone."

Elijah shook his head. "No, I can't. This is a camera, not a phone. I can't send photos from it."

"Oh, right." How could she have forgotten? "Well, how could you get copies of these photos to me to show someone?"

"Well, I'd have to go home and download them onto my mom's laptop—it's a special memory card, see, that only fits into really old computers. There used to be a cable, but it got lost. Then I guess I could either email them to you, and then you could email them to the person, or I could print them out and bring copies over to you. I invested in some really nice—"

Molly thought her brain was going to melt. "Listen, Elijah," she said, her fingers curling around the camera. "Why don't you just give it to me, and I'll—"

"Excuse me."

Molly looked up to see the father who'd previously brought the bourbon and coffee into the library looming over her desk. She gave him a tight smile. Of course. Of course someone was interrupting her right now during this crucial conversation. She worked at a service desk. She was there to help people with their book-related problems, not solve crimes. "Yes, may I help you?"

"I just wanted to say sorry again about the book." The dad looked shamefaced over what had happened. "If you want me to pay for the damage, I'd be happy to."

Molly glanced at *Six-Dinner Sid,* which was sitting, sodden and sticky, on her desk. "Okay," she said. "Great! That will be twenty-five dollars."

The man looked shocked. "Twenty-five dollars! For a kid's book? You have to be kidding me."

"Well, it's a hardcover picture book." Molly was impatient to be rid of him so she could get back to her conversation with Elijah. "In full color, and also a library edition with special binding. So actually, twenty-five dollars is a bargain. They're really—"

"Used!" The father stooped to scoop up his child, who was standing with one finger up her nose and another in her mouth. "I'm not paying twenty-five dollars to replace a *used* book! That should come out of all the money we taxpayers shell out for this place. Come on, Juniper. We're never coming back here again!"

Then he stormed off, not seeming to care that everyone could see the pint bottle of bourbon he had tucked into his back pocket.

Molly sighed and turned back to Elijah.

"I need to borrow this," she said, taking the camera from him. "I have to show these photos to someone right away, and I don't have time to wait for you to go home and print them out or email them. I'll give it back just as soon as I can."

"Sure, no problem." Elijah didn't seem to be paying attention. "Wow, Miss Molly, does that kind of thing happen to you a lot?"

"What kind of thing?" Molly was busy scrolling through her phone for John's number, which she'd thankfully added to her contacts list the first day she'd met him and he'd given her his card.

"People like that guy," Elijah said, "being so rude."

"All the time." Molly found John's number and began writing him a text.

Elijah shook his head in disgust. "Why do you put up with it?"

She glanced at him in surprise. "Because, Elijah, this is my dream job. I love it. I'm a *librarian*."

CHAPTER EIGHTEEN

John

Well, that was terrible," John said, as he and Marguerite exited Tabitha Brighton's hospital room.

Marguerite smiled. "What's the matter, Chief? You don't like picking on defenseless young girls?"

"I wouldn't call her defenseless." He thought of the way Tabitha had spewed Larry Beckwith's counterculture BS. "But I didn't like doing it, anyway."

"You knew the job was dangerous when you took it. Come on." Marguerite elbowed him chummily. "Let's go look at the baby. That might cheer you up. Seeing a happy, healthy newborn that we had a part in saving always cheers me up."

Visiting Baby Aphrodite did cheer him up, a little. Especially since the baby was swaddled in a blanket with bright yellow ducks on it—one of the many donated by the public, the nurse explained. The baby's mother—Tabitha—had directed that most of the rest of the donations be given to the island's shelter for battered women and children.

This cheered John even more. It meant that though Tabitha hadn't yet realized how thoroughly she'd been brainwashed by Dakota, she was at least somewhat civic-minded. This was a sign that she could still be saved.

It was later in the day when he received another piece of good news—at least good to him—though it came from a surprising source. Murray—who generally refused to work on Sundays, as that was when Sheriff Wagner had always allowed him the day off to visit his in-laws in Key West—shuffled into his office and said, "Chief."

John looked up from his deputies' reports that no sign of Dylan Dakota or his followers had been found anywhere in all of Little Bridge and gaped at the head of his tech department. "Murray. What are you doing here?"

"I've been here since Friday." Murray looked like it, too. His uniform was rumpled, his face unshaven, and his glasses in need of cleaning. "I hope you're going to approve the overtime."

John frowned. "Of course, especially if you've got anything good."

"Oh, I got something good, Chief. At least, I think you're gonna think it's good: Dakota's hair is all over that sweatshirt they found at the widow's house last night."

John raised an eyebrow. He'd been expecting this, but it was still good to hear. "Hair as in more than one?"

"Either the guy is going bald or someone gave him a haircut while wearing it. I'd go for the former. Of course, I'm talking a microscopic match only. We won't have DNA for a while. I'm guessing it will be the same, though. But that's not all."

"It isn't?"

"Nope. The primary prints on the box the librarian found the baby in? They're his."

John nearly dropped the cup of coffee he'd been holding. *"What?"*

"That's right." The deep lines on Murray's face crinkled into a smile. "It was a bitch because there were so many prints on it, but I managed to isolate a couple of Dakota's right where someone would be holding a box like that if, say, they were carrying a baby in it from the new library to the old one."

In a million years, John never thought he'd want to hug his chief crime scene tech, but he had to hold back an urge to do so now.

"Murray. That is great. Just great. Overtime approved."

Murray was still grinning. "Thanks, Chief. Anything to nail this guy. Can you imagine, abandoning a little baby like she was trash?"

"No," John said, going from smiling to frowning in a split second. He was actually feeling a little choked up, and not only over the prints. Murray was finally coming around to his side from Sheriff Wagner's. "No, I cannot. Thanks for this, Murray. Thanks for skipping your in-laws this weekend to help with this. We might actually nail Beckwith this time—if we ever catch him, that is."

Murray nodded and turned to go. "I hope so. And to be honest, skipping my in-laws is not exactly the biggest sacrifice."

John laughed just as his phone chimed that he had a text. He checked it, expecting to hear from Katie. She had dance practice all day, but they were supposed to catch up that night over dinner together.

It wasn't Katie, however.

Hi, John, it's Molly. I found something I need to show you. Can you stop by sometime today?

His heart rate sped up. Pete had told him to cool it and not blow things by seeming overeager.

But she was texting him. Not even twenty-four hours since they'd last seen each other, *she* was texting *him*, and asking him to stop by. It was okay for him to do so, wasn't it?

Of course it was. Pete was wrong. They were adults. There were no rules. Were there rules?

He knew there were *laws*, of course, and what to do about people who broke them. But this was different. Certainly there weren't really rules like Pete was saying, about texting back too quickly, and the jumping of bones (Lord, how he hated that expression) by certain dates, and all of that. That was simply unbelievable.

Although, to be honest, Katie had shared a few things about dating in high school, and all of them had sounded just as unbelievable as the things Pete had shared. They had sounded so awful, in fact, that John had instituted a rule of his own, and that was that Katie wasn't to date anyone until college.

But she had only laughed at him and said, "Oh, Daddy," and done precisely as she liked. So that had been a failure, much as his own dating life had been until now, so clearly he knew nothing.

But that was high school. This was the adult world.

Quickly, he texted Molly back that he had to finish up some things (Pete would approve of this) but could meet her in a few hours.

A text bubble appeared. She was texting back!

Great. I'll be helping out at the inn. Can you meet me there?

Of course he could. The inn was on his way home. And the good thing about the inn was that it had a bar. They could have a drink (surely she was allowed to drink while on check-in duty), and that would almost be like a date. A quick date, but it might count as their second.

And then when they finally managed to meet for the steak dinner, that would be their third—

No. No, he was not playing Pete's game.

See you there, John texted back.

Of course, for it to count as a date, he had to pick up flowers on his way over, even though Pete had warned him against doing this.

But Pete didn't know everything. Pete was John's age,

yet had never been in a relationship lasting longer than four months, so how were his rules working out for him? John knew from experience that women liked flowers, and also felt that Molly deserved flowers after everything she'd been through, finding an abandoned baby *and* its mother near death.

The only problem was that it was Sunday, so the island's only flower shop was closed.

But that wasn't a problem, because John knew from having dealt with a credit-card fraud case at Island Blooms that the Morettis, the flower shop's owners, lived in a sweet little cottage behind the store, while also owning several apartments above it.

So he banged on their door until they answered it and bemusedly agreed to open the shop and allow him to buy a nice bouquet of daisies. Not roses, because that would be overkill, and Molly seemed like the type who would like daisies.

While there, he also queried the Morettis about the availability of an apartment for the new children's librarian. It was ridiculous for Molly to have to work two jobs just to afford to live in Little Bridge, and the Morettis were known as being conscientious landlords, who kept reasonably priced, if fairly small, apartments.

"Molly's very quiet," he assured them, though in actual fact he'd found Molly to be quite loud when expressing her opinions, which she did quite often. "And she works for the city, so her income is steady."

This piqued Mrs. Moretti's interest. She said they happened to have a tenant they were kicking out of one of their one-bedroom apartments at the end of the month. "Rent never on time, and the parties!" She shook her head in disgust.

"Why didn't you call me?" John asked. Excessive noise without a permit was considered a breach of the peace in Little Bridge.

Mrs. Moretti shrugged. "Call you every night? What would be the point? Anyway, he's leaving now. We can take your girlfriend."

John felt himself blushing. "She's not my girlfriend. Like I said, she's the new children's librarian, and since the hurricane, as you know, affordable housing has been very—"

"Yes, yes." Mr. Moretti laughed and slapped him on the shoulder. "We know. She's not your girlfriend, but you're bringing her flowers. We understand very much."

John, still blushing, had them wrap the daisies in plain brown paper—he didn't want the bouquet to look too over the top—and left after thanking the Morettis profusely. By the time he arrived at the Lazy Parrot it was happy hour, and the guests who'd already checked in were lounging around the pool with margaritas and cocktail plates.

"Hey, sexy policeman," one of the lady guests said to him as he walked by, looking for Molly, who hadn't been at the front desk. "Are those flowers for me?"

"No," John said flatly. "And I'm with the sheriff's department, not the police. These flowers are for Molly Montgomery. Have you seen her?"

"Oh, John!"

He saw a woman wearing a florescent-green beach cover-up with matching flip-flops waving to him from across the pool and realized it was Joanne Larson, one of the Lazy Parrot's owners. He approached her, grateful to be getting away from the woman who'd called him a sexy policeman.

"Hello, Joanne," he said, when he reached her. "Molly texted for me to meet her."

"Yes, I know." Joanne was holding a tray of something beige smeared on cucumber rounds. "She told me. She'll be right back. She's helping a new guest with their luggage. Fish dip?"

John shook his head. He felt another spurt of irritation at the unfairness of the situation. A librarian shouldn't need a side hustle just to afford her rent.

Of course, if he convinced Molly to leave her live-in job at the hotel and move in to the Morettis' apartment, that would leave Joanne and Carl Larson shorthanded. The only solution he could see was to find them a new night manager. He wondered if Deputy Swanson, the officer who'd been so blithe about his tardiness in responding to the alarm at Mrs. Tifton's house, would care for the position. He certainly wasn't cutting it in law enforcement. Maybe his true calling was in hospitality.

"So Molly tells me you're going to be dancing in the mother-daughter Snappettes performance," Joanne said, helping herself to one of her own hors d'oeuvres.

John attempted to smile.

"Yes. Yes, I am. I'm really looking forward to it," he lied.

"So am I," Joanne said. "I've already bought tickets for Carl and myself, and all of our friends, too. We can't wait to see it. It's going to be a hoot and a half! Are you going to wear an actual Snappette uniform?"

"The, er, costume decisions aren't up to me, so I'm not sure. I'm certain whatever it is will be very tasteful."

"Oh, I hope not," Joanne said. "We all want to see you in a Snappette uniform. That's what we're paying for, really."

"Wait, what are we talking about?" one of the nearby guests wanted to know.

"He's going to be dancing for charity with the high school cheerleading squad," Joanne said, pointing at John.

"It's a dance team," John corrected her.

But no one cared. Everyone on the poolside deck was staring at him appraisingly, all of the ladies smiling, the men confused.

"In a *dress*?" one of the men asked, looking appalled, though he himself was holding a drink that contained a pink paper umbrella.

"Shirtless, I hope," one of the ladies said, winking at John suggestively.

"Where can I get tickets?" one of the other ladies asked from the hot tub, nudging her friend.

"It's not till next month," Joanne said.

"I don't care," the guest responded with a cackle. "I'll extend my stay, especially if there's a chance he'll be doing it shirtless."

John was beginning to feel uncomfortable. "Now hold on," he began, because he'd learned at his four-hour sexual harassment workshop that the objectification of women could also happen to men—even law enforcement officers. It was also no less harmful, even though it was occasionally reinforced by first responders themselves, like those hose draggers over at the fire station and their ridiculous yearly calendar. "Let's—"

"John!"

Thank God Molly had finally appeared, wearing a flowy white sundress and looking as fresh and as welcome as rain after a hot day.

"Hello," he said, forgetting Joanne and her guests and everything but Molly and her radiant smile. Then he remembered something else. "Here. I brought you these." He handed her the flowers.

Molly gasped as she took them from him. "Daisies!" Molly cried. "They're beautiful! And my favorite. How did you know?"

He didn't know how he'd known. He just had. He wasn't at all surprised to have been right.

He was surprised, however, when Joanne and all of her guests (the women, anyway) let out a collective "*Awwww.*" He wanted to jump into the pool, sink to the bottom of the deep end, and not come out until he'd either drowned or they'd all gone away.

"How beautiful," Joanne said, setting down her tray of fish dip and taking the flowers from Molly. "I'll put them in a vase for you. You and John go visit." When Molly hesitated, Joanne waved her impossibly long, florescent-green nails at her. "Go on. I got this!"

Molly laughed and took him by the hand, leading him away from the pool and toward a thatched tiki bar beneath the outdoor stairs she'd taken last night to get to her room.

"Here, let me get you a drink," she said. "What'll you have?"

"Beer is fine."

"Beer it is." She slipped behind the bar and pulled out a bottle from an outdoor mini fridge. "Do you want a lime with that?"

"God, no."

She laughed again and passed him the beer. "Sorry about that," she whispered, nodding toward the still-gossiping guests, many of whom continued to look in their direction. "You know how it is. This place is like Disney World to them. Everything in Little Bridge is an attraction—including the locals. Seeing me with a man who's brought me flowers is a bit like seeing the guy who plays Goofy without his head."

He looked at her. "I don't think they see you as Goofy. Maybe one of the princesses, like Cinderella."

"Oh, and are you my handsome prince, here to rescue me from a life of drudgery?"

Damn. He'd put his foot in it again. "I didn't mean—that wasn't what I—I meant because you're so—"

She laughed again, and reached out to lay a hand upon his wrist. "John, I was kidding. I wouldn't mind being rescued from having to wash so many towels. But I couldn't ask for cheaper rent or a more centrally located place to live, and Carl and Joanne really do need the help."

John nodded, thinking to himself that this would be a bad time to tell her about the apartment over the flower shop. Then it really would look like he was trying to rescue her.

Instead, he said, changing the subject, "So, you texted that you had something to show me?"

"Oh, yes." She reached beneath the bar. "I'm afraid you're not going to like it very much, though."

"Go ahead." He sipped his beer, feeling extremely contented. It was nice simply to be in her company, even with a dozen pairs of eyes watching their every move. The waterfall by the side of the pool and jets in the hot tub were making a relaxing splashing sound, and the blossoms on the night-blooming jasmine had already begun to open and release their intoxicating scent. If he didn't have to go home to see Katie, he'd happily hang out here all evening.

"One of my patrons brought this into the library today," Molly said, bringing a digital Leica out from beneath the bar. She must have noticed his expression change, since she added, quickly, "Don't worry, it's his father's, not Mrs. Tifton's. The time and date stamps on the photos on it prove it. That's why I wanted to show them to you, though—the photos that he took on it last night. You're not going to like them, but you need to see them."

Now John was beginning to feel less relaxed. His beer

forgotten, he leaned forward against the bar to peer into the camera's display screen as she switched it on. "Why am I not going to like them?"

"Because," Molly said. "They're of Katie. Katie and the High School Thief."

CHAPTER NINETEEN

Molly

At first Molly thought John might be having a heart attack. He'd gone a little pale and his breath seemed to quicken as he scrolled through the photos on Elijah's camera.

"Are you—are you all right?" she asked, wondering if she should run for the emergency defibrillator that the Larsons kept in the kitchen. She'd taken enough job-mandated first-aid courses that she knew how to use it.

She'd just always hoped she'd never need to.

"I'm fine."

The words came out tonelessly. He hadn't looked up once from the camera screen.

"That *is* him, isn't it?" Molly asked. "Dylan Dakota?"

"That's him," John said. His gaze was still glued to the screen. "And my daughter."

"Yes. I guess Katie and her friends had a little photo shoot for some kind of cheer camp they're applying to." What was wrong with him? He looked so strange. "I think Dylan must have been skulking around in a lot of people's backyards last night before he settled on breaking into Mrs. Tifton's house. I bet there are other people who probably got footage of him on their home security cameras and maybe weren't home and don't even know it yet. I was thinking that if we sent this image over to Meschelle at the *Gazette*—"

He finally looked up from the screen, and when he did, his blue-eyed gaze was troubled. "I can't."

Molly was surprised. "But, John, why not? If Meschelle runs this photo on the front page, everybody will pay attention. It's super eye-catching. This is much better than running a mug shot of the guy, which I'm sure you must have considered but can't do because his lawyers would eat you alive. And this is a current photo and shows him in the act. Someone is bound to recognize him and realize that they've seen him somewhere around. Then they'll call in and tell you where you can—"

John pointed at one of the photographs—specifically at Katie, whose hip was thrust out as she blew a provocatively sexy kiss in the direction of the viewer, all while dressed in her very short Snappette skirt and halter top. "That's my *daughter*."

Molly was still confused. "I know, but, John, I'm sure Katie will be happy to help. She's an outgoing girl. She'll love the attention."

"It isn't that," John said, staring at her as if she'd gone crazy. "I don't want *that* photo of my daughter on the front page of our town newspaper."

Suddenly, it all became clear—why he was so taken aback by the photos. It wasn't only the fact that Dylan was lurking around in the background in some of them. No, he was just as disturbed by Katie's appearance.

But while some of his daughter's poses were a little suggestive, Molly didn't think they were shocking. They were the same kinds of photos all the teens she knew were posting online.

Poor Katie. It was hard enough on the kid that her mom had left just as she was hitting her formative teen years and now she was being raised by a single father.

But being raised by the town *sheriff*? Molly hoped she hadn't gotten her into too much trouble.

"John, I'm sure Meschelle can have the photo cropped so Katie doesn't show, or blur her face out, since she's a minor," Molly rushed to explain. "There's no need to mention her name or show her at all."

He lifted his bottle to take a long swig of beer, staring at the photo and continuing to look pained. "I'll have to think about this."

Molly didn't find this response very reassuring. "Look, I know this must feel very personal to you now. How could it not? Dylan's trashing my library was very personal to me, too. But we can't let our personal feelings keep us from doing everything we can to find this guy. I really think letting Meschelle run this photo would—"

He plunked down his bottle loudly enough to cause several of the hotel guests to turn their heads to see what was going on.

"*We* aren't going to do anything to find this guy," he said. "That's *my* job."

Before she could say anything else, he was lifting the camera and turning to leave. "Sorry, but I really better go. I said I'd meet Katie for dinner. This does help." He waved the camera. "Thank you."

Molly had a sinking feeling that instead of helping, she'd made everything worse—especially any chance of their having any sort of relationship, romantic or otherwise. She struggled to find something—anything—to say to salvage the situation. "John, I'm sorry. I—"

"No, really," he said, and managed a tight smile over his shoulder as he strode off. "I mean it."

Then he was gone.

Molly was certain he hadn't meant it at all. Sighing, she turned her wounded expression toward Joanne, who was simultaneously sipping a margarita and pretending to be wiping up a spill on an outdoor table nearby, not eavesdropping.

"Did I blow it?" Molly asked her.

"Oh, honey, no." Joanne was quick to rush to Molly's side. "He's just a man, and a protective one at that. Seeing his little girl like that—so close to that fellow he's been trying to catch for so long—threw him for a loop, is all. And to find out about it from you, of all people!"

"Why is it so bad that he found out about it from me? I was trying to help."

"Well, of course you were. But he likes you—he brought you flowers, didn't he? So he wants to look good in front of you. And then you throw it in his face that he can't even protect his little girl from that piece of lowlife scum—"

"That isn't what I meant to do at all!"

"Of course you didn't. Don't worry about it. As soon as he catches that walking piece of phlegm, it will all blow over, and he'll be coming back again with flowers to apologize."

Molly shook her head, thinking of the pain she'd seen in those blue eyes. "I don't think he will."

"Oh, come on now. Why not?"

"Well, for one thing, because I wasn't doing laundry just now. I was using your old computer up at the front desk to download that camera's memory card. Because I kind of had a feeling he wouldn't agree to send Meschelle those photos." Molly shrugged sadly. "So if he doesn't, I will, Joanne. I *have* to. I can't let that guy get away with what he did to the library—not to mention that little baby and her mother!"

Joanne took a long, reflective sip of her margarita. Then, after swallowing, she said, "Well, in that case, you're right, honey. The sheriff probably won't be coming back with flowers for you anytime soon."

CHAPTER TWENTY

John

Sunday was Spaghetti and Meatball Night at the Mermaid Café, and no matter what else was going on, John always tried to make a point of taking Katie there, not only because many other local families showed up and it had a nice community feel, but because he loved spaghetti and meatballs.

Katie was not the biggest fan of either spaghetti or meatballs, however. As a child, when presented with the dish, she had usually screamed until given buttered noodles and no meatballs instead. Now, as a sophisticated young woman, she merely ordered a Caesar salad with a few strips of grilled chicken on top for added protein.

But John would not break with tradition, not even after the bombshell Molly Montgomery had dropped on him . . . the latest in a series of bombshells she'd dropped that were blowing his previously orderly life to smithereens.

How and why did she keep doing this? He had never met

a woman who was at once so attractive and so determined to destroy him. Had she come to this island for this purpose only, under the disguise of a friendly children's librarian?

It seemed so.

Now he sat in one of the Mermaid's orange-and-teal booths, watching as his daughter happily waved to her friends on the other side of the restaurant. At home, she would have been texting if he'd allowed it, but at the Mermaid, texting was *really* not allowed, as Ed, the owner, would throw out customers for cell phone use.

John waited until Katie had had a few bites of her chicken and he knew she had something in her stomach and wasn't still light-headed from all the calories she'd expended at the dance practice she'd been at all day. Then he pulled out the camera Molly had given him and said, "We need to talk about this."

Katie glanced down at the camera and said, "Isn't that Elijah's? He said his dad left it when he moved out." Her eyes widened. "Oh my God. Don't tell me he *stole* it. No way. I know Elijah's a little weird, but he would never—"

"I'm not talking about the camera." John switched on the display screen. "I'm talking about these photos."

Katie blinked down at the screen. "Yeah. What about them?"

He felt a surge of exasperation. "Katie, these photos . . . you look . . . they . . . you . . . the way you're posing . . ."

She rolled her eyes and turned her concentration back to her salad. "Dad, we were just goofing around."

"Yes, I can see that. But—"

"We're not *posting* them anywhere. Well, the headshots we're going to send with our apps to cheer camp. But the rest of them were just for fun."

"Just for fun," he repeated, looking down at a photo of all three of the girls lifting their skirts and mooning the photographer—presumably this Elijah person. They still had on their cheer shorts or whatever they were called beneath their skirts, but that wasn't the point.

"Come on, Dad," Katie said, still laughing as she speared a crouton with her fork. "Don't tell me you never did silly things in high school."

"I did," he said, thinking of an incident involving a spear gun, some eggs, and an old friend's car. "But we never filmed it."

"Well, times are different now." Katie popped the crouton into her mouth. "Everybody films everything. It's no big deal."

"It *is* a big deal," John said, flipping through the photos until he found the one he wanted. "At least this time. This is why." He showed her the picture of herself with Larry Beckwith in the background.

At first Katie's expression didn't change. She said, "So what? I'm blowing a kiss. You know we all do that in the 'Mack the Knife' number—"

Then her expression *did* change. She reached for the camera in order to bring the screen closer so she could get a better look.

"Oh my God, Dad! Who is that guy? Is he *spying* on us? That is so gross! What a creeper."

"That," John said, "is Larry Beckwith III, also known as Dylan Dakota."

"The guy you've been trying to catch for so long? The one who messed up the MTV house and the library? Oh my God, is he *stalking* me?"

Katie looked more thrilled than frightened by the idea that she had a stalker. John sighed and reached across the table to take the camera from her.

"No, he isn't stalking you. He robbed a house near Sharmaine's last night. We think he must have tried a number of homes before finding one that was unoccupied."

"So he's creeping on Sharmaine?" Katie reached instinctively for her bag, in which she kept her phone. "I have to tell her right away. She's always wanted a stalker. She's going to *die*."

"You are not going to tell Sharmaine," John said. "At least not yet. First of all, no cell phones in here, remember?"

She glanced toward the sign by the Mermaid's register:

NO SHOES, NO SHIRT, NO PROBLEM.
USE YOUR CELL PHONE? GET OUT.

Then she sighed. "Oh, right. Darn."

"Second of all," John went on, "this photo of you and Beckwith is now evidence. And there are certain people who think it should be submitted to the press so that the public can see it and help with the search for Beckwith—"

Katie gasped. Unfortunately, she appeared to be gasping with delight, not horror.

"Oh my God, Daddy, are you serious? What site? Is it BuzzFeed? When? Tomorrow?"

He frowned. This was not going at all the way he'd assumed it would go. Although he should have known: his outgoing dancer daughter would love the attention—any attention.

"The *Gazette*," he said, and was bemused to see her shoulders slump in disappointment.

"The *Gazette*? That only has like five thousand subscribers. And there's a paywall. Hardly anyone is going to see it. And I'm really trying to build my brand—so is Elijah, by the way. Do you think you could get it onto the front page of the *Miami Herald*? Or on CNN? A lot more people will see it there. And make sure you use Elijah's name as the photographer, Elijah Trujos. We all promised we would give him full credit if we used the photos for anything promotional."

John stared at his daughter. Was it possible that Molly Montgomery knew his daughter better than he did? She'd said that Katie wouldn't mind the attention, and she'd been right.

"Katie, your face is not going to be on the front page of any paper tomorrow because if I decide to turn the photo over to the media, I'm going to make sure your face is blurred out—"

"Daddy, no!"

"—for your own protection."

"But, Daddy—"

"—and I certainly won't allow them to use either your

or Elijah's names, because you are both minors, and I don't want you to be forever associated with this case or that man."

"But, Daddy, I look really good in that photo. I'm in my Snappettes uniform and everything. Think of all the donations it could bring to the team!"

John shook his head. "That is exactly what I'm worried about. Do you have any idea how many sexual predators there are who would love to see a photo like that and track down the girl in it?"

"Ugh, Daddy." Katie pouted. "I don't understand how you can be such a boomer when you were actually born in the eighties."

He pointed at her. "For that, you get no dessert, young lady."

She stuck her tongue out at him but playfully. He could tell she wasn't really mad, just like she could tell he wasn't really mad, either. They'd been a team too long to allow petty disagreements to get in the way of their affection for each other.

Unlike his relationship with Molly Montgomery, which was too new for him to let the sun set on a squabble. He had to make things right with her. But how?

"What can I get you two for dessert?" Angela, who always worked the Sunday night spaghetti and meatball shift, came up to their booth to ask.

Katie was still mock pouting. "My dad says I'm not allowed to have dessert."

"Come on now, Sheriff." Angela jerked her pen toward the counter. "Ed made a couple of his world-famous key lime pies this afternoon. You know there's nothing better than a slice of pie to fix what ails you."

John glanced at the counter and saw the pies sitting pristine and covered in peaks of lightly toasted meringue behind the glass display case. Was it really true that a piece of pie could repair all of one's troubles? Not in his experience.

But it could certainly make one feel better in the moment.

"I'll have one," John said, and began to dig around in his pocket for his wallet. The Mermaid Café was a cash-only enterprise.

"Da-aa-aad." Katie's expression was stern with disapproval. "You can't have a slice of pie. Your cholesterol. Remember?"

"I don't want a slice," John said. "I'll take the whole thing."

When Katie's eyebrows rose in shock, he explained, "It's for a friend, not me. I owe her an apology, and what better way to say I'm sorry than with one of Ed's pies?"

Now Katie began to look slyly knowing. "Her? *Her,* Dad? Is it a certain librarian you dragged me to meet the other day? Is it? *Is it?*"

"That is none of your business," John said, throwing bills onto the table as Angela went to box up his pie. "Can you find a ride home with someone here? I have to get over to the *Gazette* offices before they put tomorrow's paper to bed."

"Yes," Katie said, and nodded at a table a few booths away. "Nevaeh's over there with Marquis and those guys. They'll drop me off. Why are you so worried about me walking home alone, Dad? Because of my *stalker?*"

"Cut it out. You know I don't like you walking by yourself after dark. Be sure to put the alarm on when you get home. I might be late."

"Because after you visit the *Gazette* you'll be delivering your pie to *the librarian*?"

John shot his daughter a warning look even as he gratefully accepted the pie, wrapped in an insulated pack to keep it cool, from Angela. "Thanks," he said to the waitress. To his daughter, he said, "I love you." He leaned over and kissed the top of her head. "Be good. And safe."

"Ugh, jeez, Dad." She pushed him away, but she was grinning as she did it. "I love you, too. And you know I will."

Later, John found himself driving to the Lazy Parrot, asking himself if he was crazy. Who brought the woman they were interested in a pie? Let alone a pie and flowers in the same day. If Pete ever found out about this, he'd think he was nuts.

But John had to do something to show Molly how sorry he was for acting like such a—

Grumpy dad.

He didn't feel very reassured about his decision when he walked into the lobby of the Lazy Parrot and saw no one (as usual) at the front desk. He hadn't realized it was so late. Probably Molly was in bed already. After all, tomorrow was Monday, a workday, even for children's librarians. He should have called first.

But if he called, he might wake her. He could take a gamble, he thought, and hope she was still up and at the tiki bar—though what would she be doing there this late on a Sunday night?

He went through the lobby and out into the courtyard and instantly regretted it.

"Hello again, sexy policeman!" The tourist from before was in the hot tub—even though it was close to seventy-five degrees outside—and she was still drinking. How was that even possible? By rights she should have passed out by now from dehydration.

But no—she had a plastic cup shaped like a coconut in her hand, accompanied by a pink paper umbrella. She was staying well hydrated on something.

"Hello," John replied, just to be polite.

"Are you looking for Molly again?" the woman asked. There were several other people in the hot tub with her, none of whom, unfortunately, was Molly.

"Well," John said, trying to figure out the best reply. If he said yes, it might not look good. But if he said no, it would be a lie. "I, er—"

"He's looking for Molly," the woman assured her friends, and they all cackled in a friendly but decidedly knowing way.

Feeling foolish standing there with his pie, John began to back away. "Maybe I'll just come back another—"

"Oh, no, don't do that," the woman said. "Is that for her?" She was eyeing the insulated bag in his hands.

"Um," he said. "Yes, it is."

"What is it?"

"It's, um." John could not remember ever feeling so stupid. "It's a pie."

"A pie?"

"A key lime pie."

The women in the hot tub exchanged glances. John couldn't read them, exactly, since it was dark in the courtyard except for the light from the pool and the party lights strung across the tiki hut. But he thought they were smiling.

"Don't worry, hon," one of the women said, finally. "We'll get her for you." Then, to John's utter mortification, the women began to scream, "Molly! Molly!"

"Wait," he said. "You don't have to—"

But it was too late. He heard a door being opened somewhere above his head, and turned to see Molly on the second-floor balcony, wearing only an overlarge Denver Broncos T-shirt and what appeared to be men's boxer briefs. Even more startlingly, she had on a large pair of glasses in tortoiseshell frames.

It had never occurred to him before that Molly wore glasses, but evidently, she did. Possibly she wore contacts during the day. This would at least partly account for why her eyes always seemed so large and dark.

"What is it, Mrs. Filmore?" she called down to the women in a slightly irritated voice, then noticed John.

"Oh," she said, in an entirely different tone. "It's you."

Their gazes met, and it was as if the rest of the world melted away. The only thing that existed was her, and the smell of the night-blooming jasmine.

At least until the woman in the hot tub behind him shouted, "He brought you pie!"

John wished the earth would open and swallow him whole.

He heard Molly laugh in confusion. "What?"

He raised the insulated bag. "Key lime pie," he said. "By way of apology. Can I—may I—come up?"

It was a bold move, asking to be let into her room, especially with that bubbling vat of tourists behind him, remarking on every little thing he did. Regardless of her answer, there were going to be comments, possibly even catcalls.

"Sure," Molly said. "Come on up."

The ladies in the hot tub were quick with their "Ooooohs" and "Yeah, babys," but John did his best to ignore them, mounting the stairs two at a time and feeling glad that the darkness would—hopefully—hide the burning he felt in his cheeks.

When he reached Molly, he saw that she was grinning.

"Sorry about the Greek chorus down there," she whispered, gesturing toward the hot tub below. "They've been in there since happy hour. I switched them over to plain tonic water a while ago for their own good, but I don't think they've noticed—or that they care."

John nodded. He didn't think he'd ever seen anyone look as beautiful in glasses as Molly did. Behind the lenses of her glasses, her eyes seemed larger and darker than ever.

"I'm sorry about earlier." He thrust the pie at her. "I acted like an idiot."

Molly looked down at the object in her hands. It was difficult for him to read her exact expression because with her head lowered, her dark hair cast her face in shadow, and the only light source on the porch was coming from the open doorway behind her, the one leading into her room.

"A pie?" she asked, in what sounded to him like a skeptical tone.

"A pie." He had known this was going to be hard, but he hadn't thought it would be *this* hard. "Key lime, from the Mermaid Café. Freshly made this morning by Ed. If you haven't tried one yet, you really should, they're delicious. I just saw it and thought of you because . . . well, I thought you might like it, and also because . . . well, you were right."

Her head popped up at that. He wasn't certain because her face was still slightly shadowed in darkness, but he thought he saw her eyebrows raise. "I was what?"

"You were right. About the photos. I talked to Katie about them, and then I took them over to Meschelle at the *Gazette*. She's going to make sure that they run one on the front page tomorrow morning—"

Molly took a step backward, and at first he thought it was because she was going to ask him to leave.

But the movement brought her face into the light, and he could see that she was smiling.

"Why don't you come in," she said, gesturing toward the open door to her room, "and have a piece of this pie with me?"

John glanced at the warm, inviting glow coming from inside the room, and swallowed. He could hear Pete's voice in his head, urging him to accept her invitation.

But a stronger voice was telling him that if he did, he wouldn't come out until morning. There were things he wanted to do with Molly Montgomery that would take all night, maybe days, and he had responsibilities, to his daughter, to his community. He couldn't throw all of those away just because he wanted to—

"Okay," John said, and, smiling, stepped through Molly's door. "Thanks."

CHAPTER TWENTY-ONE

Molly

Molly couldn't believe it when she opened her door and saw the sheriff standing down there in the courtyard holding what appeared to be an insulated bag of fried chicken.

Then she'd been even more disbelieving when she learned it was not fried chicken but pie—key lime pie, her favorite.

But the absolute kicker was when he'd climbed the stairs to her room and stood in front of her and said the three words she most loved hearing in all the world—the three words she was pretty certain every librarian, or at least lover of knowledge, adored more than any other in the human language:

You were right.

They were words she'd never, ever heard her ex utter. Even on trivia nights when Eric had given an answer that was incorrect, he would argue that he was not wrong, that instead there'd been some flaw in the way the question was worded.

This should have been her first sign that the two of them were not suited for each other, because a reasonable person should always be willing to admit when they've made a mistake.

But she'd been blinded by Eric's good looks and—she might as well admit it—wealth. He'd not only had a truly incredible two-bedroom loft in LoDo, but a ski condo in Breckenridge, and time shares in both Tulum and Kauai.

It was a mistake she'd sworn she'd never make again.

So when the sheriff admitted he was wrong and she was right, what could Molly do but invite him inside?

"So I know it's not much," Molly said, rushing in ahead of him to switch off the TV so that he wouldn't see what she'd been watching—a marathon of *Forensic Files*. "But it suits me perfectly fine for now."

John took two steps inside, said, "Oh, I'm sure it's—" then froze, looking around the hotel room with the same horrified expression Molly imagined he might have worn while viewing a particularly gruesome crime scene for the first time.

Confused, Molly swept her gaze over the room, trying to see what was so upsetting him. True, the room was small. But it was a hotel room! It wasn't supposed to be huge.

And true, she had been forced to cram over thirty years' worth of possessions and belongings into the tiny space, excluding the things she'd left at home with her mother and in storage until she could find a more permanent living situation, like all her furniture and most of her cooking utensils and of course all of her winter clothes.

In fact, the only things she'd brought with her to Little Bridge, besides her summer clothes, were—

"Books," John said in a slightly stunned tone, looking around the tiny space in wonder. "You have so many . . . books."

"Oh." Molly followed his gaze and realized that if she looked at it from his point of view, the number of books she'd brought with her from Colorado might seem excessive. Because hotel rooms came with few bookshelves, her books were piled up all along the walls until they reached almost to the ceiling, stacked in every imaginable nook and cranny, including around the bed and—though John didn't know this yet—in the bathroom.

Was this particularly odd, though? Molly didn't think so.

"I know it might seem like a lot," she said, taking the pie to the kitchenette—where she'd stacked her cookbooks and of course cooking-related mystery novels, though she'd left some room for food preparation. "But I couldn't leave my books in storage until I found an apartment. What if I thought of something I'd read and needed to reread it?"

Behind her, John was wandering around, looking at the titles of all the books. "You have something against e-books?"

"Oh, no, they're fine. Lots of people like them, I know. But I love the smell of real books, you know? And the feel of paper, turning the pages over in my hands. Drink?"

He looked up from her piles of science fiction, startled. "Excuse me?"

"I was wondering if you wanted something to drink with the pie. I've got everything here." She opened her mini fridge to show him. "Beer, wine, soda, hard stuff—or I can make coffee, tea—"

"Oh, no, thanks." He seemed fixated on the books. "Don't you work in a library? Couldn't you check out whatever you wanted whenever you needed to—for free?"

"Of course. But these are *my* books. I've had some of them since I was kid. They're like friends, you know? I've never gone anywhere without them. Oh, watch the Miss Marples!"

He looked down just as his foot was about to hit a pile of books that seemed to be supporting another pile of books under one end of the coffee table. "The what?"

"Miss Marple." Now that Molly had cut two large slices of key lime pie, she hurried over to give him one. "You must know Miss Marple. She's one of Agatha Christie's most famous amateur sleuths."

John accepted the pie and sat down on the couch, which was thankfully devoid of books, although there were piles of them on either side. "I don't really read mysteries."

"Oh, I guess you wouldn't." Molly snuggled onto the couch cushion beside him. "Why would you? You live them. I bet you never watch *Law and Order* or *CSI* or anything like that, either, do you?"

He shook his head. "Those shows—they never get anything right. Do you know how long it takes in real life to get the results back on a DNA sample?"

Molly laughed. She couldn't help it. He was so funny, but didn't know it. "I can imagine reading mysteries would be a kind of busman's holiday for you. What do you read, then?"

He took a bite of pie. "Biographies, mostly."

Molly gave him a nonjudgmental smile. She didn't care what people read, as long as they read something, anything—well, aside from books about how to make bombs or other weapons that hurt people.

"What kind of biographies?" She wondered what he looked like beneath that uniform and how long it was going to be before she got him out of it.

"Historical figures, mainly," he said. He was really going to town on his piece of pie—which was no wonder, because it was delicious. But Molly wondered if his mindless eating was also partly due to nerves. "Athletes."

"Which one is your favorite?"

"My favorite biography?"

"Yes."

He gave his answer some thought. "Your boss—well, not really anymore, because she's retired, but you said she kind of hired you as her replacement—Mrs. Robinette?"

Molly nodded. "Phyllis. Yes?"

"When I was a kid growing up here, I got into trouble a lot. Nothing serious, but I might have been headed down a wrong path if I hadn't ended up in your library one day and run into your boss—Mrs. Robinette. It was raining, so it wasn't like I had anywhere else to go, and she handed me a book she said I might like."

Molly continued to smile, thinking of Elijah. "What book was it?"

"An autobiography written by a man named Dick Gregory."

Molly's smile broadened. She'd have to remember to tell Phyllis later. She'd be so pleased. "Good choice, was it?"

"I loved that book. I had no idea there could be books like that. I don't think I'd ever read a whole book before, except when required to for school. But that book—I finished it in a day. And then all I wanted to do after that was find more books like it. I even tried out for the school track team a week later because that's the sport Dick Gregory played."

Molly frowned. "But I thought you played baseball in high school?"

"I did. The baseball coach saw me running track and recruited me for the team. I guess I was pretty good, because our team made it to nationals."

She smiled and took his empty plate from him and set it, along with hers, on the coffee table. "I love hearing stories like that. All it takes to get someone to love reading is finding them the right book—a book that could even change their life."

"Is that why you're a children's librarian?" he asked her. "Did you have a book like that?"

"Of course. Only I'm sorry to say it was Nancy Drew—but an original copy, not any of those bland reprints. I found it in my great-grandmother's attic, all crumbling and falling apart, and it was like finding a secret treasure. Original Nancy drove a yellow roadster and wore a cloche and went after real gangsters with guns. I have it here if you want to—"

She'd started to get up to go to her stack of mystery juvenilia, but he reached out and grabbed her hand, then gently pulled her back down onto the couch. When she turned her head to look at him questioningly, she saw that his blue-eyed gaze seemed more intense than ever.

"How did you know I played baseball in high school?" he asked.

Her heart stuttered. *Oops*. "It's a small town. People talk."

"Do they? Or have you been asking around about me?" His lips were tantalizingly close to hers.

"No." She absolutely had been. "Why would I do that?"

"Because you like me."

"Well, I don't dislike you. I certainly respect you in a professional capacity."

"I respect you in a more-than-professional capacity."

The next thing she knew, he was kissing her, his lips tasting sweetly tart, like the pie. Not just kissing her, either, but embarking on a thorough exploration of the inside of her mouth with his tongue while his hands slipped up beneath her nightshirt. Fortunately, she wasn't wearing a bra.

She had no idea what she'd said to cause this kind of reaction from him—something about respecting him, and Nancy Drew.

But if mentioning Nancy Drew was all it took to get him to respond this way, she was going to talk about that crime-solving minx all of the time. As his lips dipped below her mouth and slid down her throat, those hard hands of his began doing things to her beneath the nightshirt that made her toes curl. Then he was pulling the too-large shirt up and over her head, exposing her breasts to his roving lips. When his hot mouth closed over one of her nipples, teasing it with his tongue, Molly couldn't help burying both her hands in his thick dark hair and arching her body against his, even as she tilted her own head back in ecstasy and . . . heard a stack of books fall over behind her. Damn! The sound of the cascading hardcovers caused him to look up in surprise, but she only pushed his head back where it belonged and said, "Don't worry about that." She'd sort the books out tomorrow.

The only problem was that his erection wasn't the only hard thing she could feel against her soft, bare curves.

"Um, excuse me." She plucked at his shirt as one of the points of his sheriff's badge dug into her. "Would you mind?"

"Sorry," he rasped, and fumbled at the buttons of his uniform.

"Let me help," she said, and soon he was gloriously shirtless above her. It was everything she'd been hoping for and more. And yet it was not nearly enough.

"And this." She pointed impatiently at his belt, on which he still wore his gun.

"Oh, damn." He drew off the belt to place it high on her stack of gothic romances, which promptly tumbled to the floor. His look of dismay was comical. "I'm sorry."

"It's okay," Molly said, and sat up to work on undoing his fly, realizing they were never going to get to where she wanted them to be as quickly as she needed to get there if she did not take the initiative.

"No, I can—"

"I've got it."

She did, too. What came spilling out when she successfully managed to undo his uniform trousers was everything Molly had been suspecting she'd find from that time she'd watched him play cornhole on the beach and had so admired his form, front and back. It was sheer perfection, and it was standing at full attention just for her.

"Oh, John," she said, and sighed, as she wrapped herself around him, delighting in his heavy, masculine warmth.

"Molly," he whispered into her hair. He sounded worried. "I don't—I don't have—I didn't bring anything because I didn't think we were going to—"

Molly leaned her head back to blink up at him. "Are you talking about condoms?"

"Yes." He leaned up on his elbows, clearly frustrated. She could feel that frustration throbbing against her bare thigh. "I didn't think I'd be having sex with you tonight. I only came to apologize and bring you a pie. I didn't bring any . . . any . . ."

Molly laughed. She couldn't help it. "Don't worry. I've got some." She leaned down and reached into her purse, which she'd thrown onto the floor along with her bra the moment she'd come home from work. From the depths of the bag she pulled something in a hot pink wrapper. "Leftover from my teens-only sex-ed talk last month."

He sounded a little out of breath as she straddled him. "Are all librarians like you?"

"Oh, yes." She ripped the wrapper open with her teeth, then skillfully unrolled the condom down the length of his penis, her breasts skimming the fine dark hair that coated his chest. "We try always to be prepared."

"I think I—" His hands had gone to her hips, and almost as if he couldn't help himself, he'd begun to push himself inside her—which was all right, because she was wetter than she could ever remember being. "I think I—"

But she never got to hear what he thought, because at that moment he entered her fully, and she cried out at the sheer physical joy of it.

But wasn't that what made the best things in life so much more enjoyable, the sweet tinged with a little tart, so that your heartbeat sped up and all your senses came alive?

And, oh, he was moving beneath her, his hands slipping to cup her breasts, and she could hardly breathe. He felt so good, her skin seemed to be tingling all over, and stacks of books were collapsing all around them. Faster and faster, harder and harder, and this was a disaster, why hadn't they moved to the bed, and oh! Books were tumbling around her, but they weren't heavy at all. They felt like feathers, golden feathers, cascading around her body, and now all she wanted was for this feeling to never end, except all good things had to end sometime, and—

When she opened her eyes, she was lying collapsed on the sheriff's damp chest. Both of them were breathing hard. And someone was banging on her door.

"Molly? Molly, is everything all right in there?"

"Oh, no." Molly lifted her head. "It's Mrs. Filmore," she whispered. "She's in the room downstairs. She must have heard the books fall."

"I'll handle her." John started to get up.

"John, no—you don't have to say a word to her."

"I'm not going to say *a* word to her." John was already reaching for his shirt. "I'm going to say *a lot* of words to her."

"John." Molly couldn't help laughing at the absurdity of the situation. "Honestly, don't."

"As sheriff of this town, it's my duty to keep the peace, even if that means shutting up noisy neighbors."

"She's not a noisy neighbor," Molly insisted. "She's a nosy tourist. She was supposed to check out this past weekend but she and her husband extended their stay because she's so obsessed with the whole abandoned baby thing. She just wants to know what's going on between us."

As if on cue, Mrs. Filmore called through the door, "I heard something falling. Do you need help?"

"No, Mrs. Filmore," Molly said, frantically looking around for her own shirt. "I'm sorry, that was just some books."

"Are you sure?" Mrs. Filmore sounded unconvinced. "I thought I heard shouting."

Meanwhile, John was tugging on his own shirt.

"No, no shouting, Mrs. Filmore," Molly said, pulling her shirt on over her head, but John was faster. He already had his uniform trousers pulled up and zipped. "Everything's fine in here. There's nothing to worry about."

"Well, I'm not *worried,* exactly." Mrs. Filmore's voice was filled with false concern. "It's just that Fluffy the Cat has been crying to be let in, and you're usually so—"

John yanked open the door and stood there, his uniform completely buttoned, everything in place except his gun belt, and smiled down at Mrs. Filmore. "Is there something I can help you with, ma'am?"

John's body was mostly blocking the doorway—purposefully, so that Mrs. Filmore couldn't see that Molly was only half-dressed.

But Molly could hear the astonishment in the woman's voice, even if she couldn't see it on her face.

"Oh, um, no, Officer," said Mrs. Filmore breathlessly. "I'm—I'm so sorry to have disturbed you. I was only checking on Molly. I heard, um, a thump, you see, and I thought—"

"Sheriff," John said.

"I—I'm sorry?"

"You called me Officer. But it's Sheriff. I'm Sheriff John Hartwell." He pointed to his badge. "See? I told you that before, downstairs."

Molly, by that time, had her boxers back on. She hurried to join John at the door.

"I'm fine, Mrs. Filmore," Molly gushed. "See? Everything is fine. We were just having some pie."

Mrs. Filmore looked past Molly and the sheriff at the coffee table, which was covered with the empty plates from which they'd had pie earlier. Of course, the floor was also strewn with books, around which Fluffy the Cat was now sauntering. He'd managed to sneak in between their legs when they weren't looking.

"Oh," the older woman said. "Well. All right, then. I'm glad everything is okay. I'll just—"

John's cell phone began to chime, shrilly. He dug it from his trouser pocket, glanced at the screen, glowered, and said, “I have to answer this. If you ladies could excuse me for a moment—”

Then, his phone pressed to his ear, he stepped out of the room and into the darkness of the hotel’s second-floor balcony to take the call.

But not, unfortunately, far enough away to prevent Molly from hearing every word he said.

CHAPTER TWENTY-TWO

John

John recognized the number on the screen of his cell and felt a spurt of irritation. Of course Tabitha Brighton's parents chose this moment, of all times, to call him back.

But he supposed it was better than calling him ten minutes earlier, when his time had been even more pleasantly occupied.

"Hello," he said. "This is Sheriff John Hartwell."

"Sheriff?" The voice of the woman on the other end of the line sounded surprised. Surprised and agitated. "I didn't realize . . . oh, dear. Not again. I'm so sorry, Officer. What's Tabby done this time?"

He did not correct her use of the wrong title. "Well, that depends. To whom am I speaking?"

"Oh, I'm sorry. I'm her mother, Beth, Beth Brighton. I'm sorry not to have called sooner, but my husband and I—Tabby's father—we've been away, and cell phone service was a bit spotty, and . . . well, you know, we just receive so many complaints about Tabby—"

"What did she do now, Beth?" demanded a voice—male—in the background. "Whatever it is, I'm not paying for it."

"Oh." Beth Brighton sounded uncomfortable. "Sorry. That's my husband, Tom. Like I was saying, Tabby's been a bit . . . troublesome over the past few years, and we felt like we deserved to get away for a bit, so . . ."

"I see," John said. "How long has it been since you last saw your daughter?"

"Oh, let me see. A year? I think it's been a year or so since she ran off."

"Ran off?"

"Yes. Well, for good this time. She's done it before, but this time it's seemed to stick. We had an argument about the SATs—her grades have never been the best, even though she's a bright girl. Her IQ is at the genius level, according to one child psychiatrist we took her to. We've just never seemed to be able to make her understand that grades are important for getting into the right college. All her friends are going to lovely schools this year—Yale, Duke, Baylor. But last spring Tabby refused to sit for the SATs. She said they didn't measure anything that's actually important, only rote memorization, which isn't real knowledge or intelligence—can you imagine?"

Remembering his own conversation with the Brightons' daughter, John said, "Yes, I can."

"Well, of course, we panicked. I mean, she's our only

child. What was her future going to look like if she didn't go to college? How was she going to be financially successful?"

John wanted to point out that he knew quite a few successful people who hadn't gone to college, and that there were many different ways to measure success other than financially, but instead he said nothing. He'd learned long ago that one of the most valuable tools in law enforcement was the skill of shutting up and listening.

"She's always been this way, really—stubborn. Did you know she refused to get braces, too? Said she didn't see why she had to conform to society's standard of beauty."

John wished that Katie had felt this way. It would have saved him thousands of dollars in orthodontia bills.

"But with the SATs, we really thought we got through to her," Tabitha's mother went on. "We took her to half a dozen life coaches and therapists, and thought she understood. And then the morning of the day of the test, I went to wake her up, and she was just . . . gone. She'd packed all the things she loved best—books, mostly—and disappeared. Without a word."

"Except for my Platinum American Express card," John heard Tom Brighton shout in the background. "I get the bill every month. I can see all the ridiculous things she's been buying!"

"Oh," Mrs. Brighton said. "Yes. The credit card. It's in Tom's name, but only his initial—T. Brighton. So we didn't cancel it, because we thought it might help Tabby. She can still use it, even if someone asks for ID. The bills we get every month—and of course calls from people like you, in law enforcement—are the only way we know . . . that we know . . ." She sighed. "Well, that she's all right."

John said, "I see," again. It was the only thing he could think to say. Truthfully, he was a little disappointed. Not about the credit card—although it had been missing from Tabitha's wallet, so he presumed one of the Sunshine Kids had stolen it . . . most likely Beckwith.

No, he was disappointed that Tabitha's relationship with her parents was so adversarial. That meant they were going to have no idea who the father of her baby was. Though Tabitha herself insisted it was Beckwith, and that Beckwith loved her and the baby, John was beginning to think this was doubtful. Why would Beckwith put his own offspring into a box and then leave her in a library restroom? He couldn't imagine any father doing this. It was possible Tabitha was so crazy about the guy, she only *wished* the baby was his.

Then again, Beckwith was the worst. If anyone was going to abandon his own newborn, it would be him.

Why, though, had he abandoned the baby and its mother only to stick around town? In a decent boat, he could have crossed the Gulf and been in Mexico by now.

Not that any of it mattered. Regardless of whether or not the baby was his, John intended to spend the rest of his life making sure Beckwith paid for what he'd done.

"Where is she?" Mrs. Brighton had apparently put her husband on speaker phone, because John could now hear him barking very clearly into his ear, "Where is my daughter, and what has she done now? If you've got her locked up, you can tell her from me that I'm not bailing her out again. I'm sick of all her wacko views. All I want is a kid who'll go to college and get a job and stop spending all my money on pizza and spray paint."

"Well, Mr. Brighton," John said in his calmest tone, "I don't know about any of that. All I can tell you for sure is that your daughter is currently in the maternity ward in the hospital on Little Bridge Island, Florida."

"Florida?" Mr. Brighton repeated with as much horror as if John had said *Hell*.

His wife was a little more on the ball. "*Maternity ward?* Is—is she all right, Officer?"

"My understanding is that she will be. Congratulations. You're grandparents. Your daughter's given birth to a healthy baby girl."

"*What?*"

Both parents were stunned into silence. As he waited for them to catch their breath, John listened to the sound of the waterfall by the side of the pool splashing in the courtyard below, along with the rumble of jets in the hot tub and the loud croaking of the frogs that lived in the bushes behind it. He decided to take the opportunity while the Brightons were still too shaken up to think better of revealing such personal information to ask, "Would you happen to know who the father is?"

"The father?" Mrs. Brighton murmured vaguely. She was still in shock at the news that she, an attractive and relatively young woman in her early forties—John had looked her and her husband up, and seen that they were wealthy suburbanites—was a grandmother. "No. No, how would I know that? I didn't even know she was pregnant. We haven't heard from her in months.

"Oh, my little girl," Mrs. Brighton cried. "I just can't believe it. My baby—has a baby!"

"Where is my granddaughter?" Tabitha's father demanded. "When can I see her? And my daughter?"

"Well, just as soon as you can board a plane and get down to Little Bridge Island," John said, hoping that neither Tabitha Brighton nor Molly Montgomery would be too displeased with what he'd done. Obviously Tabitha had the right to keep her whereabouts and the birth of her daughter a secret from her parents, with whom she'd apparently been feuding for some time.

But she had nearly died. And so had her child. These were things John felt her parents had a right to know, too.

"Fine," said Mr. Brighton. "We'll be there tomorrow. . . . Wait, where is this Little Bridge, exactly?"

It took John some time to straighten out the logistics of travel to Little Bridge Island with the Brightons, since there were no direct flights, unless they chartered a private jet. This irked Mr. Brighton, but his wife seemed eager to take the trip to see her daughter and granddaughter, no matter how many hours it took or how inconvenient it seemed.

John considered this a good sign.

What was decidedly not a good sign was when he ended the call, put his phone away, and turned to see Molly Montgomery standing in the open doorway to her room, glaring at him with her arms folded across her chest.

"What?" he asked. It was hard to tell with the light streaming from behind her, but her body language indicated that she was mad. He had a feeling that he knew why, but surely after the extraordinary sex they'd just had, she couldn't be *that* mad.

Unless it hadn't been as extraordinary for her as it had been for him. But she had certainly seemed to enjoy it. She'd been the one Mrs. Filmore had heard shouting, not him. He'd only knocked over a few piles of books . . . and of course, in the moment, nearly told her that he loved her, because—in the moment—he was sure he did.

Now he was glad he'd kept those words to himself.

"Did you honestly call Tabitha Brighton's parents?" Molly demanded in a cold voice.

Okay. So she was mad.

"Yes, I did." He stepped forward into the light so that he could see her face. Yes, she was definitely mad. Behind the lenses of her glasses, her dark eyes were pools of flames. Her lips were set into a firm line of disapproval, as well. "She nearly died. I felt they had a right to be informed."

"She's eighteen!" Molly cried. "She's an adult!"

"She's a runaway," he shot back, "who swiped her parents' credit card, fell in with a cult, got pregnant, trespassed, vandalized your library, and nearly died giving birth. If she were my daughter and someone found her in the condition that you did, I would want to know about it. So yes, I found her parents and called them."

Molly had unfolded her arms and was now pacing up and

down the length of the outdoor hallway, still sputtering. It was clear that Mrs. Filmore had gone back down to her room, but Fluffy the Cat had stayed behind and was now sitting in the doorway to Molly's room, calmly licking a front paw and regarding them both with wide amber eyes that seemed to say, *Wow, buddy. You sure screwed the pooch on this one.*

John couldn't have agreed more.

"You do realize that legally, she has a right to her privacy?" Molly demanded.

"Of course. But she isn't one of your library patrons, Molly. She's involved in a criminal investigation."

This stopped Molly cold. She swung an incredulous look at him. "Are you going to press charges against her?"

"Maybe, if that seems like the best way to get her to give up Beckwith. I think she knows where he's hiding."

"John, she's been traumatized!"

"All the more reason for her to give up the person who traumatized her. I know you think because she's eighteen, she's an adult, but she isn't acting like one."

"Well, maybe her parents are partly to blame for why she acts the way she does," Molly said. "Maybe her parents are awful, and that's why she ran away from them."

John had to admit that Molly had a point. Tabitha's parents had seemed pretty awful—at least the father.

He wasn't going to say this out loud, however. He was pretty sure she wouldn't like it.

"Don't tell me you've never called the parents of a child," he said instead.

"I've threatened to, lots of times," Molly said. "But I've never done it. Kids have a right to their own privacy—and their own autonomy."

"I agree—until they start hurting themselves, or others. And it isn't true that you've never called the parents of a child. You came to me today with compromising photos of my daughter taken by one of your young patrons."

Molly stiffened. "That was different."

"How is it different?"

"Because that was part of your investigation. That was to help solve it."

"So was calling Tabitha's parents. I have to work my cases the way I see fit. Sometimes my methods may not be pretty, but they tend to work." Except when they didn't . . . case in point, Larry Beckwith III.

"But Tabitha's parents are probably who she was running away from in the first place, John! And now you've told them exactly where to find her."

"You don't know anything about her." John thought it was possible that he was going insane. She was *making* him insane. "You sat with her while she was bleeding to death and drifting in and out of consciousness, but that's not the same as having a conversation with her, because believe me, if you had, you'd call her parents, and a social worker, and a shrink, and all the help you could get for her, because whatever has happened to that girl, it's made her *bananas*."

Molly blinked, hard. "John," she said, in what sounded to him like a tearful voice, "I think you should go now."

"What?"

"You heard me. It's late, and I have to be at the library in the morning for a staff meeting. I think you should go."

Belatedly, he realized that she was genuinely angry. And also about to cry.

"Molly, you're not actually going to let this come between us, are you? Because I thought we had a very nice time this evening—"

"We did," Molly said. "Physically. But I'm not sure we connect on more basic levels."

"What's more basic than what we did in there?" he asked, jabbing a thumb toward her room. "Where, I'd like to point out again, I think we *more than* connected."

"I'm talking about empathy."

If she'd struck him, he could not have been more surprised. "You think I lack *empathy*?"

"I don't know how much empathy you can have when you refer to a woman who's been through what Tabitha has as bananas."

He shouldn't have been surprised, he knew. She'd already called him amoral and unconscionable. Why not add lacking in empathy to the list?

But he still stood there feeling as if he'd been gut-punched, while the cat slowly began to lick its other paw. *Don't look at me, buddy,* the cat seemed to be saying. *I don't know what's going on here, either.*

"I think if you'd actually had a conversation with her," John said, desperately trying to salvage the situation, "you'd agree with me that Larry Beckwith has brainwashed Tabitha Brighton to the point that she is bananas."

It didn't work. Molly had gone back into her room to fetch his gun belt. "I don't think so," she said, when she returned.

He knew he should apologize, but . . . why? He hadn't done anything wrong! At least, not technically. He was the sheriff. It was his case!

"You can't have it both ways, Molly," he insisted. "You can't demand that I publish my daughter's photo in the paper and then also tell me not to contact Tabitha's parents. I was right to call her parents, because she needs them. She does, desperately. And when you see that I'm right, you'll . . . well, you'll be the one bringing *me* pie. *Banana* cream pie."

He smiled, proud of himself for the witticism. A little levity might help the situation. It had always helped with Katie, and even Marguerite, when they got emotional.

But he soon saw that it had definitely not helped now. He knew this the minute his gun belt came sailing at him.

Fortunately, he caught it before it hit the wooden floor. She'd practically thrown it at him, which wasn't good. It was never a good thing to throw firearms, even when they were holstered, with the safety on.

"Not going to happen," Molly said. She didn't sound tearful now. She only sounded angry. "I'm going to bed. I think you should, too. Good night."

"Good night," he said, and watched as she ducked into

her room, slamming the door behind her, leaving him and the cat outside in the suddenly still, all-consuming darkness.

The cat, unperturbed, yawned and sauntered toward him. John took a quick step backward, knowing what the cat intended to do—rub up against him and once again get its orange fur all over his uniform trousers.

"No," he said. "No way, cat."

He hurried down the steps to the hotel's courtyard, fastening his belt as he went. The cat sat at the top of the stairs and watched him go with wide, unblinking eyes. John couldn't help but think that the cat was judging him, much in the way he was judging himself. The evening that had started out as one of the best he'd had in as long as he could remember had ended in disaster.

But how? He couldn't understand it. What had he done? Violated HIPAA by calling a victim's parents?

What was so wrong with that? When it was during the course of an investigation, that was his *job*.

And yes, maybe he had mentioned that Tabitha was a little bit off her rocker. But he wasn't going to lie about the facts in a case. Facts were facts. That didn't mean he was lacking in empathy. He had plenty of empathy!

Just not for nitwits who went around breaking the law, putting the lives and property of innocent citizens at risk.

If Molly Montgomery couldn't see this, then maybe she was right, and they couldn't connect on a basic level.

Except . . .

Except.

Everything felt so right when they were together. So right and so good and so true.

Only now that they were fighting, everything felt terrible.

What was he going to do?

CHAPTER TWENTY-THREE

Molly

Molly couldn't sleep at all that night.

Which was upsetting, because she hadn't gotten much sleep the night before, either.

In fact, she realized as she stumbled down to the kitchen the next morning to help Joanne set up the breakfast buffet, she'd been sleeping pretty badly ever since she'd found that baby in her library's restroom and met the blue-eyed sheriff who was now haunting her dreams—when she did manage to snatch a few minutes' sleep, which wasn't nearly often enough.

"So," Joanne said, winking at Molly as she popped some of the Larsons' famous blueberry muffins from their pan and onto a serving plate. "How did it go last night? I heard you had a visitor."

Molly smiled wanly. "Great." It was impossible to keep anything secret in a small hotel or on an island as tiny as

Little Bridge. Soon everyone would know that she and the sheriff had slept together. It was only a matter of time.

Joanne beamed. "I knew it. I just knew you two were made for each other. You know why?"

"No. Why?"

"Because you both take your jobs so seriously. Not many people find their passions in life, but the two of you really have."

"Hmmmm." This was interesting. In fact, maybe they took their jobs a little *too* seriously. "Yes. Well."

Why had she lashed out at him that way? She didn't know. Well, she did know, but now that he was gone, it seemed so unreasonable. So he'd called Tabitha's parents. So what? He'd obviously felt that he needed to. He was right that he'd spent more time with the girl than she had. He had to know what her mental state was, and what he was doing. Didn't he?

Molly wasn't sure. He was a man, and men were so . . . well, mysterious. No matter how many books she read, she didn't think she'd ever understand them. Look at what had happened with her ex. Molly had thought she'd known him, and then he'd turned out to be someone completely different. Not that he'd cheated on her or turned out to be a gambling addict or a serial killer or anything like that. He'd simply assumed that after they were married and had kids, she was going to quit her career to homeschool them.

Not that this was such a terrible thing. In some situations, homeschooling was preferable and/or necessary. And some people—like Eric's new fiancée, Ashley, at least according to her social media posts—would be *thrilled* to commit their lives to it.

But where had Eric gotten the idea that homeschooling a not-yet-existent child was something *Molly* wanted?

Maybe she had simply never really known him, and he had never really known her.

Well, she wasn't going to make that mistake again.

It was just unfortunate that she'd already slept with the sheriff—well, not exactly unfortunate, because sleeping with him had been really fun. Better than fun. One of the best sexual experiences she'd ever had, if she were honest—before getting to know him better.

Unless . . . well, unless he was right.

But how could he be right? Who would refer to a young woman who'd been through what Tabitha Brighton had as bananas? That was just so insensitive. Who would call her parents when she so clearly had chosen a life far from them? Who would—

"Oh, would you look at this?" Mrs. Filmore and her husband were the first people in the dining room for breakfast—as usual—and so were the first people to grab that morning's *Gazette* and unfold it. "What a creepy photo!"

"What's it of?" grunted Mr. Filmore. He was never very talkative, but he was even less so before his first cup of coffee.

"Look." Mrs. Filmore held up the paper so everyone in the dining room could see it.

And there, directly above the fold, was a full-color print of the photo Elijah had taken of Katie in her Snappette uniform, blowing a kiss, with Dylan Dakota lurking in the background.

Beside the photo, in large black letters, screamed the headline:

Have You Seen This Man?

There was an article beneath it that was several paragraphs long, written by Meschelle Davies.

Molly nearly dropped the bowl of pathetic-looking fruit salad she'd made.

Katie's image had not been cropped or blurred. Her face was clearly identifiable in the photo.

"Good Lord," cried Joanne, who was serving Mr. Filmore scrambled eggs. "That's—"

"Kathleen Hartwell," Mrs. Filmore said, reading the caption below the photo. "'Sixteen-year-old daughter of Sheriff John Hartwell, with image captured by Elijah Trujos of suspected High School Thief. Anyone with information on the identity of this man is urged to call the Sheriff's Department.' Oh my goodness, isn't the sheriff the man who was visiting you here last night, Molly?"

Molly set down the fruit salad bowl with a thump. "Y-yes." She swallowed. "I . . . I . . . I better go."

"Molly?" Joanne called after her as Molly raced from the dining room. "Is everything all right?"

"Fine! I just have a meeting. I'll see you later!"

Molly felt guilty for rushing off like that, leaving Joanne to deal with breakfast service alone (though Joanne's husband, Carl, usually showed up to help later, after taking his sugar levels). But she simply couldn't face the scrutiny of the Filmores, especially with Katie Hartwell's photo staring up at her—the photo she'd insisted John give to *The Gazette.*

She understood why he'd done it. His desire to catch the High School Thief was almost pathological.

But what she couldn't understand was why he hadn't had Meschelle crop out Katie or blur her face. Though she had to admit, not doing so made the image much more startling. It was bound to get a good deal of attention. . . .

This suspicion was proved true when she arrived at the library (late, of course) and found the staff there poring over *The Gazette.*

"Oh my God," Henry said when she walked in. "Did you see this photo on the front page of today's paper? Isn't this that girl who was in here the other day with her dad, the sheriff?"

"Yes," she said, with a tight smile. "That's Katie Hartwell."

Molly regretted that she hadn't called in sick for the day. She'd thought about saying that she had food poisoning or a migraine—anything not to have to face talking about John or anything, really, to do with what had happened over the weekend.

But now she really, really regretted it.

"This photo is so creepy!" Henry declared. *Creepy* appeared to be the word of choice to describe the picture that Elijah had snapped of Katie and the High School Thief. "I feel like I've seen this guy somewhere before, but I can't think of where."

"Well," Molly said, as she went to put her purse away. "If you do, you should contact the Sheriff's Department immediately."

"Yeah," Henry said. "But I feel like if I had seen someone that grotesque-looking, I would totally remember where."

"I don't think he's actually grotesque," Phyllis said in her calm voice. "I think he merely appears that way because of the ominousness with which he's looming in the dark behind the girl. Perhaps, in another setting, he would appear more normal."

Henry shook his head, still staring down at the photo. "No. No, I've definitely seen him before. But where?"

"Maybe around the new library. We know he's been hanging out there."

Molly picked up the phone at her desk and checked her voice mail while simultaneously scrolling through the emails on her desktop computer. She didn't know what she was hoping to find—something from the sheriff, perhaps?

But he had her personal cell. If he'd wanted to get in touch with her, he'd have called or texted that number.

He hadn't, of course. She'd already checked her phone a million times. Why would he bother to contact her when she'd made it so clear she wanted nothing more to do with him?

There was one unusual message on her office voice mail, however. Molly stopped scrolling through her many emails when she heard it. A female voice, hesitant and oddly weak, said, "Hello, Miss Montgomery? Hi, this is, um, Tabitha Brighton. I'm the, um, person you found in the library? Anyway, they tell me you're the one who saved me and, um, my baby. I just wanted to call and say, um . . . thank you. Thank you very much for what you did."

There was a long pause, during which it sounded like the girl was holding back a sob. And then Tabitha said, "That's all. Just thank you."

Molly was so surprised—and moved—that she held on to the receiver for a second or two longer than necessary after Tabitha hung up, staring at her cluttered desktop, her eyes too watery with tears to see anything.

"Are you all right?"

The voice startled her, even though it was gentle. Molly turned to see Phyllis Robinette beside her, holding a cup of tea.

"Oh, yes." Molly hung up the phone and hastily wiped her eyes. "That was Tabitha Brighton, the mother of Baby Aphrodite, thanking me for helping her. I don't know what's wrong with me. I never cry . . . except of course at the end of books."

"Well, you've had a rough few days." Phyllis sank into the

chair beside Molly's desk. She was such a small woman that she easily fit into it. "I was going to say that you don't look very well. Your color is off. Is something the matter?"

Everything is the matter, Molly wanted to say. But she didn't want to burden her mentor and friend with her problems, especially since they weren't at all work-related.

"I'm fine," she lied, instead. "I just have a headache." This part wasn't a lie. She'd been feeling a headache coming on since asking the sheriff to leave last night. "And I didn't sleep well."

This wasn't a lie, either.

"Why don't you take the day off?" Phyllis leaned forward and patted Molly kindly on the knee, the only part of her she could reach from her low perch.

"I couldn't possibly. We have so much to do. The staff meeting—the move—"

"All of that will be here when you get back. We did get along here before you came, you know."

This was true.

She glanced at her desk phone, remembering what John had said to her the night before about Tabitha. *You don't know anything about her.*

Maybe she needed to remedy that.

"Well . . . I could just take the morning off," Molly said, reaching inside her desk drawer for her purse. "I could come back later this afternoon."

"If you're feeling better," Phyllis said.

Molly had already leaped to her feet. "If I'm feeling better, of course. Thank you, Phyllis."

"*The Complete Poetry* of Maya Angelou," Phyllis called after her, as Molly was hurrying away.

This froze Molly in her tracks. Slowly, she turned around. "I'm sorry, Phyllis. What did you say?"

"*The Complete Poetry* of Maya Angelou," Phyllis repeated. "That's what I'd bring for the girl to read. She's a new mother, so—assuming she's keeping the baby—won't have a lot of time to read. But she might be able to snatch a poem here and there. And Maya Angelou hits the spot for just about everyone."

Molly, feeling a little ashamed for not having thought of this herself, nodded. "Of course. And I should bring something for her to read to the baby. It's never too early to start reading to a child." Then she smiled at the older woman. "How did you know I was heading to the hospital?"

"Oh, my dear." Phyllis shook her head as she pushed herself from the tiny chair. "You are more Harry Potter than Proust—not precisely difficult to read."

Molly wasn't certain if she should feel insulted or flattered by this, but chose to feel flattered.

She had to take a ride-share service to the hospital because it was too far away to walk or bicycle to. She half expected to be turned away when she asked for Tabitha Brighton's room—she wasn't family, after all—but the kindly volunteer at the information desk looked up the room number and gave it to Molly after asking who she was and carefully checking her ID. Apparently Molly was on some kind of list of approved visitors—or rather, was neither Dylan Dakota nor a member of the press, so was allowed to roam the halls of the hospital freely.

She found Tabitha's second-floor room with ease and was about to enter without knocking (since the door was wide open) when she saw that Tabitha was nursing. An RN stood beside her, looking down on Baby Aphrodite's little dark head and murmuring, "There. There, see? You've got it. I told you that you'd get it."

Molly paused on the threshold, pleased to see both mother and baby looking so well, especially considering the condition they'd been in the last time she saw them.

Now they each had a rosy flush to their cheeks, and Tabitha was smiling, her eyes bright. Molly couldn't see the baby's eyes because her head was turned away from her, but she supposed they'd be as shiny as her mother's.

Feeling like an interloper, she raised her hand and knocked softly on the doorjamb. When both Tabitha and the nurse looked up in surprise, having been completely absorbed in their task, Molly said, softly, "Hello. Sorry to interrupt. It's just me, Molly Montgomery, the children's librarian? I hope you don't mind, but I got your message and I thought I'd stop by to see how you were doing. I hope this isn't a bad time."

Tabitha's face changed as Molly revealed who she was. Of course she hadn't recognized her—how could she? She didn't remember that dreadful time in the library—or hopefully didn't—so she'd been regarding Molly distrustfully. But now she relaxed.

"Oh, hi," Tabitha said. "I thought you were the social worker for a second. They've been threatening to send her up here all day."

Molly was a little confused—what was so wrong with social workers? But then the nurse said, "Now, then, Tabitha, we only want to make sure you and your baby have bonded, and that you have somewhere safe to go when you get discharged."

"Of course we've bonded," Tabitha said in a gently scoffing tone. "Look at us!"

It was true that Baby Aphrodite was snuggled very close to her mother, and seemed to have a voracious appetite. Molly could hear the hungry little slurping sounds from where she was standing in the doorway.

"So," she said, hesitating to come into the room since she hadn't exactly been invited, "you're keeping her?"

Tabitha looked shocked. "Of course I'm keeping her! Why does everyone keep asking me that?"

Molly felt like this response was invitation enough to enter the room. She did so, placing her purse and tote bag on the floor and taking a seat in the visitor's chair, which was beside the girl's hospital bed.

"Well, only because someone left her in my library," Molly said. "Have you figured out yet who might have done that?"

Tabitha rolled her eyes. "Well, the cops keep saying it was my boyfriend. But I know he'd never do anything like that."

"Hmmm," Molly replied, noncommittally. "Well, the police can be wrong."

"Right? I mean, why would my boyfriend do that to his own baby?"

"Because men can suck," said the nurse, whose nametag read *Cecile*.

"Not my boyfriend." Tabitha's voice was firm. "He's going to come pick us up, and we're going to live on a boat and sail around the world and homeschool Cosette."

"Is that what you've named her?" Molly asked, reaching up to touch one of the baby's tiny pink toes. She couldn't help it. The little foot was dangling out from beneath the baby's blanket just a few inches away, looking so soft and sweet and innocent that Molly had to touch it. "Cosette?"

"Yes." Tabitha had the dreamy look that all women got while nursing, Molly's sister included. But Tabitha's was especially pronounced, because she was a teenager thinking about the boy she loved. "From *Les Misérables*. That's my favorite book. Cosette knows tremendous hardship, but she's a survivor, not a victim. I want my daughter to be just like her."

"Not including the hardship, I hope."

"Of course not!" Tabitha looked at Molly like she was crazy.

"Well, she's so young, I doubt she'll remember the rough start she got in life. I'm sure you and your boyfriend will give your daughter a wonderful upbringing. Has he called you?" Molly couldn't believe she was sitting there, gently interrogating the new mother while she was nursing. What was wrong with her? "I suppose you're getting discharged soon."

"Well, no." Tabitha looked ever so slightly troubled. "But I mean, he's busy."

"Sure he is," said Cecile in a flat voice.

"No, really, he is. He's getting the boat. We talked about this. He said it would take a few days to get a good one."

"You mean steal one," said Cecile.

"It's not stealing," Tabitha insisted. "It's wrong to own property or people."

Molly exchanged a glance with the nurse, who was adjusting Tabitha's IV. The nurse suppressed a smile and turned away. It was clear she'd heard Tabitha express similar sentiments.

Suddenly Molly understood why John had insisted that Tabitha was "bananas."

But Molly had a different opinion. Tabitha wasn't mentally ill. She was simply young . . . young, naive, and in love.

"Well, of course it's wrong to own people," Molly said carefully. "But you might feel differently if someone took something that belonged to you—if it was your boat, for instance."

"Not if they really needed it," Tabitha said, shaking her head. "I'd give anyone anything I had that they really needed. I'm happy to share all that I have with those who have less."

"Yes, but what if what they took was Cosette?"

Tabitha's arms tightened protectively around her daughter. "What are you talking about?"

"I'm talking about the fact that someone took your baby away from you. You weren't okay with that, were you?"

"Of course not! But I'm talking about material things, not babies."

"You said it wasn't okay to own people."

"I don't own Cosette. She's my daughter. I'd never let anyone take her away."

Molly nodded. "Okay. I was just checking. Here, I brought something for you." She rose and reached into her tote bag and pulled out the books, then handed both to Tabitha.

Tabitha gave the book of poetry only a fleeting glance, but she gasped at the picture book. "*The Snowy Day*! Oh my God, I used to have this book when I was a kid. It was my favorite. How did you know?"

"Everyone had that book when they were a kid," Molly said. "It's everyone's favorite. It's our most checked out book in the library, even though it's never snowed once in Little Bridge. I think that's why the kids here like it so much. I thought you might like to start reading it to Cosette."

"Oh, I will." When she was smiling, as she was now, Tabitha was a very attractive girl. "Thank you. Thank you so much, Miss Montgomery!"

It was on this scene—a rosy-cheeked Tabitha flipping through the pages of her favorite picture book as she nursed her newborn daughter, Molly and the nurse standing beside her bed—that a well-dressed man and woman walked in a few seconds later, wheeling suitcases behind them, bringing with them the unmistakable scent of air travel and money.

"Tabby?" the woman said, in disbelief, nearly dropping her suitcase.

Tabitha looked up from the book, and her jaw dropped in shock. "Mom? Dad?"

CHAPTER TWENTY-FOUR

John

"The phones have been ringing off the hook" were the words with which Marguerite greeted John as he stepped into the office. "Everyone—and I mean *everyone*—on this island has seen Dylan Dakota."

"His name is Larry Beckwith."

"You know who I mean."

"Great."

John couldn't remember ever feeling this tired. He felt weary down to his bones. All he wanted to do was crawl back into his bed, pull the covers up over his head, and sleep for eight hours. Maybe ten.

But unfortunately he couldn't, because he had a criminal to catch.

Dylan Dakota had been seen at Frank's Food Emporium buying beer.

Dylan Dakota had been seen at Ron's Place drinking rum.

Dylan Dakota had been seen at an art gallery opening Thursday night admiring a watercolor by Bree Beckham and had even asked its price, though in the end he hadn't bought it.

Dylan Dakota had been seen near the bight admiring city planner Randy Jamison's yacht, and a few people had even thought he might try to steal it, but by the time deputies arrived, he was gone.

Dylan Dakota had been everywhere and seen by everyone, and yet no one seemed to know where he was right now.

John sat at his desk and rubbed his face. He wondered what he'd done to deserve a thorn like Larry Beckwith in his side. He wondered what he could do to get Molly Montgomery to like him again and to put Larry Beckwith in jail forever. He wondered if he was too old to quit law enforcement and go pitch for the Miami Marlins.

Marguerite knocked on his office door then opened it without waiting for him to say "Come in."

"Chief, I've got Dorothy Tifton on the phone, the lady whose house got robbed?"

John regarded her wearily. "I know who she is, Marguerite."

"Well, she says she has to talk to you, and you only. I told her you were busy, even though it doesn't look to me like you are, actually. But she said it was important. I bet it's something about her insurance. What do you want me to do?"

John waved a hand. "Put her through."

"Right, Chief. If you don't mind me saying so, you look like crap, Chief."

"Why, thank you, Marguerite. That is so kind of you."

"Just letting you know, Chief."

Marguerite closed the door on her way out. The call from Mrs. Tifton came through a few seconds later.

"Hello, ma'am," John said, trying to sound as cheerful as possible and knowing he was failing. "What can I do for you this fine morning?"

"Sheriff." Mrs. Tifton's voice was hardly above a whisper. "I want you to know, I've got him."

"I'm sorry," John said. "I can barely hear you, Mrs. Tifton. Can you speak a little louder?"

"No, I can't. Because I'm on the tail of that animal who broke into my house, and if I speak any louder, he might notice me."

This caused John to sit up a little straighter in his chair. "I'm sorry, Mrs. Tifton. Did you say—are you—are you with Dylan Dakota *right now*?"

"If you mean the High School Thief, that's right," the old woman whispered. "Only that's not the name he told me. He told me to call him Larry."

John was so excited that he stood up behind his desk. Stood up and threw his stapler as hard as he could at his office door. The stapler broke the glass in the center of his doorframe, on which the words *Sheriff John Hartwell* had been written. Now, thanks to the stapler, there was only a gaping hole—a gaping hole soon filled by the face of Marguerite Ruiz, wearing an incredulous expression and mouthing the words *What the hell?*

John pointed at the phone receiver he was holding to his

ear. *We have him,* he mouthed. Aloud, he said, "So where are you, Mrs. Tifton?"

"I'm at 24 Hour Fitness," Mrs. Tifton whispered. "I don't normally work out here, but I might change gyms, because they were very nice just now about letting me bring my dog in—you met my dog, didn't you, Sheriff? My dog, Daisy?"

"I did meet your dog," John said, while scrawling *24 Hour Fitness* on a pad near his phone and holding it up for Marguerite to see. She nodded, then spoke quietly into her shoulder radio. "Your dog, Daisy, is lovely."

"She is, isn't she? Anyway, I was walking Daisy this morning, like I usually do, and thought I'd stop by the Cuban coffee place, because they make the best café con leches, don't you think?"

"Of course." On the pad, John wrote, *NO SIRENS. DO NOT SPOOK HIM* and showed it to Marguerite. She nodded and again spoke quietly into her shoulder radio.

"Well, I was there ordering my coffee, and who do I see but this boy, also ordering coffee, and he starts petting my dog—everyone loves to pet my dog because she's just so cute, if I do say so myself. And I think to myself, 'Well, this boy looks just like the boy from the photo in the paper this morning.' Only he's wearing a baseball hat, maybe as a disguise, but I think, 'Well, that's not a very good disguise, because you can still see all the tattoos and the ear thingies.' And do you know what, Sheriff? I could smell him. And this boy smelled exactly like the hooded shirt you all found at my house! Not only that, but do you know what he said to me?"

"I do not," John said.

"He notices me looking at him and he says, 'I bet you're thinking I'm that guy from the paper today.' Well, I couldn't have been more shocked, because that's exactly what I was thinking! And I said to him, 'As a matter of fact, I do. You know that boy robbed me and also vandalized my library.' And he laughed and said, 'Oh, that was your library? I thought it was the people's library.' And I said, 'It is, but I'm the person who donated all the money to renovate it.' And he said, 'Well, thank you for that. We need more libraries in this world. I'm sorry my friends and I did that to your library. But you know it technically belongs to the people, and we're the people, so we have the right to do what we want.' And so of course I said, 'Young man, respectfully, I disagree.'"

John could feel himself beginning to sweat, even though he kept the air-conditioning at the sheriff's department—as opposed to his home—at a strict seventy degrees. He was clutching the phone so tightly, he thought it might break in his hand.

"And he has the nerve to smile at me and say, 'Well, you're not going to turn me in, are you?' And do you know, Sheriff, I was so scared—I mean, he scared me! Something in that smile! And his eyes—like he was dead inside. So I said, 'Of course not. You're kind to dogs, so how bad can you be?' Because he was standing right there! Petting my dog! He could have broken little Daisy's neck! What else could I do?"

"You did exactly the right thing, Mrs. Tifton," John said

into the phone. Covering the mouthpiece, he said to Marguerite, "How many?"

"We've got one car in the area, two on the way. The one in the area should be there any second."

"Who is it?"

"Martinez."

"Good." To Mrs. Tifton, he said, "So how did you end up at the gym, ma'am?"

"Well, I figured I should follow him, see where he's staying." John almost rolled his eyes. No wonder the widow and Molly Montgomery got along so well. The two of them had both read way too many detective novels. "And it turns out, it's the gym."

Of course. Of course it was. Beckwith could rent a locker for his stuff, have all the hot showers and clean towels and soap he needed, get in a good workout, and probably even sleep there in some dark space if there was no one else around—and if the night staff was female or gay, he could charm them into letting him stay, depending on how susceptible they were to his charms—all for only twenty dollars a day. It was so much cheaper than a hotel room and so much more convenient than crashing in some vacant house or building.

John could have kicked himself for not having thought of it before.

"And you're sure he's there now, Mrs. Tifton?"

"Well, I'm watching him right now on the elliptical—Oh, there's a sheriff's deputy coming in—did you send him?"

"I did. Listen, Mrs. Tifton, I want you to stay out of the way. You've done an absolutely amazing thing, but I can't afford to let you get hurt."

"Don't you worry about me, Sheriff. I'm a tough old bird. Ooh, your deputy is arresting the boy! He's putting handcuffs on him!" Mrs. Tifton wasn't bothering to whisper anymore. "I can't wait to tell all of my friends!"

"Tell them what, Mrs. Tifton?"

"That Daisy and I caught the High School Thief, of course!"

"Neither can I, Mrs. Tifton," John said, feeling better than he'd felt in a long time. "Neither can I."

CHAPTER TWENTY-FIVE

Molly

"Oh, Tabby."

The two people standing in the doorway to Tabitha's hospital room could only be her parents. Her mother even looked like her a little—but with a more stylish haircut, highlights, and decidedly inappropriate clothing for Little Bridge: a wool sweater set with twill trousers and designer boots.

"Mom?" Tabitha seemed less happy and more stunned to see them.

Molly wasn't certain what to do. On the one hand, it didn't seem right for her to intrude on this family reunion.

But on the other, if this wasn't what Tabitha wanted—and last night Molly had kicked John out because she'd been sure it wasn't—then maybe she should stay. Someone needed to look out for the girl, no matter how misguided she seemed.

"Tabby, darling." Mrs. Brighton hurried forward to give her daughter a hug and kiss.

Tabitha didn't respond. She seemed frozen in shock. The baby, meanwhile, had fallen asleep at her breast.

"Oh, what a little sweetheart," Mrs. Brighton said, and swept a gentle finger over Cosette's forehead while at the same time tugging at Tabitha's hospital gown so that her chest was covered.

"Mom," Tabitha said, finally seeming to find her voice. "Dad. What are you doing here? How did—how did you find me?"

"Well, the sheriff called us, sweetheart," Mrs. Brighton said. She moved to sit down in the chair Molly had vacated. "He was very concerned for you. And the baby, of course."

Tabitha looked stonily from her mother to her father.

"I don't understand why. We're fine."

Cecile the nurse lifted her iPad—clipboards seemed to be a thing of the past—and said, "Why don't I take the baby back to the nursery?"

"That won't be necessary." Tabitha's voice was cold. "These people are leaving."

"Now, Tabby." Mr. Brighton had the patient voice of a man used to dealing with irrational customers and hormonal women. Molly wondered what he did for a living. "Let's be rational. It's not just you anymore. You've got the baby to think of."

"I *am* thinking of her." Tabitha wrapped her arms more tightly around Cosette. "The last people in the world I want around her are you."

"And on that note—" Cecile reached for the baby. "Why don't I take little Cosette down the hall so you all can talk and she can sleep undisturbed?"

Tabitha gave the nurse her daughter—but not without saying, cuttingly, "All right. But just remember, I'm the only one allowed to take her from this hospital. Don't let *them* do it."

"Tabitha!" Mr. and Mrs. Brighton looked shocked. Even the nurse looked mildly offended.

"Around here we only allow babies to go home with their parents," she said to Tabitha. She shot the Brightons a stern look as she wheeled Cosette, in her bassinette, from the room. "Their *legal* parents, the ones on their birth certificate."

"Now, see here," Mr. Brighton began, but Mrs. Brighton put a hand on his arm and shook her head. *Not now, dear.*

This reunion was going exactly the way Molly had feared it would, which was why she'd warned John against it in the first place. She felt obligated to jump in. "Maybe I could be of some help here."

"And who are you?" Mr. Brighton demanded, his patience beginning to wear thin.

"I'm Molly Montgomery, the island's children's media specialist—"

"She's the lady who found me," Tabitha interrupted. "She found Cosette, too. If it weren't for her, neither of us would even be alive."

"Oh." Mr. and Mrs. Brighton looked at Molly with renewed interest. Molly ducked her head modestly.

"Well, I wouldn't go that far," she said.

"No, it's true." Tabitha was doing up her hospital gown now that Cosette was gone. "She's been really nice to me. Everyone here has, even though I don't necessarily deserve it."

"Oh, well—" Molly had been about to assure Tabitha that of course she deserved it when she remembered what she and her fellow Sunshine Kids had done to the media room in the new library. She pressed her lips together and said nothing.

"Can we just talk sensibly here for a minute?" Mr. Brighton said. "Of course we're very grateful to you, Ms. Montgomery, for helping our daughter and granddaughter. But what exactly is your plan, Tabby? You have a child of your own now. How do you intend to support her? Where do you plan to live? Don't you think it's time you gave up on all this 'living off the land' foolishness and came home?"

"Yes, darling, do." Mrs. Brighton reached out to squeeze her daughter's hand. "Daddy and I would love to have you and—Cosette, is it?"

"Thank you for the invitation," Tabitha said stiffly. "Really, thank you. But I already have a place to live, and that is with the father of my child."

Tabitha then launched into her speech about how she and Dylan and baby Cosette were going to sail around the world together, just as soon as Dylan could get a boat.

"Dylan says our first stop on the boat is going to be Tahiti. I've never been there, but he says you can just walk up to a tree—any tree—and if it has fruit growing on it, you can pick the fruit and eat it, and nobody hassles you for stealing their fruit. Not like here in this country."

Both the Brightons seemed somewhat stunned upon hearing this, so Molly asked, more out of politeness than anything else, "Did that happen to you here, Tabitha? People got angry because you were eating their fruit?"

"Did they ever! We walked by this key lime tree here over by the courthouse, it was bursting all over with fruit—I don't know if you've ever had key limes, but they're delicious—and Dylan climbed it and started shaking the fruit down to me, and I was catching it in my skirt, and this mean old lady came out of her house and started yelling at us to quit it because we were stealing her fruit."

"Well," Molly said slowly, "it was her tree. Maybe she was going to make a key lime pie later."

"Whatever," Tabitha said, dismissively. "There was more than enough to share!"

It was a very romantic plan, and Molly wanted to believe in it as much as Tabitha did.

There were just two problems with it. The first was that Molly knew for a fact that Dylan had left Tabitha as well as her baby for dead, which didn't exactly make him the world's most desirable partner.

And two, as Tabitha was talking, Molly's cell phone buzzed. When she glanced at it discreetly, hoping it was John—and also knowing how silly she was being for hoping it was John—she saw that she'd received a text from Dorothy Tifton:

You'll never believe it! I helped solve a crime! Yes, ME! I caught the High School Thief! I got him to confess and followed him to the gym and called the sheriff!!! They found my iPad and camera in his locker! Your sheriff is interrogating him now! Come to my place tonight to celebrate, 6 P.M.! Champagne and caviar!

This was accompanied by an actual photo, apparently taken by Mrs. Tifton, of Dylan Dakota, aka Larry Beckwith III, being led from what looked like the 24 Hour Fitness on Washington Street in handcuffs by a muscular young sheriff's deputy.

Molly felt the ground shake beneath her. As Little Bridge Island did not sit upon a fault line, it was unlikely there'd been an actual earthquake, so what she'd felt was only in her own mind.

How was she going to break the news to Tabitha that the father of her child had just been arrested? The two of them were going nowhere together, let alone Tahiti, if the sheriff had his way—nowhere except jail.

When she tuned back in to the conversation, she heard Mrs. Brighton saying, "I'm sorry, Tabitha. But raising a child—a newborn—on a boat is unrealistic. Where are you going to get diapers?"

"I'll be using cloth diapers, of course, Mother, and I'll wash them in the sea."

"Oh, for the love of all that is holy." Mr. Brighton paced the small room, ending up at the window. "Is that a *dump*

I'm looking at, for Christ's sake? Who in the name of God builds a hospital next to a *dump*?"

"Um, Tabitha," Molly said, reluctantly clicking on the photo Mrs. Tifton had sent her. She didn't want to upset the young mother. What if the shock caused her milk to dry up? This happened frequently in novels, at least in the mysteries Molly so enjoyed. But it seemed necessary to tell her. "I just received something I think you should see."

Tabitha looked unconcerned. "What is it?"

Her look of unconcern turned to deep, deep unhappiness the moment she saw the photo. *"What?"* she cried. "What *is* that? When did *that* happen? Why? Why would they arrest my Dylan?"

"Well," Molly said, "for one thing, because of what all of you did to the library. And for another, because he left you instead of getting you help while you were giving birth to Cosette. You could have died. And for another, because he abandoned your baby on a toilet, and then broke into my friend's house and stole her camera and iPad."

"He d-didn't," Tabitha insisted.

"Tabitha, he did. You know he did. You can lie to the police all you want, but you can't lie to me."

Tabitha responded by bursting into loud, hiccupping sobs. This startled everyone in the room, but none more than her mother, who moved quickly to embrace the girl, sitting beside her in the hospital bed and caressing her hair, murmuring, "Oh, sweetheart. Oh, my baby. It's going to be all right. Everything is going to be okay."

Except it wasn't. Of course it wasn't.

Tabitha's heart was broken. She'd finally realized the truth—a truth she'd probably known all along, just never allowed herself to think—and now her plans for herself and her baby lay in shatters around her. Molly looked at the weeping girl and couldn't help feeling very sorry for her. She knew now why John had called her parents. He'd had to. Of course he'd had to.

Because she had no one else. Except for her baby, she was all alone.

"They c-can't p-prove any of that!" Tabitha cried, desperately grasping at one last straw of hope. "They can't prove it, can they?"

"Actually," Molly said, her heart aching for the girl, "they can."

"What is going on in here?" Dr. Nguyen stood in the doorway with Nurse Cecile and another woman. The other woman was dressed in normal clothes, not nurse's scrubs or a white physician's coat, and was holding a clipboard. Molly would have bet her life that she was a social worker. "What have you been saying to my patient to get her so upset?"

"I'm sorry," Molly said, slipping her cell phone back into her purse. "That was my fault."

"Are you family?" the social worker asked.

"No," Molly said meekly.

"Then please leave. I need a word with this patient and her family in private."

"Of course," Molly said, and started to leave, but Tabitha's strident voice stopped her.

"No!" Tabitha cried. "If she goes, I want my parents to go!"

"But, Tabby—" Her mother drew away from her, looking stricken.

"Everyone goes!" Tabitha was practically screaming.

Dr. Nguyen's voice was crisp. "I don't want my patient upset. Everyone, please go."

Molly shuffled out into the hall with Tabitha's parents. As soon as the door was closed behind them, Mr. Brighton turned to Molly and asked, "What on earth did you show her that got her so upset?"

Molly lifted her cell phone and showed them. "That's her boyfriend. I think their trip around the world is going to be delayed for a while."

CHAPTER TWENTY-SIX

John

John sat down at the table in Interview Room 3 and studied the individual sitting across from him. He always forgot, except when he was in his presence, how small Larry Beckwith III, aka Dylan Dakota, was. Small but wiry, of course, and able to slip in and out of tight spaces undetected . . . undetected except for the destruction he left behind.

"So, Larry," John said, conversationally. "Can I get you anything? I understand you've already had your morning coffee, but how about some soda? Juice? Water?"

Larry smiled at him. He looked perfectly at ease in the stiff-backed wooden chair. And why wouldn't he? John had removed his handcuffs—Beckwith wasn't going anywhere.

"There's only one thing I want," Larry Beckwith said. "And that's my lawyer."

"Oh, right." John nodded. "You said that before, when

Martinez was bringing you in. I understand your lawyer is on his way. But it's a long drive from Miami. I thought maybe you and I could pass the time while we wait having a little chat."

Beckwith sneered. "My lawyer doesn't drive anywhere. He's taking his private jet."

John frowned. "Well, it will be a while before the jet is fueled up, the pilots get the flight plan, and all of that. Just out of curiosity, doesn't it bother you, employing a law firm that leaves such a huge carbon footprint, flying everywhere to meet their clients? That's something that would worry my daughter—she's just a few years younger than you. She's all about trying to save the planet, the polar bears, the melting glaciers. That doesn't upset you?"

Beckwith only smirked at him some more and said, *"Lawyer."*

"Yeah." John nodded again. "I get it. You don't want to talk. And that's your right—as you know, because you've been read your rights. But I'm just curious, since you have a daughter now, too. Believe me, if she ends up anything like mine, she'll read you the riot act when she's older about wasting fossil fuels."

This caused the smirk on Beckwith's face to turn into a slightly suspicious frown.

"I never waste fossil fuels. I'm as eco-conscious as can be. I can't help what my lawyers do. And I don't have a daughter."

"Oh, yes, you do," John said. "We got the results of the blood test on that baby we found last week in the ladies' room of the library. And not to go all Jerry Springer on you, Larry, but . . . you *are* the father."

All the blood drained from Beckwith's face, causing his dark goatee and neck tattoos to stand out starkly against his pale skin.

John assumed he wasn't going to say anything—except "Lawyer"—and was about to go on when Beckwith surprised him by suddenly leaping from his chair, knocking it over behind him, and bringing both fists down, hard, on the tabletop in front of him.

"No!" he bellowed. "That isn't true!"

John stayed calmly in his seat, knowing there were several people watching from behind the two-way mirror who would come rushing in to restrain Beckwith if he needed them to.

But John wouldn't need them to. He could handle this little twerp all by himself.

"Struck a chord there, did I, Larry?" he asked mildly. "Frankly, I don't get why you're so surprised. You haven't exactly been discreet about any of this. You confessed to Dorothy Tifton at the Coffee Cubano that you're the one who robbed her house and destroyed the media room in her new library. We found the items you stole from her in your locker at the gym. We have your prints and hair on everything that you touched, practically. It's almost like you wanted to get caught this time. It's so unlike you. What's going on?"

His shoulders drooping, Beckwith turned around, picked

up the chair, and sat back down in it. Then he folded his arms across the table and buried his face in them.

John expected to hear the word "lawyer" come out from beneath those folded arms. But what he heard instead surprised him:

A sigh. A sigh that sounded—if he wasn't mistaken—like defeat.

And, though John found it hard to believe, he realized he was actually making headway with Larry Beckwith III, aka Dylan Dakota.

"What happened with the girl, Larry?" he asked in his most sympathetic tone. "Why did you leave her to die?"

This caused Beckwith to lift his head. He shot John a look of astonishment. "What? I didn't!"

"You most certainly did, Larry. If that librarian hadn't walked in at the exact moment she did, Tabitha Brighton would have bled to death."

"That's . . . that's impossible!" Larry Beckwith was sitting up straight in his seat now. His face was still white as paper. "When we left her, she was fine. I mean, yes, she had just had the baby, and she was a little out of it, but . . . women have babies all the time and they're fine. Historically, women have been having babies for millions of years and gotten up afterward and gone out to work in the fields. How was I supposed to know she wasn't fine?"

John had to physically restrain himself from walking over, picking Beckwith up, and hurling him through the two-way mirror. He wanted to hurt him that badly.

The repercussions if he did so wouldn't be that severe. Yes, he'd probably lose his job, but so what? He'd always be rehired back in Miami. Katie wouldn't want to leave because of the Snappettes, but she could always go live with her cousin.

But Molly. Molly would probably never forgive him, even though Beckwith was a scumbag who deserved to suffer. He couldn't hurt Beckwith, because Molly would be mad.

So instead of throwing Beckwith through the two-way mirror, John said, with all the patience he could summon, "First of all, Larry, women throughout history have done no such thing. Without proper postnatal care, they die, even in this day and age. You aren't stupid, Larry, you know this. Even people without a college education, which you have, know this. You can't sit there and tell me with a straight face that you thought that woman was going to be fine. You took her child and left her, but that's not all. You took her cell phone. You left her there with no means to call for help."

"But I knew—" Beckwith looked almost tearful. "I knew someone would be coming into the building the next day. I'd overheard the construction workers talking, so I knew there was going to be an inspection, and that someone was going to find her."

"So rather than call nine-one-one for her yourself, you just decided to risk letting her die?"

"I was drunk, all right?" Beckwith wasn't just tearful now. He was actually crying. He reached up and angrily swiped at the tears in his eyes. "I wasn't thinking properly.

I'll regret it for the rest of my life, but—that's what happened."

John felt a sudden jolt of clarity.

No. It couldn't be. And yet the proof was right in front of him.

Larry Beckwith had feelings. He had actual feelings. And for Tabitha Brighton, of all people.

"You love her," John said, in a tone of disbelief.

"What?" Beckwith looked up from his damp fingers.

"You love her. You love that girl. That's why you stuck around after the rest of your band of merry muck-making men left. To make sure Tabitha and the baby were all right."

To John's surprise, Larry Beckwith III began to blush scarlet. "No!" he said, sullenly. "Absolutely not. I don't care what happens to them."

"Yes, you do," John said. "That's why you stayed, and that's why you got caught. You care about her. You love her."

Beckwith's face had gone crimson—whether with rage or embarrassment, it didn't matter. John knew the truth.

"I don't!" the boy cried. "I mean, obviously, I don't want her or the baby to *die*, especially if it's my baby. She told me she couldn't get pregnant—she swore to me. And by the time I figured out what was going on, it was too late. She insisted we keep it."

"That scheming hussy." John shook his head with mock sympathy.

Beckwith glared at him, but his red-rimmed eyes gave away his true feelings.

"I didn't even know if it was mine! How could I be sure?

I hardly knew this girl. She just showed up out of nowhere, claiming she'd read about me on Facebook, wanting to join the group. But really it was *me* she wanted."

John, still feigning sympathy, shook his head. "That must have been terrible for you."

"I'm serious!" Tears streamed down Beckwith's face. "Do you know what my dad is going to do to me when he finds out about this? Cut me off. He didn't mind the other stuff, but getting a girl pregnant?"

"Absolutely," John said with a straight face. "She deserved to be left like that."

"That's not what I'm saying." Beckwith shook his head with enough force that tears streamed back toward his ears. "We made sure, you know, the baby got born all right and left it in a safe place, where someone decent would find it—people who go to libraries are all smart, you know—civic-minded? People who read books are found to be more empathetic than those who don't. They have some idea, at least, of how to raise a kid. And then we ran."

"It was the least you could do," John said, and meant it. It was the very least the kid could do.

"Right? But somehow . . . I don't know. I couldn't—I couldn't leave."

"When you say 'we,' who do you mean?"

"Aw, those idiots from last year." Beckwith rocked back in his chair, thoroughly disgusted with his own choice in friends. "You remember."

"From the MTV house?"

"Yeah, same group, more or less." Beckwith, having once

claimed he wouldn't say a word until his lawyer showed up, now couldn't shut up. He seemed to be finding catharsis in spilling his guts to the sheriff. John wondered if he knew every word he said was being recorded, observed by the state's attorney as well as numerous other individuals, and jotted down by John himself in his notebook. "Bunch of followers. Not an original idea or spark of imagination in a single one of them. At least Tabby really believed in the movement, though, you know? And in me." Beckwith's voice caught on a sob. "She always believed in me."

John nodded, jotted the words *Is this guy for real?* in his notebook, and underlined them. "Maybe that's why you couldn't leave."

"What?" Beckwith looked up from the pity party he was having for himself. "What are you talking about?"

"I'm just circling back to my original question. After you so generously abandoned your own baby in a place where she would be found by someone more civic-minded than yourself, and then left your girlfriend to die—"

"Hey, I told you, I didn't leave her to die!"

"I'm sorry, let me rephrase that. When you left her bleeding to death in an empty building and took her cell phone so she couldn't call for help—"

"God, would you stop ragging on me?" Beckwith pleaded. "I've already got a father to do that, okay? I don't need you doing it, too. I know I screwed up, all right? And guess what, I never wanted to be a father myself, but I guess if I have to, I want to be a good father, not like mine, who's never done anything but tell me what a loser I am, practically from the day I was born. Nothing I've ever done was good enough. Not like he was ever there for me—"

"Well, fortunately you're going to be there for your child," John said, closing his notebook with a snap and rising to his feet. "You're going to be doing it from jail, but you're going to be there for her. She and her mother can come see you every Sunday during visiting hours. I'm pretty sure you know that, though. That's probably the real reason why you let yourself get caught. So you wouldn't have to take any more parental responsibility toward her than that."

"No!" Now Beckwith, who'd been completely unresisting up until then, took a lunge at him. "That isn't true!"

John pushed the much smaller man back down into his seat.

"Oh, pipe down, Larry," he said irritably. "It's true and you know it. Your days of living off Daddy's money, not to mention other people's property and hard work, are over, and you knew it the minute you heard you yourself were a father. That got you so scared you decided you'd rather go to jail than face up to life as a parent. So suck it up. You got what you wanted. And no lawyer in the world is going to be able to bail you out of this one."

With that, John turned and left the interview room, only to run into Pete Abramowitz in the hallway.

"How was that?" he asked the attorney.

"Magnificent." Pete was grinning. "He's in there sobbing like a toddler right now."

"Because I said he likes a girl." John felt disgusted with himself and the world in general.

"Well, hearing that kind of thing has to be hard on a sociopath."

"Good," John said. "Don't accept a plea."

"No worries. I'll make sure he gets the max. You do realize he won't be in your jail for long though, right? Once he's convicted, he'll probably get sent to prison upstate."

John thought with relish of all the seaweed that needed removing on Little Bridge's beaches, and how unhappy Beckwith was going to look in an orange jumpsuit, raking it.

"I know," he said. "But I'll enjoy his stay while it lasts."

Pete winked. "Okay, then."

It was at that moment that Marguerite came up to them and said, "Excuse me, Chief? There's someone waiting to see you in your office."

John tried not to make a face. It wasn't the sergeant's fault. "Marguerite, I thought I told you, no interviews with the press until—"

"It's not press, Chief." Marguerite was having a hard time suppressing a grin. "It's Molly Montgomery, the librarian and, uh . . . she's holding a pie."

CHAPTER TWENTY-SEVEN

Molly

Molly was examining the five-foot-long stuffed dolphin sitting in the corner of John's office when the door suddenly opened and he walked in. She straightened guiltily, though what she had to feel guilty about she didn't know. There was no law against looking at other people's stuffed dolphins.

"Oh," John said, when he saw her. "Someone donated that for Baby Aphrodite. I was going to take it over to the hospital, but I keep forgetting."

"Cosette," Molly said, automatically.

John appeared confused. "What?"

"Cosette. Tabitha named the baby Cosette, after the character in *Les Misérables*."

"Oh." John stood there in the doorway looking, as always, tall and dark and impossibly handsome in his uniform. It was all she could do to keep herself from throwing her arms around his neck then and there and kissing him.

But of course that's not what she'd come there to do. She'd come to apologize. Hopefully kissing might follow, if she was lucky.

It would all depend on what happened in the next few minutes.

"Well," he said, closing the door behind him. The door had a large piece of plywood in the middle of it where Molly imagined there'd once been a plate of glass. She supposed something had happened to break the glass—possibly it had been shattered by the elbow of an unruly perp who'd needed subduing.

John headed toward his desk, which Molly saw was scrupulously—some might say even compulsively—tidy.

"I guess Cosette is better than Aphrodite," he said. "Easier for other kids to spell when she gets to school, anyway."

"Yes." Molly stood there awkwardly, wondering how to begin. She wasn't used to being wrong, so this was difficult. Not that she was *wrong* wrong, but she didn't want to go around being the word police. *That* was wrong. People had the right to express their feelings. "Listen," she began. "I want to apolo—"

"No, *I* want to apologize," he interrupted. "I never meant to—"

"No, let me go first." Molly approached his desk, refusing

to allow its tidiness to intimidate her. "I've just come from the hospital. I met Tabitha—and her parents."

"Oh." He hadn't sat down, or offered her a seat, either. They each stood, the desk separating them. "That must have been . . . interesting."

"It was. You were right." Molly plopped the pie she'd purchased from the Mermaid Café onto the center of his desk. "Banana cream pie. Tabitha is a deeply confused girl. I wouldn't personally call her bananas, because I find that term insensitive. But she's got a lot of growing up to do, and she definitely needs her parents, even if she's intent right now on pushing them away."

"Well," John said, looking down not at the pie, which was covered in a clear plastic lid glistening with condensation, but into Molly's eyes. "I just got through interrogating her boyfriend. And he's a real treat. I don't blame her for being so messed up after what he's put her through, even though—get this—the guy is in love with her."

Molly's jaw dropped. "What?"

"Yeah. Don't get me wrong—he's completely conflicted about the whole fatherhood thing—who wouldn't be? Parenthood is the toughest job in the world. But he loves her. That's why he let himself get caught, and confessed, even. He feels terrible about what he did, even if that doesn't excuse it, or mean he isn't going to be punished for it."

Molly shook her head in wonder. "Well, Tabitha will be happy to hear that. She thinks he's coming to get her and the baby, and take them sailing around the world."

"That isn't going to happen. Not for fifteen to twenty years anyway. Maybe a little less, with time off for good behavior."

Molly shook her head. "People do crazy things for love."

"Oh, yeah?" His grin pulled at her heartstrings. "What's the craziest thing you've ever done for love?"

Molly looked down at the pie between them. "Probably this."

His glance fell down to the pie, then moved swiftly back up to her eyes. His grin faltered, and he reached a hand out across his desk to grasp one of hers. "Molly," he said, in a voice gone suddenly hoarse.

Molly clutched his fingers in her own, unnerved as always by the brightness of his electric-blue eyes, and felt her pulse race. She began to babble. She couldn't help it.

"I'm not saying I love you, of course," she prattled. "It's much too soon for that. But I certainly like you—*more* than like you. And I'd enjoy spending more time with you, if that's something you'd be interested in."

His fingers tightened over hers. "That's something I'd be *very* interested in," he said. "I more than like you, too, Molly."

Then he pulled her toward him by the hand, gently, so that their lips—nothing else, only their lips—were touching across the desk. It started out as the sweetest kiss Molly had ever experienced, full of forgiveness and hope.

But the longer it lasted, the more desire crept in. He really was, Molly decided, the best kisser she'd ever met.

And since this time they weren't being interrupted by a knock or a cell phone ring, when he slid a hand around Molly's waist to pull her closer, she didn't mind leaning so dangerously near the pie that she almost put a knee in it—it was worth it, if she could feel more of this man who had the ability to melt her insides at his slightest touch.

Who knows how much more intimate things would have become between them if the door to his office hadn't been flung open suddenly and a young girl's voice hadn't said, "Hi, Dad—Oh!"

Molly tore herself away from the sheriff and threw herself into a nearby office chair.

"Oh, Katie." John sat down quickly behind his desk. "Is school out already?"

"It's a half day." Katie looked suspiciously from her father to Katie. "Teacher conferences. What were you two doing just now when I walked in?"

"Dance lesson," Molly said, just as John said, "Kissing."

Molly threw John a disbelieving look, but he only returned her glance with a *So, what?* shrug.

"She's going to have to know the truth sometime if we're going to do this," he said to Molly, who felt herself turning red. To Katie, he said casually, "Miss Montgomery and I are dating. And it's polite to knock before you enter a room, Katie."

Instead of looking horrified or bursting into tears or doing any of the things Molly most feared a teenage girl might do upon hearing her father was seeing a woman other than her mother, Katie Hartwell laughed and dropped into the visitor's chair opposite Molly's.

"Ha, I knew it," she said, letting her legs dangle over the arm of the chair. "So where are we going for dinner?"

CHAPTER TWENTY-EIGHT

Molly

WELCOME TO SNAPPETTES
MOTHER/DAUGHTER NIGHT!
Snappette Mothers Dancing with
Their Snappette Daughters

–Admission $15–

–All proceeds go to support the Snappettes Dance Team–
Saturday Night @ 8 pm
Little Bridge High School Auditorium
–Go Snappers!–

Feeling nervous, Molly chose to save a row in the middle of the auditorium—not too close, but not too far back, either—for all the friends she had who'd bought tickets but hadn't yet arrived. Draping the long scarf she'd worn—on which was printed images of books, of course—across the row so everyone would know the seats were taken, she selected the aisle seat for herself, so she could make a quick escape to the lobby or to the stage, just in case . . . well, just in case.

Molly had never before considered the importance of being able to make a quick escape from a theater—or of sitting with her back to the wall of a restaurant, and not the window or door. But these were all things that were becoming second nature to her now that she was in a relationship with a lawman.

She seemed to know more than half the people in the audience, and they recognized her, as well, waving to her as they sat down. Molly waved back. She was beginning to appreciate how nice it was to be the only children's librarian in a small town—and the sheriff's girlfriend.

"Scoot," Henry said as he appeared at the end of the row holding two bags of popcorn. He had no appreciation of Molly's role as the town's only children's librarian, or the sheriff's girlfriend. "If you're going to hog the aisle seat, you have to be prepared to move over for everyone else."

Molly twisted in her seat so that Henry could move past her. "How crowded was it out in the lobby?" she asked anxiously.

"Packed." Henry moved her scarf and plopped down into the seat beside her. "The whole town is here, practically."

"Oh, God." Molly took the bag he offered her and began

to shove the overly salted popcorn into her mouth. "What if he's terrible?"

"You and Katie have been rehearsing with him for like what, twelve weeks?" Henry rolled his eyes. "He can't possibly be terrible. And even if he is, isn't that kind of the point? He's the comic relief."

"I don't want him to be the comic relief! The girls and I want him to be *good*."

"I'm glad you became a librarian, because you have no understanding of theater whatsoever."

"Who has no understanding of theater whatsoever?" Patrick O'Brian and his husband, Bill, were standing at the end of Molly's row, dressed, as usual, to the nines. Patrick was holding a bouquet of roses. Molly's stomach lurched.

"Oh, no," she said. "Who are those for?"

"Your honey bunch," he said. "To celebrate his dramatic debut. Scooch over so we can get in. Or did you drape that scarf across those seats for someone else?"

"They're for you guys." Molly stood up to allow them to squeeze past her. "But please don't give those roses to John in front of everybody. It's the girls everyone should be celebrating, not him. The girls and their moms have worked really hard on this show. John's only in one number, they're in six."

"Oh, sweetie." Bill smirked at her as he went by. "John's the one getting these. Especially if he wears a Snappettes uniform. He *is* wearing one, isn't he?"

Molly looked heavenward. Everyone had been asking her about the Snappettes uniform, and if John was wearing one.

"You'll have to wait and see," she said, giving her standard reply.

"Well, he'd better. The entire reason this place is so crowded is because people want to see their elected sheriff wear a tiny pleated skirt."

"Well, that is sexist and wrong," Molly said. "You people are supposed to be here to support the Snappettes, not to see your sheriff in drag."

"Honey, we're multifaceted. We can do both."

"You guys need to stop."

"Is he still proposing to you, at least?" Bill asked.

Molly stared at him. "Why on earth would he do that?"

"Because of the song." Bill sang a snippet of "Single Ladies," including the part about how if you liked it, then you should put a ring on it. "Rumor has it that after the song, he's going to come down off the stage and propose to you, with a ring and everything."

Henry barked with laughter at Molly's suddenly crimson face while Patrick took the opportunity to punch his husband in the shoulder.

"What?" Molly cried, completely mortified. "That is not going to happen. Who told you that?"

"It's all over the Little Bridge Island Facebook community page," Bill said, while Patrick punched him again.

"It's not," Patrick said quickly. "Molly, it's not."

"I hadn't heard that," Henry said, indignantly. "But then, I only go on Insta."

"It's not true," Molly said. How could it be true? She and John didn't keep anything secret from each other. Of course they'd talked about marriage, but only jokingly. And he would never propose to her in such a public manner. He'd know how much she'd hate that. "We've only been seeing each other for a few months."

"Uh, almost *four* months," Henry corrected her. "But I agree, it's too soon." He glared at Patrick and Bill. "Guys, it's too soon."

"Well, personally, I think it would be adorable," Patrick said. "And I think that left hand of hers is calling out for a nice six-pronged square-cut two-carat diamond solitaire with a platinum band—"

"Would you please stop?" Molly begged.

"Molly!"

Hearing her name, she looked across the auditorium and saw Mrs. Tifton—her dog, Daisy, in her arms—waving to her. She was sitting with Phyllis Robinette and a number of her other friends from her yoga class in a special reserved section—reserved because Mrs. Tifton, upon learning of Katie and the Snappettes through Molly, had become a major donor to the dance team.

Major? She'd basically paid for the team's choreography and uniforms for the next five years.

Molly waved back, hoping the widow didn't mind too much that she'd declined her invitation to sit with her. Mrs. Tifton's seats were so close to the stage that Molly feared John would think she was sitting there to coach him through his routine.

Or, now that Molly had heard the latest rumor about

the two of them—and, Little Bridge being such a small town, there'd already been several, including one that she was carrying his twins, though that had been the day she'd worn an empire-waisted blouse to work, a mistake she'd not make again—that she was sitting there so she'd be in easy proximity to accept his proposal.

The lights flickered, giving them the five-minute warning that the show was about to start. Molly looked around, the butterflies in her stomach feeling as if they'd turned to elephants. "Where's Meschelle?"

Henry glanced around the auditorium. "There she is. Meschelle!" he shouted, and waved at the journalist. "Over here! We saved you a seat!"

Meschelle sauntered over, carrying another one of her colorful bags, this one covered in real seashells. "Thank you for screaming my name in front of everyone," she said to Henry when she reached them. "I so appreciate that."

"Oh, you love it," said Henry.

"You're not covering this for the paper, are you?" Molly asked Meschelle uneasily, since she saw that Meschelle had her phone in her hand.

"Why wouldn't I? It's a total feel-good story. People love this kind of stuff."

Molly's heart lurched. Surely Meschelle meant only the performance, not anything she might have seen on Facebook.

"Yes," Molly said, "but don't you think John's been in the news enough lately?"

"For what?" Meschelle was arranging her enormous tote

neatly at her feet. "That High School Thief stuff was ages ago."

"Yes, but what about the baby thing? And reuniting her with her mother?"

"Again, ages ago, Molly. I don't think you understand how quickly news cycles turn over."

"Speaking of the baby thing." Henry pointed to two women coming down the far aisle of the auditorium. "Isn't that her? Tabitha whatever-her-name-is?"

Molly craned her neck to look and was pleased to see that it really was Tabitha, looking happy, glowing and healthy, baby Cosette strapped snugly to her chest in a sling. Behind her trailed Mrs. Brighton, looking a little less happy, but nevertheless better than the last time Molly had seen her, at Story Time in the new library. She'd traded her sweater set and boots for an expensive designer shift, boho-chic jewelry, and sandals.

"Yes, that's Tabby," Molly said. "And her mother."

"Wait, she didn't go back to Connecticut? She's *living* here now?" Meschelle's fingers flew over her phone's keypad, as if she was already getting started on her follow-up story.

"For now." Molly couldn't help smiling. "Tabitha plans to stay as long as her boyfriend is in jail here. And because she's staying, her mother's staying, to help with the baby."

"But that could be years! You know how slowly the court system moves here."

After exchanging cheerful waves with Tabitha and her mother, who'd noticed her in the crowd, Molly turned back toward the stage, a small smile on her face as she thought of the pie she and John had nearly overturned the day of Larry Beckwith's arrest. They'd consumed a lot of pie in the days since. "I know. People do crazy things for love."

She only hoped John wouldn't take that to the extreme this evening.

"What about Tabitha's father?" Meschelle demanded.

"Mr. Brighton? Oh, he's back in Connecticut, working and taking care of the house. I think he realizes this whole thing can't last." Molly waved her hand at Tabitha and her mother, who'd taken their seats and weren't looking her way, to indicate what she meant by "this whole thing." "Their hope is that eventually Tabby, who is a very smart girl, is going to come to her senses and want to go back to Connecticut with them to raise her daughter, and maybe even go to college. Mr. B is keeping the home fires lit until that happens."

"Well, that's good," Meschelle said, with an approving nod. "That Larry guy is a jerk."

"True," Molly said. "But he's still her baby's father."

"Are his parents helping out with child support, at least?"

Molly nodded, thinking of the Beckwiths, who'd shown up at Story Time as well. "They're as excited about their new granddaughter as the Brightons."

"Well, that's good, at least," Meschelle said with a sigh.

The house lights dimmed, plunging the school auditorium into darkness.

"It's starting!" Henry dug his fingers excitedly into Molly's arm.

"Ow. If you're going to be doing that the entire time—"

"I won't." Henry pulled his hand away and plunged it back into his popcorn bag. "It's just that I can't wait to see you as a blushing bride-to-be."

Molly glared at him. "Really? You, too?"

He looked apologetic. "Sorry. The whole thing is just a rumor, I swear."

"It had better be." Molly couldn't imagine anything worse than being proposed to in a public forum, like on a stadium kiss cam or in front of a flash mob. Or the way Bill had suggested John might do it.

Please, she prayed. *Please, John, don't do this.*

A hush fell over the auditorium as the blue velvet curtains were parted just enough so that a muscular young woman wearing a red leotard, short white skirt, matching white fringed vest, white cowboy boots, and a red cowboy hat could slip through and address the audience.

"Welcome, everyone," she said in a loud, clear voice, "to the annual Mother-Daughter Snappettes Reunion Show, this year featuring something we've never had before—a dad!"

The applause was thunderous. There was hooting and even some whistling. Molly began to feel that perhaps there was enough good cheer in the room that no matter how John's performance went, it would be well received.

The young woman—Leila DuBois, whose mother owned the steak house where Molly had gone with John for their first ever proper date—waited for the applause to die down before continuing. "And now, without further ado . . . we welcome you . . . back to the future!"

Loud, thumping music filled the auditorium—so loud that a few startled residents threw their hands over their ears—and then the curtains behind Leila parted to reveal the entire dance team, dramatically lit in pink and blues, already posed with their backs to the audience, their pom-poms raised high.

"Five, six, seven, eight . . . !" shouted their coach.

Then the dance team, Leila and Katie among them, began to lead the audience on a journey through the past five decades, accompanied by their mothers (and, in some cases, grandmothers) and other alumni who'd agreed to join them. They started with snippets of top songs from the sixties ("Louie Louie," "Respect") and seventies ("Sweet Home Alabama," "I Will Survive") and moved quickly through the eighties and nineties ("Celebration," "Girls Just Want to Have Fun," "Like a Virgin," "Losing My Religion," and a rousing rendition of "All I Wanna Do"), complete with quick costume changes, very theatrical lighting, and even some crowd-pleasing tumbling.

By the time they got to the aughts, Henry's eyes were streaming from laughter (he'd seemed to particularly enjoy the team's dramatic take on "Losing My Religion," which they'd interpreted literally, employing nuns' habits and crucifixes). Molly saw that both Patrick and Bill were smiling like lunatics, and even Meschelle had lowered her cell phone and was actually paying attention, a slightly stunned look on her face.

"What," she murmured, "even *is* this?"

But of course nothing could have prepared any of them for John's number. Molly knew what to expect, because she'd attended multiple dress rehearsals, often stopping by the high school after work so they (sometimes with Katie, sometimes not) could grab dinner.

But had they really made some kind of change to it that she did not know about? If they had, Molly was going to be really mad. It was perfect as it was, and the show wasn't supposed to be about John. It was supposed to be about the Snappettes, through the ages.

So when the lighting changed and she heard the first chords for "Single Ladies," she raised her hands to her face in nervous anticipation. She was both dreading and excited for what was about to happen.

The crowd screamed when John—nearly a foot taller than everyone else onstage—came bounding out onto the stage with all the other dancers. Although he wasn't wearing a traditional Snappettes uniform, he still looked very much like part of the team in his red sweatpants, white T-shirt with a sequined *S* emblazoned across the chest, and confident attitude. The red sweatband around his forehead had been Molly's idea, and in her opinion, it really brought the whole look together.

She'd been right about it, too. All around her, the audience was going wild, people cheering and calling, "Sher-RIFF, sher-RIFF!"

But John wasn't distracted. The *S* on his shirt catching the stage lights and shimmering, he stuck every step of "Single Ladies" along with the girls, right on cue.

What he did *not* do during the number was leap off the stage and race toward her with a ring to put on her.

Thank God.

Then, suddenly, the entire audience was leaping to its feet in a standing ovation. The show was over, and Molly was very, very relieved, in more ways than one.

"I'm going to kill you for scaring me like that," she said to Henry, as they both applauded.

He looked crushed. "I don't know what happened. The rumor mill is usually right!"

"Oh, sure. Like it was about me carrying his twins when all I did was wear a high-waisted blouse and eat a whole Harpooner burger from the Mermaid Café for lunch one day?"

Henry sighed. "I'll never listen to a single scrap of gossip ever again."

"I'll believe that when I see it."

Everyone agreed, as they filed out, that the show had been outstanding—the best Snappettes performance of all time.

"The sheriff was so good," people kept saying to Molly.

"This is exactly what the town needed," others were saying. "It's good for everyone to have something to come together over, something we can all agree on, despite our differences. And we can all agree that the Snappettes are amazing! And so is our sheriff!"

Molly beamed. It was nice to hear that something she'd helped work on with two people she loved so much had succeeded.

She looked for both John and Katie in the crowd—they were supposed to meet after the performance to get a celebratory dinner together—but she didn't see them.

"Oh, Molly, there you are!" Joanne and Carl Larson caught up with her in the lobby. "I was hoping we'd see you here. Wasn't that wonderful?"

"Hello!" Molly exchanged hugs with her former landlady and employer. "Yes. How are you both doing?"

"Great! You need to thank your sheriff for us, Molly." Joanne was grinning as she squeezed Molly's hand. "We didn't think anyone could take your place, but Eric Swanson is working out swell."

"That's good," Molly said. She'd felt guilty about leaving the Larsons, but when the opportunity to move into a sweet little one-bedroom apartment above Island Blooms had become available, she simply hadn't been able to turn it down. She'd been running herself ragged trying to work nights at the inn while putting in full days at the library, especially after the new library opened. There'd been so much extra work to do.

Fortunately, John had recommended one of his deputies to the Larsons to take her place at the Lazy Parrot, and the transition had worked out perfectly.

"I'm glad Eric's doing well," Molly said.

"More than well." Carl was practically radiating high spirits. The Snappettes could do that to people. "That guy's got a real feel for hospitality. I don't know what he was doing in law enforcement in the first place."

"That's so good to hear! I have to go now, okay? I'll see both of you later." Molly happened to spy John—who'd changed back into his regular street clothes—in the crowd behind Carl and Joanne. He was holding the bouquet of roses that Patrick and Bill had given him and throwing her desperate looks while trying to fend off a large group of other well-wishers.

"Oh, of course, honey." Joanne gave her one last hug. "Give Fluffy the Cat my love. We miss him over at the inn, but he just loved you so much—it's better that he's with you."

"I will! And thanks!"

And then Molly was across the lobby and at John's side.

"You were so great!" she cried, rising on tip-toe to give him a modest peck on the cheek. She didn't want to scandalize any of the "cottontops"—as John affectionately referred to Little Bridge's more elderly citizens—by doing what she wanted to, which was throw her arms around him and kiss him on the lips.

"Thank you, Molly," he said, behaving as circumspectly as she was—but only, she knew, because they were in public. "I have to admit, I was pretty nervous."

"Glad it wasn't me up there," Randy Jamison, the city planner, said, slapping John on the back. "Of course, it wouldn't have been, because I'd have to be dead before I'd be caught up on a stage like that."

"That could be arranged," Pete Abramowitz said dryly.

"What was that?" Randy asked.

"Nothing." Pete winked at Molly, who grinned back at him.

"Do you want to get out of here?" John leaned down to whisper in Molly's ear.

"Sure, if you want to. But what about Katie?"

"Oh, she and the other girls are heading off to get pizza. They're starving."

Molly slipped her fingers in between his. "You must be, too. You expended a lot of energy up there."

He grinned down at her. "I think I have a little left."

"Miss Molly! Sheriff Hartwell! Miss Molly! Over here!"

Molly turned toward the sound of the all-too-familiar voice and saw Elijah standing by the lobby's drinking fountain, his father's Leica in his hands.

"Hi," he said. "Hey, sorry to disturb you, but can I get a photo of you two together?"

"Elijah," Molly began, rolling her eyes.

"Just real quick. It's for the school paper. I'm the official school photographer. It's for the last edition, before school lets out for the summer."

"Sure." John, suddenly magnanimous, wrapped his arm around Molly's waist and pulled her toward him, then plastered his "sheriff's smile" on his face. "How's this?"

"Oh, great," Elijah said, snapping away, making generous

use of his flash. "That's just great! You two make a real attractive couple—did anyone ever tell you that?"

"Elijah," Molly said in a warning voice.

"No, I mean that most sincerely. I'm sure a lot of people say that, but I truly mean it. I'm taking photography next semester, did you know, Miss Molly? I'm going to be the next Angel Adams."

"Ansel Adams," she corrected him.

"Yeah, whoever. Anyway, I don't want to take any boring landscape photos like he does. I want to be a crime scene photographer. All because of you, Sheriff. And you, too, Miss Molly." Elijah tipped an invisible hat toward Molly. "I won't be seeing too much of you at the library this summer, Miss Molly, because I'm going up to Tallahassee to visit my dad for a few weeks. But I'll be back in the fall. I'll see you then."

"See you then, Elijah," Molly said, and was relieved when he hurried off to go take photos of Katie and her friends.

Only then did she turn to John and say, "Tallahassee? His father lives in Tallahassee. Isn't that where . . . ?"

"Yes." John's bright blue eyes were alight with mischief. "Rich Wagner, the sheriff I replaced after he turned out to be hiding a second family in Tallahassee, is Elijah's father."

Molly couldn't believe what she was hearing. "But Elijah has a different last name."

"He took his mother's maiden name after he found out the truth about his father." John shrugged. "He wanted to hide his relationship to the man. Most of the kids at school knew the truth, anyway—but not Katie. She was in Miami when that happened. And not you—you just got here."

"Oh, the poor thing." Molly stared after Elijah, remembering how much time he'd spent in the library and his mother's concern for him. "He certainly seems to be coming out of his shell now, though," she said, as she watched him flirt with Katie and her friends.

"That's all because of you," John said, giving her an affectionate squeeze as he followed the direction of her gaze. "He's a different kid now than from even a few months ago, wouldn't you say?"

"It's all because of *us*," Molly said. "You're the one who let the paper run his photo. You gave him back a sense of self."

John grinned. "Yeah, maybe. I guess we make a pretty good team, huh?"

Molly side-eyed him. "Don't get cocky."

After saying their good-byes, they strolled hand-in-hand through the quiet, night-darkened parking lot. The high school had been built just yards away from the ocean, so all Molly could hear was the sound of the waves slapping against the seawall and the gentle breeze rustling through the palm fronds near the auditorium's entrance. The summer air was balmy and sweet, and the moon, just rising over the ocean's dark surface, cast everything in blue-and-white shadows.

"You really were amazing," she said, as they approached

his enormous gas-guzzler of an SUV—which both she and Katie had convinced him to exchange for a hybrid as soon as he got approval from the mayor.

"I was all right. The last part didn't go the way it was supposed to."

Molly shook her head. "Yes, it did. You didn't miss a step."

"No, there was this whole part that the girls and I threw in at the last minute that we ended up not doing."

"Why not?"

"Because I didn't think you'd like it."

Molly froze, realizing what he was referring to—what he *had* to be referring to. She dropped his hand and stood by herself in the middle of the parking lot, eyeing him suspiciously. "Wait a minute. Are you telling me the rumor is *true?*"

He grinned at her from about five feet away, one hand in the pocket of his jeans, the other still holding the roses. "Why? What have you heard?"

She put her hands on her hips. "I heard you were going to jump down off the stage and come up to me in the audience and put a ring on it."

His grin turned into a smile that crinkled the skin around those too-bright blue eyes. "That was the plan, yeah."

Her heart seemed to skip a beat. "So what happened?"

"You're not really the public display of affection type."

"You're right," Molly said, her heart thumping . . . but this time with pleasure, not dread. "I'm not."

"So I thought I'd do it in private, instead. I wasn't planning on it being in a parking lot, but I can't wait anymore." From the pocket of his jeans, he extracted a small velvet box, then opened it and held it toward her. "I'm not saying today, or tomorrow, or anytime soon. I know it's only been a few months. I'm just saying sometime in the future. Will you?"

Trying to remain dignified and to suppress the silly smile that was threatening to break out across her face, Molly took a few steps toward him and examined the ring without touching it.

"Is that a six-pronged square-cut two-carat diamond solitaire with a platinum band?" she asked, fighting hard not to hyperventilate.

"It is." John sounded surprised. "How did you know?"

"Oh," she said. "Just a guess. Are those roses really for you, or are they for me?"

He gave her a sheepish grin. "They were supposed to be for you, after you said yes. Patrick was going to shower us with them. But I told him—I told everyone—that that plan wasn't going to work. I know it's soon, but Katie said I needed to follow the advice of the song and not let you get away, and I happen to agree." The grin faded, and his expression turned serious. "So what about it, Molly?"

Molly stopped trying to act dignified and let out a joyous laugh. It was loud enough to startle the seagulls that had been roosting quietly nearby, as well as the last few stragglers who'd been heading toward their cars. Even John seemed startled.

"Is that a yes?" he asked, looking alarmed.

"Yes," she cried, and threw her arms around his neck and kissed him on the lips, not caring this time what anyone thought. "I love you."

He must not have cared, either, since he said, "I love you, too," and kissed her back.

Acknowledgments

So many people helped me in the creation of this book, I can hardly begin to thank them all! But here goes:

First and foremost my friend Nancy Bender, who gave me the idea not only for this book, but the entire Little Bridge Island series.

Michael Nelson and Allison Merkey of the Key West Public Library, who were so generous in answering my many questions about the library and its inner workings. Special thanks to Allison, who first met her husband, a sheriff's deputy, at the Key West library, and so is the true inspiration for this story. (But of course this book is entirely fictional. Any errors or missteps are entirely my own.)

I would also like to thank my agent, Laura Langlie, and everyone at William Morrow for their energetic support of this and all my books, especially my editor, Carrie Feron, assistant editor Asanté Simons, publicity director Pam Jaffee, and marketing director Molly Waxman.

Special thanks to friends and readers Beth Ader, Emily Bender, Jennifer Brown, Gwen Esbensen, Mark Gambuzza, Abigail Houff, Michele Jaffe, Rachel Vail, and my amazing media managers, Janey Lee and Heidi Shon.

Thanks also to the many, many readers, especially in the city of Key West, who have so generously supported me and the Little Bridge Island series.

And of course I could not forget the countless librarians who have helped me over the years by not only finding amazing books for me to read myself, but for putting my books into the hands of millions of readers. You are all truly heroes.

And last but not least, my husband, Benjamin, who has put up with me for thirty years and ninety books!

About the Author

Insights,
Interviews
& More . . .

About the author

Meet Meg Cabot

Lisa DeTullio Russell

MEG CABOT was born in Bloomington, Indiana. In addition to her adult contemporary fiction, she is the author of the bestselling young adult fiction series The Princess Diaries. More than twenty-five million copies of her novels for children and adults have sold worldwide. Meg lives in Key West, Florida, with her husband.

A Conversation with Meg Cabot

***Q: How did you come up with the idea for* No Offense?**

A: I was taking a walk with my friend Nancy, who pointed to a cute little house here in Key West (where we both live) and said, "I just love that house. It's where the sheriff and the librarian live."

I froze in my tracks. "What?" I cried. "How could there be a sheriff and a librarian living together in this town and no one told me before this? How did they meet? Do they solve mysteries together?"

Nancy was unable to answer any of these questions, so I went home and immediately outlined this book and pitched it to my editor (who fortunately loved the idea).

I did find out later that the Key West librarian in question met her cute sheriff husband under entirely crime-free circumstances that bear no resemblance whatsoever to this story, and that no, they do not solve mysteries together (however, he does show up at her library frequently—to take her to lunch). Like the sheriff and librarian in this book, they do not agree on everything. ►

To me, that's what gives a romantic relationship just the sizzle it needs to work!

Q: How did you get so many details about librarians—and sheriffs?

A: I love librarians! One of my aunts went to Indiana University in Bloomington, Indiana (where I grew up), to study library science at the same time I was attending elementary school, and I absolutely worshipped her.

After that, I haunted my local library weekly, and my school libraries every day (yes—I was that kid who ate her lunch in the library). Librarians were the ones who encouraged my love of reading, gently reassuring me that it was okay to venture out of the children's section and into YA and then the adult section. Without them, I'm positive I wouldn't have become the writer I am today.

Since becoming an author, I've been privileged to speak at numerous libraries and even attend librarian conferences, where I've met hundreds, if not thousands, of librarians. For this book, I interviewed a number of librarians (including the two mentioned in the acknowledgments) and read numerous nonfiction books on libraries and library science (*The Library Book* by

Susan Orlean is a favorite). Any errors you might find, however, are my own, or were for the selfish purpose of propelling this narrative.

As for details concerning law enforcement, I can only say that I've watched every single episode of *Law & Order* ever made . . . just kidding (not really)! My brother is a police sergeant, and I bombarded him, along with members of Key West's local law enforcement (who shall remain nameless so they don't get blamed for any of my errors), with questions. Many of them now run when they see me coming.

Q: Both Molly Montgomery, the librarian in* No Offense*, and Sheriff John Hartwell love to read and mention the titles and authors of numerous books throughout this novel. Are these books real, and if so, are they books you enjoy, as well?

A: Yes, all but one of them are real books, and have also been favorites of mine at different periods in my life. I recommend all of them (except *The Wilderness Survival Handbook* by Sternberg, which I made up), either to read yourself or to give as gifts to younger readers (please check for age appropriateness before gifting). ▸

Q: In your last book,* No Judgments, *you gave readers recipes for some of the food your characters enjoyed in the story. Do you have any for us now?

A: The salad-dressing chicken that Katie Hartwell makes for her sheriff father in *No Offense* is an old standby! It's so good, no one will ever know you didn't slave over it all day.

What you will need:

- Chicken (I prefer dark meat with the skin on, but it works just as well with white meat without skin.)
- A big sealable plastic bag or a large bowl
- Baking tray
- Aluminum foil
- Tongs or forks
- Meat thermometer (if you want to be completely safe)!
- Salad dressing of your choice (I prefer Italian, but you can try it with your favorite salad dressing and see how it goes. Many people swear by Dijon honey mustard. Some people also add barbecue sauce in addition to salad dressing. It's entirely up to you.)
- If you prefer to make your own marinade, a recipe I've used before is:

¼ cup key lime juice (regular lime or even orange or lemon juice can be substituted)
3–4 tablespoons cider vinegar
1 teaspoon garlic powder
1 teaspoon onion powder
a pinch of dried basil
a pinch of dried oregano
a pinch of dried thyme
a pinch of cayenne (optional)

How to make the chicken:

1. Take the chicken out of the packaging and put it in the bowl or sealable plastic bag.
2. Pour a generous amount of salad dressing into the bag, enough to lightly coat the chicken. Seal the bag.
3. Massage the salad dressing into the chicken, making sure you get the dressing to coat all parts of the chicken. If you're using a bag, you can massage the chicken through the bag.
4. Don't forget to wash your hands if you just massaged the chicken in a bowl with your bare hands.
5. Put the chicken into the refrigerator and wait two to twenty-four hours. ▸

You can try cooking it before two hours is up, but it won't have had as long to marinate and won't be quite as good.

6. Once the chicken is marinated, preheat the oven to 375°F.
7. Place aluminum foil over a baking tray and pour chicken from bowl or bag onto tray. Be sure to save the excess salad dressing! You'll need it later.
8. Put the chicken in the oven and bake 20 minutes. After 20 minutes, remove the tray from the oven and flip the chicken pieces over with your tongs or fork, then coat them with the leftover salad dressing from the bag or bowl.
9. Put the tray back in the oven and bake for another 30 minutes or until cooked through (chicken should be 165°F internally).

Enjoy your salad-dressing chicken! ~